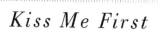

*Kiss Me First*

# Kiss Me First

A NOVEL

## LOTTIE MOGGACH

DOUBLEDAY
NEW YORK LONDON TORONTO SYDNEY AUCKLAND

Copyright © 2013 by Lottie Moggach

All rights reserved. Published in the United States by Doubleday, a division of Random House, Inc., New York. Published simultaneously in the United Kingdom by Picador, an imprint of Pan McMillan, Ltd., London.

www.doubleday.com

DOUBLEDAY and the portrayal of an anchor with a dolphin are registered trademarks of Random House, Inc.

*Jacket design by Ben Wiseman*
*Jacket illustration © Graeme Montgomery/Trunk Archive*

LIBRARY OF CONGRESS CATALOGING-IN-PUBLICATION DATA
Moggach, Lottie.
Kiss me first : a novel / Lottie Moggach. — First Edition.
pages cm
1. Young women—Fiction. 2. Identity theft—Fiction. 3. Identity (Psychology)—Fiction. 4. Internet fraud—Fiction. 5. Suicide—Psychological aspects—Fiction. 6. Suspense fiction. I. Title.
PR6113.O36K57 2013
823'.92—dc23
2012046724

ISBN 978-0-385-53747-6

MANUFACTURED IN THE UNITED STATES OF AMERICA

10 9 8 7 6 5 4 3 2 1

First United States Edition

*For Mum and Kit*

*Kiss Me First*

*It was a Friday night,* about nine weeks into the project. Tess's voice sounded normal, but I could see that she had been crying and her narrow face was pale. For the first few minutes of the conversation, she leaned her head back against the wall behind her bed, gaze turned to the ceiling. Then she righted it and looked straight at the camera. Her eyes were as I'd never seen them: both empty and terrified. Mum sometimes had the same look, toward the end.

"I'm scared," she said.

"What about?" I asked, stupidly.

"I'm so fucking scared," she said, and burst into tears. She had never cried in front of me; in fact, she had told me she rarely cried. It was one of the things we had in common.

Then she sniffed, wiped her eyes with the back of her hand, and said more clearly, "Do you understand?"

"Of course," I said, although I didn't entirely.

She looked straight into the camera for a moment and said, "Can I see you?"

At first I thought she meant, *Could we meet up?* I started to remind her that we had agreed that shouldn't happen, but she cut me off.

"Switch on your camera."

After a moment, I said, "I think it's best if we don't."

"I want to see you," said Tess. "You get to see me." She was staring right at the camera, her tears almost dried up. She gave a small smile and I felt myself soften. It was hard to resist, and I almost said, *Okay, then,* but instead I said, "I don't think it's a good idea."

She looked at me a moment longer. Then she shrugged and returned her gaze to the ceiling.

I will be honest here: I didn't want Tess to see me in case I failed to meet her expectations. This isn't rational, I know: Who knows what she thought I looked like, and what did it matter? But I had examined her face so carefully, I knew every nuance of her expressions, and I couldn't bear the thought that, if I turned on the camera, I might see a look of disappointment pass over it, however briefly.

Then, still looking at the ceiling, she said, "I can't do it."

"Of course you can," I said.

She didn't speak for more than a minute, and then said, uncharacteristically meek: "Is it okay if we stop for today?" Without waiting for an answer, she terminated the call.

||||||||||

I admit that that particular conversation has replayed in my head several times since.

All I can say is, I said what felt right at the time. She was upset and I was comforting her. It seemed entirely natural for Tess to be scared. And when we spoke the next day, she was back to what by that stage was "normal"—calm, polite, and detached. The incident wasn't mentioned again.

Then, a few days later, she looked into the camera and tapped on the lens, a habit she had.

"Do you have everything you need?"

I had presumed that we would go on communicating right up until the last moment. But I also knew it had to end.

So I said, "Yes. I think so."

She nodded, as if to herself, and looked away. At that moment, knowing I was seeing her for the last time, I felt a sudden, intense rush of adrenaline and something akin to sadness.

After quite a long pause, she said, "I can't thank you enough." And then: "Good-bye."

She looked into the camera and made a gesture like a salute.

"Good-bye," I said, and: "Thank you."

"Why are you thanking me?"

"I don't know." She was looking down at something, her leg or the bed. I stared at her long, flat nose, the curve of her cheekbone, the lines around her mouth as delicate as fallen eyelashes.

Then she looked up, leaned forward, and turned off the camera. And that was it. Our final conversation.

*There is no Internet here,* not even dial-up.

I didn't anticipate not being able to get online. Of course I had done my research, but the commune has no Web site and I could find little practical information elsewhere beyond directions on how to get here. There were just useless comments in forums, along the lines of Oh, I love it, it's so peaceful and beautiful. I know that communes are places where people go to get "back to nature," but I understood that they are also where people live and work on a semipermanent to permanent basis, and so assumed there would be some facility to get online. Spain is a developed country, after all.

I understand that Tess had to head to a remote spot, but three-quarters of the way up a mountain, without a phone mast in sight— that's just unnecessary. Of all the places in the world, why did she choose to spend the last days of her life *here*?

4

I admit, though, that the location is not unpleasant. I've pitched my tent in a clearing with extensive views over the valley. The surrounding mountains are huge and colored various shades of green, blue, and gray, according to distance. At their feet is a thin silver river. The farthest peaks are capped with snow: an incongruous sight in this heat. Now that we're going into evening, the sky is darkening to a mysterious misty blue.

There's a woman here dressed like an elf, with a top exposing her stomach, and sandals laced up to her knees. Another one has bright red hair twisted up on either side of her head, like horns. Lots of the men have long hair and beards, and a few are wearing these priest-like skirts.

Most of them, however, look like the people begging at the cash points on Kentish Town Road, only extremely tanned. I had thought I might not look too out of place here—Mum used to say I had hair like a hippie, center parted and almost down to my waist—but I feel like I'm from a different planet.

Nobody here seems to do very much at all. As far as I can see, they just sit around poking fires and making tea in filthy saucepans, or drumming, or constructing unidentifiable objects out of feathers and string. There seems to be little that is "communal" about it, aside from a collective wish to live in a squalid manner for free. There are a few tents like mine, but most people seem to sleep in tatty vans with garish paintings on the side, or among the trees in shelters constructed out of plastic sheeting and bedspreads. They all smoke, and it appears obligatory to have a dog, and no one picks up their droppings. I've had to use half of my supply of wet wipes cleaning the wheels of my suitcase.

As for the human facilities, I was prepared for them to be rudimentary but was shocked when directed to a spot behind some trees signposted SHITPIT. Just a hole in the ground, with no seat and no paper, and when you look down you can see other people's waste just lying there. I had promised myself that, after Mum, I wouldn't have dealings with other people's excrement and so have decided to make my own private hole in some nearby bushes.

It is, of course, everyone's prerogative to live their lives in whichever way they choose, as long as they do not hurt others. But—like this?

Back in London, I felt near certain she had come here. It all seemed to add up. But now I'm starting to have doubts.

Nonetheless, I told myself I'd spend a week here making inquiries, and that is what I shall do. Tomorrow I'll start showing her photo around. I've prepared a story about how she is a friend who stayed here last summer and whom I've lost track of but believe is still somewhere in the area. It's not actually a lie. I just won't mention that I'm looking for proof of her death.

It's almost half past nine now, but it's still sweltering. Of course, I had researched the temperature, but I wasn't fully prepared for what ninety degrees Fahrenheit feels like. I have to keep wiping my fingers on a towel to stop moisture from getting into my keyboard.

It was even hotter in August last year, when Tess would have been here. Ninety-five degrees; I looked it up. She liked the heat, though. She looked like these people, with their sharp shoulder blades. She might have worn a little top like the elf woman—she had clothes like that.

I've opened the flap of my tent and can see a rash of stars and the moon, which is almost as bright as my laptop screen. The site is quiet now, except for the hum of insects and what I think—I hope—is the sound of a generator somewhere nearby. I'll investigate that tomorrow. Although I have a spare battery for my laptop, I'll need power.

You see, this is what I'm going to do while I'm here: write an account of everything that has happened.

I got the idea from Tess. One of the first things she sent me was an "autobiography" she once wrote for a psychiatrist. It provided a certain amount of useful information, although, like everything Tess did, it was full of digressions and inconsistencies, the facts clouded by retrospective emotions. This isn't going to be like that. I just want to lay down the truth. I've told the police a certain amount, but they don't know the full picture. It feels important that there is a definitive record.

There are some things I haven't told anyone about, like Connor. Not that I've had anyone to tell. I don't suppose the police would have been particularly interested. Besides, even if there had been someone to tell, I don't think I could have. Whenever the thought of him, Connor, came into my head—which was fairly regularly, even in the midst of the police business, even when I thought I was going to prison—it was as if I were allergic to it. I would feel very ill for a moment and then my head would reject the thought, as if it were trying to protect me from the attendant strong emotions.

I'm not yet sure what I'm going to do with this. Nothing, probably. I'm certainly not going to put it up online. I know that's what we "young people" are supposed to do, but it never appealed to me. Volunteering unasked-for information, presuming others will be interested in one's life, seem both pointless and impolite. Of course, on Red Pill we'd present our opinions, but that was different. There it was a rational discussion about a philosophical topic, not a splurge of whatever random thing came into our heads. It's true that some people did use the site as a kind of confessional, posting long accounts of their "journey" and what terrible childhoods they'd had, using it as an outlet for their angst. But I didn't join in with that. I never said anything personal. In fact, apart from Adrian, I don't think anyone there knew what age I was, or even that I am a girl.

|||||||||||

So, the first thing I want to say is that it's not true that Adrian "preyed" on the "vulnerable" and "socially isolated." The police psychologist, Diana, kept going on about it too, making a big deal about Mum dying and me living alone. But first, by the time I had found the site, Mum had been dead for almost three months, and second, it wasn't as if I'd never gone near a computer when she was alive. It's true that my online activity did increase after she died, but that seems a natural consequence of having so much more free time.

It is possible that, had Mum been alive, things might not have gone exactly the way that they did, because she wouldn't have let me go and meet Adrian on Hampstead Heath that day. But who's to say I wouldn't have lied to her? I could have told her that I had an eye test, or some other excuse that justified a few hours away from home. I was not in the habit of deceiving her, but one of the things this experience has taught me is that concealing the truth is some-times necessary for the greater good.

So it's impossible to prove whether or not I would have become involved with Adrian and Tess had Mum still been alive. Therefore it's pointless to speculate.

As for "socially isolated": It's true that after she died and I moved to Rotherhithe, I didn't see many people. Mum and I had lived in the same house in Kentish Town all our lives, and the new flat wasn't near anyone I knew. I didn't even know Rotherhithe existed before moving there. When Diana heard that, she seemed to think it was significant, and asked why I had deliberately moved somewhere remote. But it wasn't like that; I ended up there by accident.

When Mum was given her year prognosis, we decided we would have to sell the house and buy me a flat to live in after she died. The reasons were financial. There was a big mortgage on the house and credit card debts, and, although I had been caring for her up till then alongside the NHS nurse who came in every day to administer her medicines, we decided we would have to get another, private person in for her final months. The progression of her MS meant that she would soon need lifting in and out of bed and onto the toilet, and I couldn't do it on my own. Also, I would have to get a job in the future, and because I didn't have a degree, we decided that I would do a distance course in computer software testing. Mum had a friend whose son, Damian, had just started his own software testing company, and she arranged for me to work for him from home on a freelance basis, provided I had completed this course. I would need to study for three hours a day to get the qualification, so that was further reason to get some help.

Mum and I did our sums and worked out how much we would have for my flat. The answer was, not very much at all. Kentish Town was too expensive, so we looked at areas farther out, but still, the only places within our price range were Not On: former council flats on the top floor of intimidating tower blocks or, in one case, on the North Circular, the filthy six-lane road where Mum and I got the bus to the shopping center. I would often not make it past the front door before telling the estate agent I had seen enough.

Back at home, I would tell Mum about the viewings, making her gasp at descriptions of filthy hall carpets or a car balanced on bricks in the driveway. Penny, the woman we'd employed to be Mum's caregiver, eavesdropped on our conversations, and one day looked up from the property pages of her *Daily Express*.

"It says here that the area around Rotherhithe is a wise buy," she said, accentuating the last two words as if it were a phrase she had never heard before. "Because of the Olympics."

I ignored her. She was a silly woman, always offering her banal opinions and fussing around with her lunch, and I had quickly learned to pretend she wasn't there. But she kept on butting in, going on about Rotherhithe. Eventually, Mum and I agreed that I would go and see a place within our budget in the area, just to keep Penny quiet.

The flat was on the first floor above an Indian restaurant on Albion Street, just behind the Rotherhithe tunnel. There was a huge sign above the restaurant with the (unattributed) statement that it was "the best curry house in Rotherhithe." Albion Street was small but busy; teenagers on bikes barged through shoppers on the crammed pavement, and thudding music issued from a barbershop. The pub on the corner had Union Jacks covering the windows, so you couldn't see inside, and men stood outside drinking pints and smoking, even though it was only three in the afternoon. When I found the front door to the flat, the paintwork was shiny with grease, and on the step below lay the remains of a box of fried chicken, a pile of half-gnawed bones.

It was all highly unpromising, but because I had come all this way—it had taken more than an hour by tube from Kentish Town—I decided that I should at least have a quick look inside.

The flat had clearly been unoccupied for some time; the front door resisted opening due to the large pile of post banked behind it. On entering I noticed a strong smell of onions.

"It's just for a few hours in the afternoon," the estate agent said, "while they get the curry started."

He led me first to an unremarkable bedroom, and then to the kitchen. The particulars had mentioned an "unofficial" roof terrace, which turned out to be just a bit of asphalt outside the window overlooking the backyard of the restaurant. The yard appeared to be used as a rubbish dump and was full of drums of cooking oil and catering-sized Nescafé jars. A solitary bush grew out of a crack in the concrete. When the estate agent led me back into the narrow hall, he grazed against the wall with his car keys and left two gouges in the soft plaster.

Last, we went into the front room. It was dim, despite its being a bright day outside. The reason for that, I saw, was that the restaurant's sign jutted up over the bottom half of the flat's windows, blocking out the light.

We stood there for a moment in the gloom, and then I said I would like to leave. The estate agent didn't seem surprised. Outside, as he was locking the front door, he said, "Well, at least you wouldn't have to go far for a curry."

I didn't reply. On the tube back, though, I started to think that the comment was actually quite amusing, so when I got back home I repeated it to Mum.

I had, of course, intended for her to laugh. Or at least smile; she was wearing her respirator all the time by then, and was short of breath. But instead she said, in her Darth Vader voice, "That's nice."

"What?" I said.

"Useful," she said. "For when you don't want to cook. You were never very good at cooking."

This was not the reaction I was expecting. The anecdote was

meant to be humorous, because I didn't eat spicy food. That was the point. When I was eleven, I had a chicken curry at my friend Rashida's house and went bright red and was sick. Mum had to come and pick me up.

I am not proud to say I got angry. I remember looking at her with the respirator clamped to her face, the tubes up her nose, and having this ridiculous notion that rather than helping her live, the tubes were actually sucking out her brain cells, emptying her out to a shell.

"I hate curry!" I said, and then, louder, "You know that! I was bloody sick at Rashida's; don't you remember?"

I didn't usually swear, and certainly not at Mum, so that tells you how upset I was. I remember Penny, who was as ever planted on the sofa, looking up from her sudoku, and Mum's face sort of folding in on itself.

I stormed off into the kitchen. I know now—I knew *then*—that it was an irrational reaction, but I wasn't thinking straight. With the benefit of hindsight, I think that her forgetting things was a taste of what life was going to be like when she was gone, when there would be no one left who knew these little facts about me.

I stayed in the kitchen for a few minutes, to calm down. By that point it wasn't really a kitchen anymore, more like a cupboard for Mum's equipment and pills. I remember staring at the boxes of nappies stacked up on the dining table—the same table that Mum used to lay for breakfast each evening before bed, where I had taught her how to play chess, where she had plaited my hair before my interview at Caffè Nero—and I had what I suppose you could call a realization. I won't go into details because, as I say, I intend this to be a factual account, not personal. Suffice to say, I realized that every hour I spent looking at flats would mean one less hour spent with Mum, and besides, it didn't really matter what my new flat was like. I hadn't heard of the mediocrity principle then, which states that nowhere is more special than anywhere else, but I think that's what I was applying.

I went back into the living room. Mum's head was flopped over to one side, her eyes closed. She wore these red satin pajamas to assist her movement, and the front of the top was darkened with drool. Penny was ineffectually wiping her chin, and so I took over and stroked her hair and apologized, and then I held her dead-bird hands and said that, actually, the flat was lovely, perfect, and we should definitely buy it.

So that's how I came to live in Rotherhithe.

At the funeral, friends of Mum—including some distant relatives from York whom I'd never even met before—said that they would come and visit me in my new place, and to get in touch if I ever needed anything. But I didn't encourage them, and no one pressed the issue. I suppose they didn't want to intrude, and presumed that my own friends were looking after me.

Rashida was the only person I wanted to tell, because she had actually met Mum. We became friends in year eight, and because her dad rationed her computer time, she used to come over after school to play on mine. Mum would bring us Boasters covered in whipped cream and tell Rashida about how she had once hoped to go to India but then got pregnant with me and so never did, and that she hoped I would go there one day instead. Back then, before she got ill, I'd show my impatience when she repeated herself and said silly things. "But I don't want to go to India!" I'd say, and Rashida would giggle and whisper to me, "Neither do I."

I hadn't spoken to Rashida for a few years, but had kept track of her on Facebook and knew she had moved to Rottingdean with her fiancé, a management consultant. I sent her a message telling her Mum had died, and she said she was sorry, and that if I was ever in Rottingdean I must visit her and Stuart. I noticed that she had posted a new picture showing off her engagement ring, and she had done her nails like the girls at school, with a stupid white stripe across the top, which was disappointing.

I didn't tell anyone else, but I announced my change of address on Facebook. In reply a girl called Lucy, whom I'd worked with at Caffè Nero, sent a message saying she was now managing a sandwich shop nearby in Canary Wharf, and that we should meet up. But Lucy was always quite odd. On her breaks she used to go to the Superdrug down the road and steal makeup testers. She was always asking whether I wanted her to steal me something and got offended when I said no, even though she could see I didn't wear makeup.

I had seventy-three other friends on Facebook, girls from school mostly, but they weren't proper friends. Our entire year was "friends" with one another. It was like at Christmas, when everyone would give everyone else a card whether they liked them or not, just so they'd get one back in return and could compare the thickness of their hauls over lunch. A couple of them used to be actively mean to me and Rashida, but that tailed off in year ten, when they got interested in boys and turned their attention to the girls who were their competition.

Every so often, someone would post details of an open-invitation party. Once, I went along to one, organized by Tash Emmerson. This was in 2009; Mum suggested it when we realized that I hadn't been out for seven months. The party was in a cavernous bar in Holborn with horribly loud music; I remember this one song that went, over and over again, "Tonight's going to be a good night," which was ironic. A glass of orange juice cost £3.50. Everyone was talking about their experiences at "uni," which I couldn't contribute to, and when they weren't doing that they took photos of one another. I felt so drained just being around them I had to prop myself up against a wall in the corner.

What was odd was that a lot of them were keen to have their photos taken with me even though, as I say, we could not be described as proper friends. I remember Louise Wintergaarden and Beth Scoone advancing on me at the same time from both sides and throwing their arms around me, as if we were really close. After the picture was taken, they dropped their arms and walked off without a word. Then it was Lucy Neill and Tash and Ellie Kudrow. When they put the photos up on Facebook, they didn't even bother to tag me. I showed one of the pictures to Mum and she said the girls looked really tacky, with their bleached hair and orange faces, and that I looked like Cinderella sandwiched between the two wicked stepsisters. I didn't tell her that under one of the pictures someone had commented, Ah, the old stand-next-to-a-munter trick? I didn't care, but I knew she'd get upset.

After that I didn't go to any more parties, but I read everyone's updates. I didn't understand what they were on about most of the time. It'd be gossip about people I didn't know or references to TV programs and celebrities and YouTube clips I didn't recognize. Sometimes I'd follow the links they were all getting so excited about, but they'd always turn out to be some idiotic thing, like a photo of a kitten squashed into a wineglass or a video of a teenager in Moscow singing badly in his bedroom. And always, these pictures of them dressed up to the nines, sucking in their cheeks, cocking one leg in front of the other like horses. It was like they had all had a lesson I hadn't been invited to—nor wanted to be invited to—in which they learned that hair must be straightened, that nails must have that white stripe across the tip, and that you had to wear your watch on the inside of your wrist and your handbag in the crook of your elbow, with your arm stuck up like it's been broken.

It was the same with their status updates. Sometime they'd post these elliptical messages, which didn't make sense by themselves, like Sometimes it's better not to know or Well, that's fucked it then, without making clear what they were referring to. Their lives were filled with banal drama. I remember that Raquel Jacobs wrote once that—OMG!!!—she had dropped her Oyster card down the toilet. I mean, who needs or wants to know that? It seemed incredibly stupid and pointless, yet they all responded to one another as if these things were interesting and important and funny, using all this made-up language like whhhoooop, or misspelling words like hunny, or abbreviating words for no reason, and putting XXX at the end of everything they wrote.

It wasn't that I wanted to be like that myself. But I just didn't understand how everyone seemed to have mastered it, to know what language to use and to respond instantly to comments in the "right" way. Even people who were really stupid at school, like Eva Greenland, seemed able to do it.

Very occasionally, someone would post a proper question, such as what were the advantages of using an external hard drive with their PC versus an inbuilt one. Those I would reply to, and sometimes got a response. Esther Moody wrote back Thnx u r star xxx, when I advised her how to change her Google settings from AutoFill. However, the vast majority of what they wrote was nonsense and had no relevance to my life.

I suppose what I'm saying is that if I was "isolated," it was through my own choice. If I really wanted to, I could have met up with Lucy from Caffè Nero, or gone along to another one of the open parties from Facebook. But I had no desire to.

I liked being by myself. Before Mum had become ill it'd been perfect. I'd spent evenings and weekends upstairs, reading or on the computer, and she'd be downstairs, cleaning or watching TV or doing her miniatures; then she'd call me every so often for meals and cuddles. It was the best of both worlds.

I had inherited the furniture from the old house, which had been put into storage; before she died, Mum had arranged with Penny that, when I moved into the new place, her son would pick it up in his van and bring it over. But Penny and I were not on good terms by the end. We had a ridiculous argument over her sudoku book, when she discovered that I had filled in some of the puzzles. I explained to her that I had only done the advanced ones that I knew she wouldn't be able to complete herself, but she took offense.

Then, when Mum died, Penny kept going on about how odd it was, because Mum hadn't displayed the signs of imminent death the day before: "Her feet weren't cold, and she had a whole Cup-a-Soup."

Anyway, the upshot was, her son never got in touch about the furniture. That was all right, though, because I found that I didn't even want it. Once I took the tube to the storage unit and saw it all there—the coffee table with the smoked-glass top; the white chest of drawers, still with the rubber bands around the handles that we put on to help Mum open them; the black leather lounge set; the dinner gong; the tall, framed family tree that she spent £900 getting done and proved that a distant relative once married the aunt of Anne Boleyn. I remember especially the glass corner cabinet, which

Mum used to display her miniatures. It had been in the house ever since I could remember, and I had always loved looking at the things in it. But now in the storage room, it was just a bit of cheap shelving, and the miniatures were in one of a pile of taped-up boxes. I thought that even if I brought the shelves and the box back, and wiped them clean and arranged the miniatures in exactly the same way as Mum had them, it still wouldn't be the same. I decided to leave everything there and just keep paying the £119.99 monthly storage fee.

Instead, I bought everything new from the huge Tesco Extra in Rotherhithe. I didn't need much: a blowup mattress and sheets, a little desk, a beanbag, a sandwich toaster. I put my books in stacks against the wall, arranged by color, and kept my clothes in bin bags; when they got dirty I put them in another bin bag, and when that was full I took it to the launderette. I was working from home anyhow, so I didn't need to dress up.

I passed the computer course easily and began my new job for Damian, Mum's friend's son, as soon as I had settled into the flat. It wasn't hard. Every few days he'd send me a link to a beta site that needed testing, and I'd run it through a quality-assurance program, checking for faults and bugs and weak spots, and then send back a report. I got paid per job; most would take less than a day, but the more complicated ones might require two. After I had finished my work, I would stay on the computer, playing games or, later, posting on Red Pill. I had set up my desk next to the window and quickly realized that there was a big advantage to the restaurant sign blocking the lower half of the glass: It meant there was never any glare on my laptop screen.

⫿⫿⫿⫿⫿⫿⫿⫿

Afterward, the police kept asking me exactly what led me to Red Pill. I told them I couldn't remember, that I just followed a random link, but of course I knew exactly how I got to it. I just didn't want to tell them.

As I say, after I moved into the flat my time playing games increased, to around eight hours a day. There was one game in particular, World of Warcraft. I suppose it was as if that were my full-time job, and I fit my testing work around it. I enjoyed how quickly time went by when I was playing: Whole afternoons were effortlessly dispensed with, like eating a doughnut in two bites. I soon reached level sixty and was invited to join a nice guild, which got together for raids two or three times a week. On several occasions I was nominated as leader, and it was during one preraid meeting, discussing strategy, that another player started a debate about how the decisions one took in the game revealed one's own philosophy. For instance, whether, after a raid, you distributed the gold you personally gained among the other members or took it all for yourself. I hadn't previously thought of the game in those terms and found it interesting, and he suggested that I check out this Web site, RedPillForums.com. A very cool philosophy site, he wrote. It'll blow your mind. He e-mailed me a link to a podcast on the site by the man who ran it, Adrian Dervish.

Although I ended up listening to nearly a hundred of Adrian's podcasts, I can remember that first one clearly. I made notes on it—I make notes on all the important things that happen—but I don't need to look them up now. The title was "Is This a Laptop I See Before Me?" and Adrian's opening words were "So, folks, today's question is—how much can we really know?" He then gave a whistle-stop tour of classic epistemology, starting with Socrates and ending at *The Matrix*, which happened to be one of my favorite films. He'd pose a statement—"I'm a hundred percent sure that I'm speaking into a microphone right now"—and then say, *"But! What does 'a hundred percent' actually mean?"* The best way I can describe it was like a never-ending game of Pass the Parcel: Each idea was unwrapped to reveal another inside. I remember that as the podcast went on, he started chuckling over those *but*s, as if this were the best fun a person could ever have.

There was something immediately compelling about Adrian's voice. He was American, and his accent was warm and intimate. He would be saying these mind-expanding things but in a cozy way, using these quaint words like *folks* and *gosh*. "This is really something to get your philosophical chops around," he'd say. Or, "If you thought that was interesting, golly, just wait till you hear what I've got for you next." After a few minutes, I stopped the podcast, got down on the floor, and brought my laptop close to my head to drown out the noise on the street below before listening to it all over again.

After that first podcast, I made myself a grilled cheese sandwich and then came back and listened to another four, back-to-back. As I did so, I explored the site. Its motto was "Choose the Truth." The name Red Pill was another reference to *The Matrix*: The film's characters, unaware that they are in a virtually simulated world, are invited to either take a blue pill to stay ignorant or a red pill to be faced with reality, however upsetting it might be.

I investigated the forums. In one, members were debating the "laptop" podcast. I remember being impressed by their ability to articulate and argue persuasively. I'd read a viewpoint and think it was entirely reasonable, and then someone would challenge it and make a counterargument that seemed equally convincing.

For instance, I remember one member—Randfan, I think it was— posting his opinion that only a cretin would claim to be certain that anything in the material world actually exists. We know our percep- tions and that is all we can ever know. In reply, Juliusthecat said, But how do you know that is the case? Or rather, how do you *know* that you know that this is the case? They'd discuss these vast, abstract ideas as if they were everyday topics of conversation, as casually as Mum and Penny used to talk about which supermarket had the best deals that week.

As well as forums for "pure" philosophy, there were others dedi- cated to more specific and contemporary subjects, such as whether taking someone out for dinner was the same as using a prostitute, or the ethics of downloading music. There was also a place for people to post their personal real-life dilemmas and get rational advice. One member, for instance, wrote that she had made a new friend at work who had seemed like-minded, but had then discovered this friend believed in angels, and now she didn't know how to talk to her anymore.

On the home page was a statement from Adrian, in which he introduced himself as the founder of the site and stated that although he was interested in all philosophy, he was a libertarian at heart. I'm embarrassed to say that I didn't know what that word meant. I hadn't even heard it before. He explained that libertarians believed that people owned their own bodies, and the products of their labor, and were against force: essentially, that we should all be free to do whatever we wanted as long as it didn't hurt anyone else. There didn't seem anything to disagree with about that.

Some members were obsessed with the political and economic sides of libertarianism, full of plans to banish governments and railing against taxes, but they tended to stay in their respective forums, so it was easy to avoid them. People pretty much stuck to one or two topics that most interested them: I found I spent most of my time in ethics, but there were forums for religion, arts, logic and math, and so forth.

The site was an antidote to the rest of the Web: to the rest of the world, really. Only rational thinking was tolerated, and anyone who wavered off course was immediately called on it. There was no casual use of words—*literally* meant *literally*—and unlike in other forums, proper punctuation and spelling were expected.

That's not to say that it wasn't a supportive community. Banishment was enforced only if a member was fundamentally opposed to a basic tenet of the site—if they weren't an atheist, for instance—or as a last resort for persistent troublemakers, like JoeyK.

You could see it coming when someone was going to be banished. He, the member, would start to get all cocky on the forum, challenging Adrian just for the sake of it, thinking he was being clever. Adrian would patiently engage with him, rationally argue, but if he continued being difficult and hogging the board and ruining things for everyone else, Adrian would have no option but to ask him to leave. As he said, if someone disagreed so strongly with what he was saying, there must be a better place for them. There were plenty of other philosophy sites out there.

After a few weeks of listening to the podcasts and lurking on the forums, I took the plunge and joined. I chose a user name, Shadowfax, and spent some time deciding which of my favorite quotes I should have as my "sig." In the end I went for Douglas Adams's *Don't believe anything you read on the net. Except this. Well, including this, I suppose*, which always made me laugh.

I posted my first comment on a discussion about altruism: whether an act can really be selfless, or whether we're just doing things that ultimately benefit ourselves. The posters were in general consensus that nothing we did was selfless, but I felt differently. I put across the point that when we are close to other people, the distinction between what is "best for me" and "best for others" is artificial. What is "best for me" is often to sacrifice some self-interest in order to help others. Within seconds, someone replied, broadly agreeing with me but pointing out something I had missed, and soon others joined in and it became a full debate. Hobbesian2009 wrote, Good entrance, Shadowfax! Most newcomers to the site, you see, just posted a timid introductory message, rather than launching straight into a debate. I had made something of an impact.

Two weeks later, I decided to start my own thread. I spent a while choosing my subject; it had to be attention grabbing but not so outrageous or provocative that I looked like a troll. I decided upon a subject that had been on my mind for a while: whether it was okay for a person to do nothing with her life except what she wanted to do—for example, play World of Warcraft—as long as she could support herself and didn't harm anyone else.

Immediately after posting, I had an unsettling few minutes when I thought that no one was going to pick it up, but then I received my first comment. The thread got seven responses in all, which I learned was pretty good. Most regulars were wary of newbies, waiting for them to prove their commitment before they engaged with them. To my surprise, Adrian himself joined the discussion, posting his opinion that those who were lucky enough to be in a secure position should use some of their privileges to help others who had a worse start in life.

I won't say I found debating on Red Pill easy from the start, but it did come quite naturally. What I liked about it was that, once you had the tools, you could apply them to almost any subject, including those you had no experience in. For instance, I was a significant contributor to a discussion on whether it's more ethical to adopt children than give birth to them. For the next few weeks I contributed to debates and spent most of my evenings on the site. I got to know the regulars. Although the site had nearly four thousand registered members across the world, there were only around fifty people who regularly contributed to debates, and so they quickly became familiar.

It was quite a tight "clique," but one you could get into by demonstrating intelligence and logic. They gradually came to accept me, and a happy moment came when once, in response to a newbie asking about an ethical matter, Not-a-sheep wrote, Shadowfax, we need you! because I was known to be strong in that particular area.

I also started reading. Adrian posted a list of books—"the canon," he called it—that he said were essential grounding for anyone who wanted to get the best out of the site, like Plato's dialogues, Hume, Descartes, and Kant. I ordered a few from Amazon. I read a lot before, but only really sci-fi and fantasy novels, and I found them hard going at first, but I persevered and set myself an hour's reading time every evening, making notes as I went along.

I had received several PMs—personal messages—from Adrian himself. The first was a welcome message when I joined up, and then another after three months on the forum, congratulating me for surviving the initiation period (most members drop out before then, apparently). Then, after nearly six months of regular posting, I got a PM from him asking me to apply to become an Elite Thinker.

The way the site worked was that once you'd posted your fifteenth comment, you graduated from being an NE, which stands for Newly Enlightened, to a full-fledged member. Most people remained at that stage, but a small number were invited to take an online test for Elite Thinkers. This meant that Adrian deemed you capable of more advanced thought, and, if successful, you got access to a special forum where discussion was on a higher level. It was a subscription, twenty pounds a month.

In the PM, Adrian said he had been particularly impressed by my participation in a debate over the difference between shame and guilt. *You've really wowed me, Shadowfax. You're one hell of a smart cookie.* It was quite a thrilling moment, I must say.

Of course I said yes. Adrian sent a link to the test, which was in two parts. The first asked me to respond to a series of ethical dilemmas of the sort I was used to debating on the site—whether I would kill one person to save five others, for example. The second part of the test was more of a personality test, a list of statements that required simple yes or no answers. *It's difficult to get you excited. You readily help people while asking nothing in return. You can easily see the general principle behind specific occurrences.*

A few hours after I submitted the test, Adrian e-mailed to say I had passed, and I was admitted into the Elite Thinkers. From then on, I spent most of my time on the ET forum. There were around fifteen members who were very active, posting several times a day, and I was one of them.

|||||||||||

Then came the day of *that* message.

It arrived late one afternoon, when I was in the middle of an overdue testing report. Since discovering Red Pill I had let my work slide somewhat, and the previous week Damian had sent a stiff e-mail advising me that, although he was sensitive to my grief over Mum's death, he was going to have to let me go if I didn't meet deadlines.

So I was trying to get this report finished, but nonetheless couldn't resist opening Adrian's PM. It was immediately clear that this was something different from his usual messages. On the site I was always known by my user name, Shadowfax, but here he used my real name. He must have gotten it from my credit card details.

The message read:

Leila, I've been watching your progress on the site with great interest. Fancy a F2F?

A face-to-face meeting. He named a place near Hampstead Heath to meet, and a time, which happened to be the following morning.

I remember my fingers going limp on the keyboard. My first thought was that I had done something wrong, but I soon rationalized that. Adrian was an important man; why would he bother to meet up just to tell me I was to be banished, when he could do it online? Besides, I hadn't, to my knowledge, done anything to displease him. On the contrary, he regularly congratulated me on my posts and had only the day before told the forum that I had a "first-class mind."

The only other options were, in a way, more daunting. Either he was considering making me a forum moderator, and the meeting was an interview, or he wanted something else from me. The question was—what?

‖‖‖‖‖‖‖‖

That's enough for tonight. It's four forty a.m., and my eyes have started to sting. The skin of the tent is growing lighter, and after the lovely coolness of the night I can feel the temperature starting to rise.

*This morning I woke violently* after only a few hours' sleep, feeling like I was being baked alive inside my tent. My body was leached of water, my skin covered in a greasy film. I unzipped the tent flaps and stuck my head outside, but the stagnant air offered little relief, so I dragged my inflatable mattress out into the shade of a nearby tree and tried to get back to sleep.

However, it felt odd being so exposed and I couldn't settle. After an hour I decided to get up and start my inquiries.

First, I went to the lavatory, and as I was coming back out of the bushes a tiny old woman with very short gray hair approached me, gesticulating. She had a thick foreign accent and it took me a moment to realize she was cross because I wasn't using the same place as everyone else. "You stay here, you follow the rules," she said in a harsh tone. I decided it was best not to respond, and then asked her whether she had been at the commune the previous summer.

"Yes, I was," she said, frowning. "I have been coming here for the past fourteen years. I helped make this wonderful place, and that's why—"

"Do you recognize this woman?" I said, showing her Tess's picture.

She barely glanced at the photo. "I don't remember," she snapped, before walking briskly away.

Making a mental note to ask her again when she had calmed down, I began at the north end of the site and approached every camp, showing Tess's photo to each adult I encountered and asking whether they remembered her from the previous summer. The response was disappointing. One man with five rings in his lip thought he might recognize her from "somewhere" but was unable to provide any further information. Another was adamant that Tess was a Spanish girl called Lulu who had been running a bar in Ibiza for the past seven years.

What struck me was the lack of curiosity. I didn't have to use my prepared story at all. No one asked me why I was looking for her. It's as if a missing person is a totally normal event in this world. People seemed much more interested in how I had gotten to the commune from the airport. When I said I had taken a taxi, one man asked how much it had cost, and when I told him his eyes widened and he waved his hands in dismay and exhaled loudly. "A hundred and forty euros!" He repeated it to the woman who was next to him, plaiting her hair. "A hundred and forty euros!"

That's another thing about this place. I had braced myself for "hippie talk," ready to bite my tongue during discussions about "spirituality" and "star signs" and "massages" and so on, but the conversations I've overheard have not been like that at all. People here just seem to talk about how much things cost, or where they've come from, or where they're going next.

I suppose this lack of interest in one another makes sense in terms of Tess. She knew she could come here and not be quizzed, that no one would ask awkward questions.

As I was heading back to my tent, I again heard that lovely generator hum that I had noticed yesterday evening, and followed the sound to a van parked on its own, away from the others. The door was open and inside was a woman breast-feeding a baby, and a little boy attacking a melon with a knife. There was a fan whirring, positioned near the baby. The woman had her bosoms exposed, so I averted my eyes and asked her about the specifications of her generator. She seemed surprised and said, "I don't know," so I went outside and had a look. It was only twelve hundred watts, and I guessed that, if we were to plug both the fan and my laptop into it, the fan would suffer a slight reduction in power. I thought the effect of this would not be felt so much at night, when the temperature was cooler and they were asleep, and perhaps I could use it to charge my laptop then.

I explained all this to the woman and asked her whether I could attach my converter.

"As long as we won't boil, I don't see why not," she said.

"Were you here last summer?" I asked, thinking of Tess.

"No, this is our first time," she said, and gave a little laugh. "Yours too, I'm guessing. My name's Annie, by the way."

Compared with the rest of them Annie looks quite normal. She's large and pink, and although her blond hair is messy, it's neither matted nor shaved. Her clothes are almost respectable, except the armholes of her vest are so baggy they show the sides of her bra.

I thought I might as well move my tent to be near the generator immediately. Rather than dismantle it, I just removed the outside pegs and dragged the whole structure, my things still inside, the hundred or so yards to a spot beside Annie's van. She and the children were now outside, under a makeshift canopy.

"Oh, you're going to camp right here?" Annie said.

It seemed the obvious thing to do if I was going to connect to her generator; I don't know why she asked. I nodded, and set to work repegging the tent while Annie and the boy watched.

"Do you want Milo to help?" she said. "He loves putting up tents."

Before I could say anything the little boy had skirted over and started jamming in the tent pegs, using both hands and muttering to himself. He had the same color hair as Annie, and I noticed when he knelt down that the soles of his feet were black.

After my early start and all the morning's activity, I fancied a lie-down. Inside the tent the air was hot and horrible, so I asked Annie whether I could place my mattress under the shade of her canopy and lie there.

"You're not shy, are you?" she said, but made a sweeping gesture, which I took as a yes. I pulled over my mattress, lay on my back with my arms folded across my chest, and closed my eyes. I didn't feel so self-conscious now that it was only Annie and Milo around, and soon drifted into an odd half-sleep. The noises around me—the birdsong, the dog barks, the drumming, even the voices of Annie and Milo a few feet away—were muted by the heat, and merged to form a sort of ambient sound track to my thoughts.

I don't normally remember my dreams, and certainly don't attach any meaning to them. But this one was more a series of disconnected images. Some of the scenes had an obvious source: the flight over to Spain yesterday, my first-ever air journey; the plane the same orange as a Doritos packet; the hellish throng at Luton departures hall, at the sight of which I nearly turned around and went back to Rotherhithe. But then there were also random scenes from elsewhere: walking through Marks & Spencer on Camden High Street with Mum slightly ahead, a familiar shape in her beige jacket; Tess's body twirling from a tree somewhere deep in the forest.

The sound of crying pierced my sleep and I woke to find Annie feeding the baby and Milo stirring something on a little stove. She said it was six p.m. and asked whether I wanted some dinner. I've brought a week's supply of bread and biscuits, so I don't strictly need anything else, but I accepted her offer.

"It's just a veggie chili," she said, "not very impressive." She was right.

We sat on rounds of tree trunk that had been sanded and varnished to become rudimentary seats. Annie explained that she made them to sell to tourists at markets. I said that if tourists were flying home, the stools might cause a problem with their luggage allowance: I noticed at the airport yesterday that there is a maximum weight limit. "Oh, I suppose the people will just have to stay in Spain, then," said Annie, not sounding at all bothered about the potential loss of a large section of her customer base.

Milo wolfed down his food and started playing with a wooden toy on a string, throwing it into the air and attempting to catch it again, so I was left trying to make more conversation with Annie. Luckily, she did most of the talking. She volunteered the information that she was from Connecticut in America and had decided to come to Spain as a fortieth birthday present to herself.

I was surprised to hear she's forty—only a year older than Tess would be now. She seems so much more mature. When she smiles there are at least ten wrinkles around each eye, whereas Tess had only four, and on her reddened chest there are a number of circular lines, like rings on a tree.

She asked me what I needed a laptop for, and I told her I was writing a film script. Then Milo started babbling some nonsense and I pretended to listen to him instead, which was a relief, because I didn't want to say much more.

So, that has been my day. Now it's dark and quiet outside, and I'm in the tent. Here continues the official account.

IIIIIIIIII

Adrian asked to meet at South End Green in Hampstead, which was, by great coincidence, a place I knew well. It's a little square in the shadow of the Royal Free Hospital, which had been one of Mum's treatment centers. I had spent hours looking down at the square from windows high up in the hospital, while Mum was undergoing tests, and sitting in the nearby Starbucks, which had acted as an unofficial waiting room for relatives of patients, full of pale people not drinking their coffees.

I arrived thirteen minutes before our meeting time and sat on a bench, relieved to take the pressure off my feet. I was wearing a pair of Mum's shoes, high heels, and they were a size too small for me. It was a warm day and the other benches were occupied by a mixture of tramps and hospital patients out for some fresh air, although the buses that circled the square gave little hope of that. Some of the patients were by themselves, others accompanied by helpers or nurses. One man, I remember, was dragging a drip after him—his skin was yellow as margarine—and there was an ancient old woman being pushed around in a wheelchair, her head lolling as if her neck had been deboned.

At the other end of my bench, a tramp was swigging out of a can.

As I sat there, sweating, another man came and sat beside me. He was quite young, but looked gray and hollow eyed. He lit a cigarette and smoked it very quickly, staring straight ahead as he did so. Then he stood up, dropped the butt on the ground, and walked away, leaving his cigarette packet on the arm of the bench. I leaned over and picked it up and called after him, "You left these!" He didn't turn around, so I stood and walked after him with the packet, presuming he hadn't heard. When I caught up with him, he turned around and gave me a funny look.

"It's empty," he said.

He carried on walking.

I put the cigarette packet in a bin and sat back down on the bench. Then behind me came a familiar voice.

"You are a good person, Leila."

I turned and there he was, smiling down at me.

I had seen pictures of Adrian before, of course, on video links on the site. I even recognized the shirt he was wearing, one of my favorites: blue corduroy the same color as his eyes, with a crescent of white T-shirt at the neck. I remember thinking that he looked out of place in the deathly little square, too healthy and wholesome with his plump, rosy cheeks.

On seeing him, I automatically stood up. He continued. "I saw what you did with that guy's fags just then." The word *fags* sounded odd in his warm, American voice. "Most people wouldn't have done that, you know."

"Wouldn't they?" I said.

"No," he said, and then he walked around the bench so he was next to me, looked into my eyes, and held out his hand. I shook it, and he said, "Extremely pleased to meet you, Leila."

The tramp sitting beside us let out a wail and hurled his can to the ground for no apparent reason. Adrian raised his eyebrows and said, "Shall we find a more salubrious spot? Do you mind walking?" And then: "What lovely shoes—they won't hurt your feet, will they?"

Adrian led the way, weaving through the buses on the road and onto the pavement. We walked in silence for a few minutes, past a line of shops, until we reached the edge of a large expanse of green.

"Ah, Hampstead Heath," said Adrian. "London's lung."

We continued onto the grass, past squatting dogs and office workers sitting with sandwiches, their faces tilted up to the sun. Adrian asked whether I had come far, and in reply I asked whether he lived here.

"Ha! If only. Do you know Brixton?"

I didn't, of course, but I thought it was some distance away and wondered why he had suggested meeting here, so far from both of our houses. I opened my mouth to ask, but he jumped in with another question, about my views on the upcoming London 2012 Olympics: "Are you pro or anti?"

I hadn't really considered the subject and didn't have an opinion to hand, so I was relieved when, in the next breath, he continued. "That's if the world still exists by then, of course. What do you think of these 2012 Armageddonists, convinced that mankind's number is up?"

This area I felt more confident about. Enthusiasts of these doomsday scenarios were prevalent in chat rooms, and I was aware of their nonsense arguments. I felt pretty certain of what Adrian's opinion on them would be too—after all, their beliefs could hardly be described as rational—so I took a chance and answered in no uncertain terms.

"I think they're mad."

Adrian hooted with laughter.

"Indeed, indeed. In fact"—he lowered his voice—"I've always wanted to invent my own conspiracy theory, just to prove that these morons will swallow anything. I could make one up right now: say, Obama caused the banking crisis. Give me the morning to build a Web site, throw together a video, and tweak Wikipedia, and by five p.m. I bet you I'd have a thousand true believers under my belt."

I knew nothing about Obama or banking, so was pleased that a smile seemed to suffice as a reply. Adrian then smoothly changed tack, asking me whether I'd been sporty as a child or more of a bookworm, like him—"I'm guessing from the quality of your brain it was the latter"—and from there the conversation flowed, each answer I gave leading to another topic, often only tangentially related to the last.

In that way, within about fifteen minutes we had covered a large amount of conversational ground, and Adrian knew more about me than anyone else in my entire life. Apart from Mum, of course, but with her it was different; our conversation spread over weeks and months and years and was mostly concerned with practical, everyday matters. Here with Adrian, it was all brand-new, about ideas and opinions I didn't even know I had until I heard myself voicing them. As we leaped from one subject to another, it felt a bit like that game the others played at junior school, where they tried to step on every tiled square in the playground in as short a time as possible.

Despite its speed, the conversation didn't feel effortful or one-sided, like Adrian was asking questions just for the sake of it, but rather that he was genuinely interested in my replies. There wasn't time to reflect or consider whether what I was saying was "right," but from his positive responses it seemed like it was—he would agree with me and offer up some related experience or thought of his own—and rather than feeling flustered by this rapid-fire experience, I felt instead quite exhilarated.

Then, about twenty minutes into our walk, as we were passing through a shady wooded area, he said something quite surprising that momentarily rippled the fluency of our exchange. We were discussing vegetarianism—he was one too, it turned out—and he mentioned that there was a good restaurant nearby, in Hampstead.

"You haven't been?" he said. "Oh, you must. I used to take my wife, Sandra, there; it was our favorite place. Not least because they were always very accommodating about her wheelchair."

I hadn't been aware he had a wife, let alone that she was disabled. Before I could reply, he added, "RRMS."

He immediately followed this by remarking upon the adorableness of a dog that was gamboling nearby, before asking me whether I liked animals. And so he guided us onto another topic, and that of his wheelchair-bound wife was left behind.

It was only later, when I had time to review and process the whole experience, that the full implications of this exchange became clear. Adrian had a wife, whom he talked about in the past tense, who had had multiple sclerosis.

This second coincidence made our encounter seem all the more extraordinary—yet another similarity between us. It struck me how he used the acronym for relapsing remitting multiple sclerosis without explanation, as if he knew I would know what it meant, although I hadn't mentioned the fact that Mum had suffered from the condition, either during our conversation or on the site.

It was around then that I noticed my shoes were rubbing my heels quite painfully, and I was forced to slow my pace. Adrian noticed my discomfort immediately.

"Oh, you poor thing," he said. "What you women suffer for beauty. Shall we sit?"

He motioned toward a nearby bench overlooking a pond. We sat, he at an angle beside me, one arm slung across the back of the bench. He smiled broadly at me.

The newspapers were obsessed with how "ordinary" Adrian was in appearance. One journalist described him as looking "like the deputy manager of a Dixons," which seems nonsensical: How is a deputy manager of a Dixons "supposed" to look? He wasn't very tall—about five feet, eight inches—and quite thickset, but not fat. It's true that his facial features weren't particularly striking—full, pink cheeks, a largish nose, small, deep-set blue eyes—and his most noticeable attribute was his hair, which was almost black and combed back from his forehead. In real life, it had a slightly odd, springy texture that wasn't obvious on film.

Yet there was something about him, his confidence and the way he focused his attention on you, that made him compelling and attractive. I was used to it on the videos, where he would stare into the camera as if he were an old friend, but it was the same in real life too.

"So, Leila," he said. "You're no doubt wondering why I requested this meeting. Let me make it clear from the outset. Like I said in my note, I've been monitoring your activity on the site, and you've really impressed me. Now, tell me—what is it you do for an occupation?"

When I told him about my testing work, he smiled and leaned toward me in a conspiratorial manner.

"Don't tell anyone, but despite the fact that I run a Web site, I'm terrible with computers. Ironic, huh?" He laughed. "You should give me lessons. Do you give your parents lessons?"

I explained that Mum was dead and that I had never met my father, because he and Mum had separated when she was pregnant.

"And what about siblings?"

"I'm an only child."

He smiled. "Well, I hope you see us all on the site as a kind of substitute family."

"Oh, I do, I do!" I said. I remember thinking that I didn't sound like myself, far more bubbly, like a girl on TV.

"You know, Leila, every single day you or one of the members on the site will say something wise and wonderful that blows me away. Literally makes me whoop with delight." He lowered his voice. "I'm going to confess something to you. I like to think I'm an upbeat kind of fellow, but very occasionally I find myself getting a little depressed by the state of the world. By the banality and woolly thinking that seem to be the norm. Do you know what I mean? Do you ever feel that?"

I nodded enthusiastically. "Oh, yes, definitely."

"But at times like that," he continued, "I just have to go to the site and see clever, passionate truth seekers such as yourself, engaged with the things that really matter in the world, and I know that things will be okay."

He smiled at me. I remember the sun was on his face, making it glow. I think it was only then that the reality of the situation really struck me. This brilliant man, whom everyone at Red Pill clamored to impress, was, at this precise moment in time, entirely focused on me. I could see the pores in his cheeks and smell the mint on his breath. When I looked down at his feet, I could see a sliver of the socks he was wearing under his slip-on shoes. I was up close, with complete access. Randfan, for one, would have killed to be in my position; the previous week he had told the forum that he had gotten one of Adrian's favorite mottoes—*It is not the attainment of the goal that matters; it is the things that are met along the way*—tattooed around his calf.

Although there were several people around us, their presence receded and it felt as if we were all alone, just me and him. My anxiety about the interview had also disappeared—at that point, remember, my best guess was that this was about me becoming a moderator on the forum. I was, at that moment, perfectly happy. The best way I can describe it is feeling I was in a space that was exactly the right size for me.

"So, Leila," he said, leaning back. "What do you think of the site? Please be honest. I really value your opinion."

I had anticipated this question, and told him that I thought Red Pill was an oasis of reason, a forum for intellectual inquiry, and so on. As before, Adrian seemed fascinated by my opinions. "Really?" he said. "Gosh, that's good to hear." He then told me a bit about the background of the site, most of which I already knew: how he started it in America, how libertarianism means something slightly different over here, how the Americans are more interested in the economic side of it, while in the U.K. we get more animated over the philosophical aspects.

He leaned forward. "I would never say this to anyone else, but I'm slightly more drawn to the moral side of things myself. Not to say that the economics are not important, of course. But it's *how best to live* that really gets my juices flowing."

"Me too!" I said.

"For instance, the right-to-die debate we had the other week," said Adrian. "You were very passionate about that. Would it be fair to say that's an area you're particularly interested in?"

"Yes," I said. I felt on firm ground here. "I believe that deciding upon the time and place of your death is the ultimate expression of self-ownership. It seems clear to me that anyone who professes a belief in personal freedom cannot be opposed to suicide. Freedom to choose how and when we die is a fundamental right."

"And are there conditions attached—morally speaking?" asked Adrian. "Should a candidate be suffering from a terminal illness before we condone his or her actions?"

I shook my head. "Life is about quality, not quantity, and it's up to each individual to judge whether hers is worth living or not."

As we were talking a toddler came down the path on wobbly legs. She was wearing a sun hat and cackling with delight, turning around to look at her father, who was some way behind. When the child was just a few feet away from our bench, she tripped and fell heavily on her face. After a moment, she lifted her head, gravel stuck to her cheek, and let out a ghastly wail.

Adrian winced visibly at the noise.

"Shall we walk?"

Without waiting for an answer he stood up and moved off, stepping around the crying child. I followed, and we walked in silence for a moment, down a path that led between two ponds. One of them was filled with people swimming, and laughter and shouting floated across the brown water. Adrian looked over at them and smiled, his jovial mood seemingly restored after the interruption.

"Tell me, Miss Leila, are you familiar with the claim argument?" he asked.

*Now we're back to the proper interview*, I thought. Unfortunately, I didn't know what he was referring to. I thought I could work it out rationally if I had a minute, but Adrian didn't seem to mind my lack of response and carried on.

LOTTIE MOGGACH

"It says that not only do we not have the right to prevent those who wish to end their lives from doing so, but that we actually have a duty to help them, if asked."

"Like in euthanasia?" I said.

"Well, yes," said Adrian. "But it's more encompassing than that. And it may not have to do with the actual act of suicide itself. Put it this way—should there be a situation when someone whom you judge to be of sound mind asks you to help her in some way or other to end her life, then—so says the claim argument—it is your duty to do so."

"Okay," I said. "I understand." I was still preoccupied with not knowing immediately what the claim argument was.

"In fact," said Adrian, "it's kind of like turning the common idea of euthanasia on its head. Some people are physically able to carry out the act themselves, but are prevented from doing so by the hurt it'll cause their family and friends," he said. He paused to take a breath. "Okay, so here's a hypothetical dilemma for you. A woman has an affliction that is not in itself terminal but is ruining her quality of life and is, essentially, incurable. After considerable thought she has come to the conclusion that she wants to end her life. But she knows her friends and family would be deeply hurt and upset, and for that reason she doesn't. Yet she desperately, desperately wants to kill herself and has felt convinced of this for many years. She comes to you and says that she has thought of a way she can carry out this act that will not upset her family and friends, but she can't achieve it without your help. What would you do? Would you help her?"

I nodded. "Of course. Under the claim argument it'd be my duty."

He smiled at me, dazzlingly. "You really are an extraordinary

42

young woman, aren't you? I bet people around you haven't appreciated this as much as they should."

I felt my cheeks flush. We had reached a small meadow running steeply down to a pond. Groups of merry people were dotted around, heads and brown limbs just visible above the long, golden grass, but I could view them only in a disconnected way, as if I were walking past a vast painting. My conversation with Adrian was the only thing that seemed real.

"Not everyone can deal with advanced theories like the claim argument," said Adrian. "It's beyond even some RP members. They say the right things, but really, they can only go to a certain level; they can't deal with the full implications and reality. They still cling to illusions and societal norms. They can't push through the resistance; they're not truly free. It's a rare, special person who is, Leila." He paused. "Are you free?"

We were now at the bottom of the meadow, standing by the pond. I watched a man throw a Frisbee into the water and a tubby black Labrador belly-flop after it.

"I don't know," I said finally. "I mean, I don't think I'm there yet. I know I've got lots of things to learn, but I really want to learn. I want to be free."

Adrian smiled and squeezed my shoulder. He motioned for us to start walking again, and that was when he told me about Tess.

Actually, he didn't mention her name then. He just said that a woman had come to him, desperate to kill herself, but not wanting her family and friends to know. And she had the idea to employ someone to pretend to be her online, so that no one would be able to tell she was not still alive.

|||||||||||

Of course, I didn't say yes immediately. Adrian insisted I take a week—"at least"—to consider the proposition.

"This is a huge ask, Leila. *Huge*," he said that day on the Heath, stretching out his arms for emphasis. "It will take up a lot of your time. It will require a heck of a lot of preparation and mental strength. You will have to commit to the project for at least six months. And because, alas, not everyone shares our enlightened views, you will not be able to tell anyone about what you're doing."

I nodded, deep in thought.

"There will, of course, be some form of financial remuneration," Adrian continued. "We can discuss that at the next stage. I'm afraid it won't be a vast amount—the woman is not rich—but she wants to pay you for your time." He paused. "If, in theory, you were to decide to help her, how much would you want for it?"

The question was wholly unexpected, so I had not given the matter any thought. However, at the time I moved into the flat I had done a breakdown of all my bills and food costs and calculated that I needed approximately eighty-eight pounds a week to live on. From what Adrian had said, working for Tess would be a full-time occupation and I would need to stop my work for Testers 4 U, so this would be my only income.

"Eighty-eight pounds a week?" I said.

Adrian raised an eyebrow and nodded. "That sounds eminently reasonable. I'm sure she'll be happy with that."

As we parted at the tube, he put both his hands on my shoulders and gazed into my eyes for a few moments, without saying anything. Then he smiled and released me.

"Good-bye, Leila."

The train back to Rotherhithe that day was packed. I had no

choice but to stand pressed against a man's bare, sweaty shoulder, with a group of tourists squawking in my ear. In normal circumstances I would have gotten off at the next stop and waited for another train. But that day I didn't mind. It didn't affect me. It was as if, during our meeting, Adrian had given me a protective cloak.

For the next three days I thought about the proposal, examining it from all sides. I wrote a list of the pros and cons, as I did when I had to make decisions about Mum. But this situation felt different, as if I was just going through the motions of deciding. By the time I got on the tube that day after the Heath, I knew I was going to say yes.

"I don't know anyone else who has both the mental capacity and the compassion required to help her," Adrian had said. He promised to be there whenever I needed him. "You won't be alone. I'll always be watching out for you. Your well-being is my primary concern."

We discussed the fact that, due to the risk of judgment from the less enlightened, we should avoid making reference to the project on Red Pill, even in PMs. Adrian said that if I wanted to be involved with the project, I should let him know by changing my Red Pill "sig" to a quote from Socrates. If I decided against it, it should be one from Plato. It would be a secret signal between us. "And from then on, once the project begins, we'll communicate by other means," he had added. "You are, I trust, on Facebook?"

I was keen to find an appropriate Socrates quote to use. After some consideration, I decided upon *They are not only idle who do nothing, but they are idle also who might be better employed.*

For all my certainty, my hands were shaking as I pressed the button to confirm it.

|||||||||||

In our first session, Diana, the police psychologist, said, "But did you not think, *How can this possibly work?* Even in the most practical terms—how were you going to dispose of the body?" I told her that such details were not in my remit, and that my job started only after the act had taken place. This was true, but naturally one of the first questions I asked that day on the Heath was how the woman's body would not be found and identified. Adrian explained that there were ways of committing suicide that meant it could be months, if not years, before the body was discovered, and when it was, no one would think to identify the body as this woman, because she wouldn't have been reported missing. "There are more than five thousand cases of unidentified bodies each year in this country alone," he said. "This would simply be one of them."

Of course, I asked Adrian other questions that day on the Heath—lots of them. He acknowledged that the project sounded audacious and untenable.

"But that's the beauty of it," he had said. "Remember Occam's razor? Even if people did think that something was slightly amiss, they wouldn't assume that she had killed herself and asked someone else to impersonate her, would they? They'd think of a more obvious explanation."

The idea, in a nutshell, was this: The woman—Tess—would inform her family and friends that she intended to move abroad to start a new life in some distant, inaccessible place. She would hand over to me all the information I would need to convincingly impersonate her online, from passwords to biographical information. Then, on the day of her "flight," she would disappear somewhere and dispose of herself in a discreet manner, handing the reins of her life over to me. From then on I would assume her identity, answering e-mails, operating her Facebook page, and so forth, leaving her loved ones none the wiser that she was no longer alive. In this way, I would help to facilitate her wish: to kill herself without causing pain to her friends and family, to slip away from the world unnoticed.

"Naturally, your immediate concern will be whether she is of sound mind," said Adrian. "Well, I've known Tess for a while now, and I can assure you she knows exactly what she's doing. Is she a colorful character? Yes. Crazy? Absolutely not."

After that reassurance, my thoughts then turned to practical matters. As long as I had the relevant information to hand, I thought, the logistics of imitating this woman online seemed fairly straightforward: answering the odd e-mail, a few status updates a week. Adrian told me the woman was quite old, in her late thirties; hopefully that meant she wouldn't even write in text-speak.

Rather, my worries were about the premise and the conclusion of the operation. Was this "new life abroad" a plausible move for Tess in the first place? And, vitally, how long would the project last? After all, I couldn't impersonate this woman indefinitely.

Adrian reassured me on both counts. Tess was ideally suited to the project, he said, in both her situation and character. And my involvement would last for only six months or so, during which time I would gradually distance Tess from her correspondents, reducing contact until her absence was barely noticed. "Think of it as acting like a dimmer switch on her life," he said.

Of course, I didn't know then that it was the middle bit—those e-mails and status updates—where the problems lay. And that I would never really reach the end.

|||||||||||

Now that the decision had been made, I was eager to get started. I sat at my desk and waited for Tess to instigate contact, for what turned out to be a very long two and a half days.

I didn't know how she would approach me. Facebook or e-mail was most likely, I thought, but as I had given Adrian my mobile number, there was also the possibility she might call. I opened the necessary tabs on my laptop, laid my charged phone beside it, and tried to get on with other things. I finished off a testing report and surfed the Web aimlessly, following random links, but the virtual traffic that passed in front of me felt as distant and uninteresting as the sounds of cars thundering into Rotherhithe Tunnel outside the window.

Despite my attempts at normality, the waiting made me incredibly anxious, and I can admit now that by the end of the second day I became slightly irrational. The thought began to form that maybe it was all a trap, and that any moment the police would be hammering at my door.

I know now, of course—I knew then—that my reason had been decimated by the prolonged state of heightened tension. But once the idea entered my head, I stopped even surfing random sites and just sat at my desk focusing on nothing, listening to the sounds outside. Every time blue lights filled the window—which is common in Rotherhithe—my insides lurched. At one point, a group of children started to play football against the side of the restaurant, and each thud of the ball made me jump as if it were the first time I had heard it.

By the following morning, having slept for only a few fitful hours, I was feeling even more unsettled and frayed. I decided that I could bear it no longer and had just begun to compose a message to Adrian, resigning from the project, when I glanced down at the bottom of the screen and there it was: a [1] in my e-mail in-box.

I immediately snapped back into focus. The e-mail was from an account called smellthecoffeesweetheart@gmail.com. I assumed then that Tess had set up a new, anonymous account specifically for the project, but it turned out she had used the address for years. The phrase didn't have any specific meaning; it was just a quote from a film that was on in the background when she was setting up her Gmail account in 2005.

The subject line was blank, and so too was the body of the e-mail. There were four attachments—three documents and a JPEG.

First, I opened the photograph.

Naturally, I had formed an idea of Tess from the information Adrian had provided. Not that he had told me very much: She was thirty-eight, lived in Bethnal Green in East London, and was currently working in an art gallery. Because of what she wanted to do, I was expecting a middle-aged woman with dead eyes and a face drained by despair.

But the woman in the picture was not like that at all. For a start, she looked young. Or, rather, you didn't think about her age when you looked at her, because she was so attractive. She wasn't beautiful like Princess Buttercup, but she was . . . "sexy," I suppose.

The photo was almost full-length, and showed her standing in a kitchen. Although there was no one else in view, she appeared to be at a party: The counter she was leaning against was covered with an assortment of bottles and scattered wedges of lime, and an empty blue plastic bag that was still holding the shape of its former contents.

Tess was wearing what looked like a giant white T-shirt, except she was wearing it on its own as a dress, with a gold belt. It had slipped off one shoulder, and you could see a little bump along her collarbone, like a button, like girls have in magazines. She was very tanned—she was, I would discover, half Chilean, and even in winter her skin was the color of strong tea. Her bare legs were thin and unmuscled, like she'd hardly used them. Schoolgirl's legs, Mum would have called them, although mine were never like that, even when I was at school.

Her hair was almost black, thick and shoulder length with a fringe. Her eyes were dark brown and unusually far apart. She was looking at the camera, but her head was turned slightly so you could see her long, flat nose and distinct jawline. She was smiling, but it wasn't a normal photograph smile, rather as if she had just done something naughty and no one knew except her and the photographer.

Did I really think that at the time? Or am I saying that because I discovered later that she *had* just done something naughty? The occasion was her friend Tina's housewarming party in August 2007, and the photograph was taken a moment after she had come back from the lavatory, where she had taken cocaine with the man behind the camera, Danny.

And maybe she didn't strike me as "sexy" the first time I saw her, and I'm saying that because I know she was considered so by other people

I am trying my hardest to be objective and accurate about the chain of events and my perceptions of them, to not muddy them with all the knowledge I accumulated afterward, but it is difficult. Perhaps it's safest to just say that, at the time, my first impression of Tess was that she didn't look like someone who wanted to die.

After scrutinizing the photo, I downloaded the documents. I've still got them on my computer. The first was a letter titled "Read First." This is it verbatim:

*Hi, Leila,*

*Fuck me. I honestly cant put into words how I feel that you've agreed to help me. It's like you've agreed to save my life. I know that sounds crazy in the circumstances, but its true. Im sure Im going to thank you a million times throughout all of this, so Ill start now. THANK YOU!*

*I guess the frst thing is to work out how we're going to do this. Its all new to me—obviously—but I'm thinking maybe the best thing is for me to send u an initial load of information, everything i can think of right now, and then you can ask me questions and fill in the gaps about all the things ill doubtless overlook. Is that ok?*

*Do u have a rogh idea of how long ur going to need? Obviously u got to feel like ur totally ready, but just so u know, Im really keen for it all to happen ASAP. I dont know how much Adrian told u but I've waited for this for sooooo long. I mean, are you able to start immediately?*

*Another thing—adrian and me were thinking that it might be best if u and I dont actually meet in person, and just did all the preparations thru email. It miht keep things cleaner and make it easier if your less emotionally involved.*

*So im sitting here thinking—why r u doing this for me? Well, I know why, Adrian says youre a special person. I hope its ok for u. A warning: Im a complete fucking nutcase. Sorry.*

*Ok. So what I thought Id do first of all is send u this kind of autobiography thing that a shrink made me write once. Its a few years old so just imagine that things are worse now but itll give u a general picture. Then we can take it from there.*

*I cant believe that this is finally happening. I havent been this happy in fucking years. THANK YOU!!*

*Tess xxxx*

*Ps Its funny I saw my Mum yestrdy and she was being a cow as usual and I thought, why am I going to all this trouble to stop you being hurt? Why dont I just top myself like a normal person instead of this doing this elaborate sceme? But I just couldnt. I guess I dont hate her that much.*

The next document was her CV. It gave her full name and address and date of birth, and an extremely varied list of jobs with no discernible connections, from managing a band called Grievous Mary to her current occupation, working part-time as an invigilator in an art gallery in South London (I Googled the job and it seemed to involve little more than sitting on a chair). She had not had what you'd call a steady career path, to put it mildly.

Last, I opened the "autobiography" that she had written for a psychiatrist. I will run this one through the spell-check first; it's quite long and Tess's "unique" writing style can be wearing:

Okay, so—childhood. Nothing to see there. It was okay. I was a happy kid, nice big country pile, all right parents. I remember Mum being a bit uptight, not wanting us to hug her if she was dressed up or to touch her antiques in case we mucked them up, but she did what was required of her. She wasn't toxic then. I know this goes against everything you lot believe, but I don't think early childhood counts for so much. Adolescence, that's the formative time—when you realize your parents don't control the world and you start to see things as they really are, and they start to see you as you really are, not an extension of them. Or maybe I just had a defective gene that was dormant until I was a teenager. I don't know. Anyway, all I can say is that I felt I was a pretty normal, happy child. If anything, it was my brother, William, who was the troublesome one. He was three years older, and he used to bully this boy Sean, who lived on our street, making him eat wood lice, that sort of thing. Getting into fights, stealing money from Mum's purse to go on the slot machines in the Three Tuns. And look at him now, a master of the universe with his neat little wife and pheasant hunts.

So it was all progressing as normal and I don't know what happened exactly, or when, but I know that by fifteen I was a shadow of my former self. I know that's a cliché but I can't think of a better way of putting it. The first time I remember really feeling it was the evening of my friend Simone's birthday—everyone was going to this pub that would serve us and there was this boy going who fancied me; he was one of the cool lot at school. But instead of being there I was in my bedroom, door locked, lying in bed. I told my parents I had the flu, but really it was this profound sense of hopelessness. It's hard to explain. It was like I was unaware I had been walking around all that time with a noose around my neck, and then suddenly a trapdoor had opened under me and I was hanging.

And then, a few days later, my mood suddenly lifted. Like I had been given an adrenaline injection straight into my heart. I didn't just feel better; I felt absolutely brilliant. The world was mine for the taking. I thought of that boy—I can't remember his name now—and decided to jump on my bike and go around to his house without phoning or anything. His mum answered the door and said they were having dinner, and I insisted she get him, and when she did and he came to the door, looking all bemused, I didn't say anything but just snogged him, right there and then, in front of his mum. I was irresistible and brilliant and everyone responded to me and wanted to be near me. And then I'd feel the trapdoor start to open under my feet and I would crawl home, lock the world out of the room, and fall into the pit.

That was the pattern for a few years, on and off. I knew that teenagers were meant to be moody, so I presumed that's what it was, and my parents presumed so too, I think. But my brother hadn't gone through all of this. He slammed doors and grunted and was a little shit, but he could always be pulled out of his moodiness by a bribe or watching *The A-Team*.

When I was about seventeen, I started to know that something was really wrong with me, that this wasn't normal. I started to put myself into dodgy situations, staying out all night and shagging anyone who asked. Once I gave a blow job to my friend Kelly's father, when I was staying over at her house. I was brushing my teeth and he passed by the bathroom and paused to look at me, and I took him by the hand and led him in. Another time my friends and I were at the pub in Edgware, and at eleven they had to go home—we were meant to be revising for our A levels—and I phoned Dad and made some excuse about staying with one of them, but instead I got a cab into Soho and asked someone on the street where the best place to go was, and ended up in this underground club, drinking whatever was given to me and talking to these crazy old guys wearing fedoras and cravats. One of them started stroking my tits and we went in the corner of the club, which was dark but not that dark, if you know what I mean, and we shagged there, standing up. I stayed out until the tubes started running again at six a.m. and then went straight to school and slept on a bench for two hours until the bell rang.

I didn't give a fuck about schoolwork. I failed two of my A levels but managed to get an A in art, and got a place at Camberwell to do a foundation course, which, as you can imagine, was the perfect—and worst—place for me. At art school being crazy wasn't just tolerated; it was encouraged. On my first day there I shaved all my hair off in the middle of the cafeteria and everyone instantly knew my name. I put on this club night called Topless where, yes, you've guessed it, everyone had to go topless. God, I was such a twat. I sang in a crap band, and then managed an even crapper band, Godless Mary. Boys really liked me. I was the last to leave every party. During the manic periods—I knew when they were coming on because my cheeks would feel thick and tingly—I really threw myself into my work, was wildly productive, not leaving the studio for days, not sleeping, producing ten paintings in a night sometimes, listening to the whole of the Ring Cycle at full blast, chain-smoking so much that, by the morning, I could barely croak "Hello" when the cleaner came in.

Then, when things went dark, it was like my head had been filled with concrete. All I could do was sleep, and when I wasn't asleep, I'd lie in bed thinking the most terrible things, concocting violent fantasies of death for myself and people I knew who had slighted me in some way.

Sometimes, there'd be this crossover between the high and the low; I'd be manic and irritable at the same time. I'd phone people and yell at them, and, later, when the Internet started, write long e-mails to friends who I thought had let me down somehow, or to shops who had sold out of the teacups I'd seen in a magazine and desperately wanted.

The only thing that would ease things slightly would be a hot bath, so I'd have these baths that would last half a day, using up all the hot water for the house I was sharing and then getting out when the water cooled to boil more in kettles and saucepans.

My housemates got tired of me pretty quickly, and there were arguments and finally they asked me to leave. So I moved in with the boyfriend I was with at the time, Jonny, and within about a week we had a huge row about God knows what, and I threw all his stuff out the window and wrote *CUNT* across his car in nail varnish. Yes, I am a fucking cliché. I didn't remember it the next day—Jonny had to remind me.

Sometimes I would crave peace so strongly I would jump on a train and go to some shitty depressing seaside place and book into a B and B, the kind with porcelain cats and frilly loo seat covers, just to be myself, and then spend all night awake under the clammy nylon sheets and have to run out in the early hours of the morning because I didn't have any money to pay for it.

Fuck, I want to kill myself just writing all this down. That's a joke, ha, ha. Well, not really.

I thought about suicide all the time. I thought it was the answer—literally. I used to sit in my room and imagine I had this calculator and I would type in all these details of my life and then I would press the "equals" button and the word *SUICIDE* would appear in the panel, in those red LED letters. I tried once at college, storing up all the pills I could get my hands on, and then went into a hospital and locked myself in the staff toilet and took them, my thinking being that no one would be shocked by dead bodies there, and it would be easy to dispose of me. But of course, I didn't think that if they found me, they'd have all the equipment they needed to pump my stomach, and that's what happened. Logic has never been my strong suit.

After that my parents came and took me home and they were totally confused and upset by this creature they had created. Well, Dad was confused but as dopey and nice as ever, but Mum freaked out. Like she was disgusted. She could barely touch me; all she could talk about was how I needed a haircut, or some new fucking lapis lazuli supplier she had found in Thailand, or anything that wasn't about what I had just done. It wasn't that she was upset about it, couldn't bear it—she was angry. That's when I realized she was toxic. It was this sudden realization, and all my past came into focus. It was like, if I behaved myself and was pretty and nice and agreed with her, then everything was okay; it fit into her image. But now that I was ill it was as if I was damaged goods, and she kept saying that it wasn't her fault; I didn't get it from her side of the family, her perfect Chilean aristocratic family. I remember once she told me I was wasting my youth on being fucked up, that when she was my age she had been married twice and had two children. I told her that it wasn't my life's ambition to get married and knocked up at seventeen, leave the poor guy when he turned out to be less successful than I'd hoped, travel to London and find a nice, dopey rich guy to take me and my toddler son on, and spend the rest of my life dominating him and spending his money and flouncing around like some cut-price Frida Kahlo. With the mustache but without the talent. As you can imagine, that didn't go down very well.

I had counseling, which was fucking useless—no offense—and various combinations of drugs. The pills zombied me out, made me into this numb person who didn't really feel anything, sadness or happiness or anything. On pills I'm not a person; I'm, like, a log. There was a sort of novelty at first in having this "normal" life, going to the pub, watching TV, being able to sleep for eight hours like the rest of the world. But I missed the mania. It was fun, you know? And it was a big part of me. Without it, it was like I was an impoverished aristo living in a huge pile where most of the rooms were shut up and covered in dust sheets, while I was confined to a chilly parlor. I was just existing, not living.

Then the medication stopped being as effective, and I started to slide back, and then they tried other combinations and it went on for months, for years, trying these drugs, getting bad side effects or just missing the high and going off them, getting into trouble, having these amazing nights, these crushing lows. I'd get jobs, lose them, have boyfriends, fuck them up, move into places, have to move on. It was all so fucking repetitive.

Around then I realized something—that whatever anyone said to me, whatever pills I took, whatever therapy I had, the best it could do was mask the problem. Whatever this thing was in my head, it would be there forever. Therapy's bullshit; labels are bullshit. The other day you were saying something about "beating" manic depression, like it's a dragon to be slain or something, but I don't feel like that. It's this thing that is part of me, ingrained into my character, and I will have to live with it until I die. There's no way out. This is it. I read this quote once from this woman, which was "No hope of a cure, ever, for being me," and that's exactly how I feel.

Every day, when I wake up, I have to make the decision whether or not I can bear to live with that. The thing is, now I know the script. I know what happens to me. When I'm drugged I might feel on an even keel but I'm only half alive. I'm just existing. All my fire and creativity go. And then when I'm in a manic phase I'm too alive. But as I get older the manic phases are decreasing and the depressive ones are becoming more frequent.

I haven't got a career to speak of—nice middle-class girl, all that money on education, all those possibilities. I've squandered it entirely, as my mum would say.

If I'm not on pills, then I'm crazy and I hurt people and I want to die. And if I am on pills, then I lack my fire, and I don't feel things deeply; I'm just shuffling through life like everyone else, using up resources, eating food and shitting it out. They make me not think properly about things—I have the same opinions as the newspapers, take the line of least resistance. The other day in the pub my friends were having an argument about whether you should tip in restaurants even if the service is crap, and I couldn't be bothered to take a position. I used to be a waitress—it's a subject I should feel strongly about—but I just don't have the will and energy to engage anymore. I'm living a mundane life, just for the sake of it. And what's the point of that?

And when I look at the future, I can only see more of this same old shit, but with me older. When I look at my face in the mirror now, I can see the beginnings of major lines—you know, the ones old women have, like Mum would have if she hadn't had so much surgery—and the future is just there, laid out in front of me. I've probably got a few years left in me before my face starts to fall and I become middle-aged. Men's eyes have already started to slide over me. I imagine my face as the subject of a time-lapse film, those lines rapidly getting deeper, mouth turning down into a frown, gums receding, white hairs sprouting. And then finally crumbling into dust. No, how could I forget—before that, senility. All that life and experience and memories turned to mush, and ending up pulling down my trousers in the newsagent, like dad. I'm going to be buried alive by my body and I don't want it.

You asked me the other day about children. I'm not going to have them; I wouldn't trust myself with them. I can't look after myself; how could I have children?

And you know what? I've had my fun. For all the shittiness, for all the people I've hurt and time I've wasted, all the nights in stinking Soho clubs, the mistakes I've made, at least I've lived, which is more than you can say for lots of people. But now I know what it's like and I don't want to do it anymore. I don't see it as a sad thing, particularly. I just don't see the point in repeating the same things over and over again, becoming more and more invisible, going to sleep and waking up, always doubting my own instincts, feeling either half-alive or out of control. I just don't want to do it anymore.

It finished there. After a moment, I opened a new document on my computer. I had noticed an inconsistency in her account. In the CV she had called the band she managed Grievous Mary, while in the autobiography it was Godless Mary. I made a note to ascertain from her which name was correct. Then I e-mailed back to acknowledge receipt of the documents and tell her we could proceed.

*Two things happened* this afternoon: a couple who seem relatively sane said they might remember Tess, and I got online.

My day got off to a better start. To avoid repetition of the unpleasant awakening the morning before, I had gone to sleep with the tent flaps open, lying on my back with my head positioned half outside and my eye mask around my neck. When the brightness of the sun woke me I slithered out of the tent and repositioned my mattress under the shade of the tree, whereupon I put on my eye mask and immediately went back to sleep. It was a minimal disruption, and I awoke again at two p.m. feeling quite rested.

After three biscuits and a quick wash with my wet wipes I took Tess's photo and did a round of the site. Some new arrivals were setting up camp near the main clearing. It wasn't immediately clear which of the couple was the male and which the female; both had long, limp dark hair and were skinny, the girl with not much in the bust department. The man had big black plugs in his earlobes, the size of a one-euro coin.

I asked them whether they had been here the previous summer. They said yes, so I showed them the photo. They consulted each other in a foreign language, and finally the man said that they did remember an Englishwoman on her own who looked similar, but her hair was longer and they were pretty sure that her name wasn't Tess. Something longer, beginning with "S."

Of course, I had anticipated that Tess might have used a different name when she was out here. I asked them to remember any more details of her clothes or what she had said. They couldn't, but said they would tell me if anything came back to them. I won't get too excited, though. More evidence is needed.

Afterward, I went back to my mattress under the tree, and had just dozed off when I felt a little tug on my hand. It was Milo. He said, "Annie says, do you want to come with us?" Over at the van, Annie had slid the back door shut and was in the driver's seat. She said she was going into the main town to go to the bank, and thought I might like to come along and get some food.

"A woman can't live on biscuits alone," she said.

"Will there be an Internet café there?" I asked.

"Should think so," she said. "It's a big tourist dump by the sea."

I sat in the front with Milo; the baby was in the back. I'd been in a van before, when we moved Mum's furniture to the storage center, but this was different. For a start it was ancient and the air inside was hot and unsavory, like plastic, milk, and old socks baking in an oven. The floor was thick with books, leaflets, and CDs, and the windows were plastered with tatty, bright stickers. There was a strange, furry thing dangling from the mirror, and when Milo saw me inspecting it he told me it was the foot of his pet rabbit.

"It was a natural death," said Annie as she wrenched the steering wheel with what seemed like a huge amount of effort. The van made worrying noises from deep inside, like the sound of Mum clearing her throat in the morning.

As we began crawling down the bumpy path, Annie said, "So, what's the deal with this friend you're looking for?"

I had already given Annie the story once, of course, when I had shown her Tess's photo on the first day, but started reciting again how I was looking for an old friend who I believed was still in the area. She cut me off.

"No, I know that you're looking for her. But why?" She glanced over at me with a sly little smile. "Do you love her?"

When I didn't answer, she said, "It's okay if you do, you know."

I thought it best not to dignify her question with a response, so I said nothing and looked out the window. It worked, and she changed the subject, offering up information about herself. Although I wasn't particularly interested, when I realized I didn't have to say anything back I relaxed a bit, and there was something quite soothing about looking at the scenery and hearing the lilt of her voice as we drove along.

Her American accent reminded me of Adrian, and when I closed my eyes I was taken back to his podcasts, although, of course, what Annie was saying was not nearly as interesting. She talked about her life back in Connecticut, where she had a small business making handmade wooden furniture and shared a house with another single mother, and about Milo's father. She had "given him the heave-ho" when Milo was two, but he saw his son sporadically.

"Bet you're wondering about the little one, huh?" she said, gesturing to the baby strapped to a seat in the back, although I hadn't been. She said that she had wanted another baby but didn't want the hassle of a man, so she'd had a "well-timed screw" with a stranger. She confided that she sometimes worried about whether the children would be damaged by not having a father figure in their lives.

"I don't think fathers are that important," I said.

"Oh, really?" she said.

I told her that I had never known my father, that he had disappeared when my Mum was still pregnant, and it hadn't done me any harm at all.

Annie made a "hmm" noise, and then said, "Did your mum mind not having a partner?"

"Not at all," I said. "We had each other. She always said she didn't need anything else as long as she had me."

Annie asked me about my father, and I told her what I knew: that he used to work in Ireland selling cars, that his dream was to own a racehorse, and that he had elegant hands, like mine.

As we drove, I noticed the landscape changing. Now that we were out of the hilly area and onto level ground, the trees had been replaced by large low-level tents made out of tatty white plastic, one following on from another so that they seemed to form one never-ending structure. I asked Annie what they were, and she said they were greenhouses, growing salad for supermarkets.

"It's where your tomatoes come from," she said. I could have told her that I didn't eat tomatoes, but I didn't.

When Annie stopped the van for Milo to have a pee, I got a closer look at the greenhouses. The plastic was opaque but you could see shadows inside, and in places the sheets were torn or had come away from the structure so you could glimpse behind. I saw endless rows of leaves and shapes of black men, stooped amid the greenery. It must have been unbearably hot in there. What was especially noticeable was the silence. The manual labor sites I've passed before are always quite noisy, but there I could hear no sounds of voices or music, just the soft hiss of the water sprinklers. Annie had told me that there was a drought in the area—the river near the commune had almost dried up—so it seemed odd that these greenhouses were using up so much water. Immoral, almost.

Back in the van, Annie explained that the workers were African, mostly illegal immigrants. The coast on this part of Spain was almost the nearest part of Europe to Africa, she said, and the immigrants would get on boats and cross over secretly at night in search of a better life. Some would venture farther into Europe, but most stayed here, working in the greenhouses, because they had no papers.

After an hour and fifteen minutes we reached the town. Annie parked crookedly by the road and said we should meet back there in an hour, and then she took the children off with her to the bank. I walked in what felt like the direction of the town center. It was a sprawling, dusty place, with low-level buildings, and seemed oddly quiet and deserted. I found a sign with a picture of waves on it, which I took to be the sea, and followed it. Toward the beach the buildings grew in height, which seemed wrong to me, like tall people standing at the front of a crowd and blocking the view for everyone behind.

The streets were busy nearer the seafront, full of holidaymakers. They couldn't have looked more different from the people in the commune. Their clothes were normal, shorts and vests, and they were either very white, very pink, or overly tanned, but not in a way that made them look more attractive. People were sitting on tables outside cafés drinking beer, although it was only four thirty p.m. Shops sold cheap plastic beach equipment and blared out pop music. One, oddly enough, was full of toasters and microwaves. All the signs on the shops and restaurants were in English, and the rows of newspapers outside the shops were in English too.

I don't know whether I was just relieved to be out of the commune, but I found it all quite pleasant. There was a breeze coming in from the sea, carrying on it a comforting blend of smells—chips, suntan lotion—and everyone looked familiar, like the people in Tesco Extra, only happier and more relaxed.

After a few minutes wandering around, I found an Internet café. I paid two euros and logged on. At the terminal next to mine, a hugely fat woman with a breathing problem was looking at pictures of lawn mowers on eBay. First I went to Facebook, but when I put in my details I found that I had forgotten my password; it had been supplanted in my head by Tess's. It took three tries to remember that it was Mum's second-favorite TV program, *inspectormorse*.

Once I was in, the scroll of status updates on my page had so little meaning to me they might as well have been in Russian. Even the faces and the names of my "friends" seemed unfamiliar; even when I used to see them in person at school I didn't really know them, and now they might as well have been total strangers. Tash, Emma, Karen—random names affixed to random silly young girls, all liking this, linking to that, getting excited about something or other.

I logged out and checked my e-mail. Fourteen messages, but they were all spam.

After that, I just sat there, staring at the Google toolbar on the screen. I had spent days thinking about getting online, but now that I was, I couldn't think what to do. I could hardly start a game of Warcraft; even if I remembered my log-in details after all this time, I had only forty-eight minutes before I had to meet Annie back at the van, barely enough time to get my avatar into his armor. I had a fanciful image of him being uncooperative and bolshy, hurt after all my months of neglect, refusing to put his arms into his chain-mail vest, letting the sword fall from his fingers when I placed it there.

I logged off, with seventeen minutes still remaining on my time. Next to the Internet place was a small supermarket, and I went in. Inside it was freezing cold, and goose bumps sprang up on my arms. It was a bit like a Londis, except half of the shop was taken up with alcohol. I was worried all the products would be Spanish, or strange foreign food, but most were English, things I recognized, like Heinz tomato ketchup and Walkers Crisps. I bought three family-sized bags of crisps and two packets of Hobnobs.

After the shopping I still had almost half an hour to go before meeting Annie, so on impulse I decided to have a waffle in a café, attracted by the large color photographs of the food displayed outside. The waitress spoke English. On the table next to me was an old man in a wheelchair, being fed what looked like a sausage sandwich by a woman of his age. It made me wonder whether Mum and I should have made more of an effort to have a holiday in the final years. The subject had come up, but we decided that it would have been too complicated, traveling with all the equipment and all the lifting. Seeing this couple beside me, however, made me think that it could have been possible. We wouldn't have been able to go anywhere hot like Spain, because MS had made Mum intolerant of heat, but perhaps we could have tried Cornwall. There was a series she liked that was filmed in a village there, and she had always wanted to visit it.

At five thirty p.m. I met Annie at the van and we drove back. Arriving at the commune car park, I heard music coming from a van I didn't recognize: new arrivals. I asked Annie to let me out and went over to them. The door was open, and a group of young men were lounging around inside, a mass of brown, hairy legs. They were foreign—Italian, I believe—and, although they had what I think of as the "commune look"—messy hair and bare chests and wooden bead necklaces—they didn't yet have the moldy appearance that the others here have. I gave them my Tess story and showed her picture. They gathered around to peer at it. One of them then said, "Ah, yes, Luigi remembers her; don't you, Luigi?" and then did a sort of sideways kick aimed at his friend next to him on the settee. They all started laughing, and one of them said something in Italian I didn't understand and swiveled his hands in what I suspect was a rude gesture. I had to question them further, quite sternly, to ascertain that no, they did not know Tess, but were simply having a joke.

I noticed that they were drinking wine from a bottle, and so, as I left, I informed them that the commune was alcohol-free.

I spent the rest of the evening under the tree, then had some food and a wash with my wet wipes. Now it's nine forty-six p.m. and I'm back in the tent. Outside, the sound of drumming has stopped, and the insects have taken over.

|||||||||||

Once I embarked on Project Tess, it didn't take me long to realize that, if we were ever going to get the job done, I would have to take matters into my own hands. Over the next few days, she forwarded to me seemingly random e-mail exchanges, photographs, and diary entries, with no supporting information or context attached. It was like someone packing for a holiday by sticking her hand in her wardrobe, pulling out the first thing her fingers touched, and flinging it into a suitcase. There was no system to it at all.

Just one example: Early on, she sent me a photo of herself and another woman labeled *Me and Debbie*. But there was no context— when the photograph was taken, who "Debbie" was, the history of their relationship—without which the photo was near to useless. And when she did explain things, they often didn't make sense. For instance, on questioning, Tess revealed that she and this Debbie had been close friends for a while until, out walking one day, Debbie had neglected to stop and stroke a cat they passed on the street. Tess seemed to think that this was a sufficient cause to terminate an otherwise good friendship. As I say, one's natural presumption is that people do things for a reason, that there's consideration and meaning behind their actions, but with Tess, more often than not there wasn't.

Furthermore, the information she provided was riddled with inconsistencies. The Grievous/Godless Mary question was only the start of it. (It turned out to be Godless.) She seemed hazy on details, as if they didn't matter. *Oh, sometime in the summer,* she'd say; *Jim Something*. Part of it was her "flaky" personality; part, I suspected, her condition. I had done some research into bipolar disorder, and depleted memory was a common symptom. It was exacerbated by drugs, in Tess's case lithium. *Energy is profoundly dissipated; the ability to think is clearly eroded,* I read. I resolved to contain my irritation and take control of the situation.

I made up a spreadsheet of what I would need from her, and in what order. The first request was for basic practical information: full names, addresses, phone numbers, and dates of birth of herself and her family, plus bank account details and other things of that sort.

A fairly simple request, you'll agree. But even this she seemed to find difficult. For instance, she claimed to not understand the need for her National Insurance number—*My brother's hardly going to ask for it, is he?*—and then, when I pressed her, she said that she didn't know it and didn't know where to find the information. To speed things up I told her to phone the tax office. When a day had passed and she hadn't done it, I phoned them up, pretending to be her, and got it myself.

I also asked her for the passwords to her e-mail—she had two, the smellthecoffeesweetheart Gmail one, which was her primary account, and an old Hotmail address—and her Facebook account. Thank goodness she wasn't on Twitter; after a few weeks of enthusiasm in July 2010, she had lost interest. Of course, I would need these passwords when I started the task properly, but for now my plan was to comb through her accounts and glean information.

My first step was Facebook, for an overview of her life. To all appearances, her page looked perfectly normal. Her profile picture showed her in a gallery—the Louvre in Paris, I later learned—affecting the same pose as the statue she was standing next to, one hand on her forehead as if in a dramatic swoon. She had 367 friends, which, looking at her friends' profiles, seemed about average for her generation. She subscribed to a long list of groups, and the random nature of the subjects—showing solidarity with Tibetan monks, saving an old music hall in East London, campaigning for Pizza Express to reinstate their original tomato sauce recipe, supporting obscure bands, books, restaurants, and ventures, as well as a myriad of whimsical "causes" such as Stop Aisling Wearing That Yellow Parka! and I Like the Way Huw Edwards Pronounces the Word *Liverpool*—made me suspect she was rather nondiscriminatory in the things to which she pledged allegiance.

She was tagged in 140 photos, far fewer than most people my age, but seemingly average for hers. Tess and her friends didn't pose nearly as much, either. The majority of shots depicted "spontane-ous" moments at parties and picnics and pubs, and even in the posed scenes, the subjects tended to be smiling at the camera in a natural way, or pulling silly faces, rather than tilting their heads and sucking in their cheeks like the girls from my school. The other big differ-ence was the children; Tess's friends' albums were filled with end-less, near-identical images of themselves, their partners, and their friends in the company of small children, and several of them even had photos of babies as their profile shots.

Although Tess had no special fondness for children herself—*ankle biters* and *little squits* were some of the ways she referred to them during our conversations—she had not escaped this seemingly compulsory interaction with them: I counted twenty-eight photos of her holding friends' babies. The child who featured most regularly, from a newborn baby to a five-year-old, was Tess's godson, Mowgli, who belonged to one of her best friends, Justine.

Some of Tess's own pictures were nonpeopled shots, like close-ups of grass and sunsets, a pair of hands, drops of water on a bath-room sink—proof of her "artistic nature." More interestingly, there were also some grainy pictures posted from long ago, in the pre-digital era, which must have been scanned in. One showed Tess as a young woman, somewhere around my age—"early twenties, prob-ably" was all she could give me when I pressed her on a date. The scene it depicted was a jolly one: Tess and two girlfriends in some front room, giggling as they got ready to go out. It took a moment to identify Tess; all three looked very similar, with frizzy hair and flat stomachs, each wearing trainers, a little top like a sports bra, and tight, brightly colored leggings or shorts. I presumed that they were preparing for some team exercise, but when I asked her about it later, Tess, laughing, said, "Ah, sweet!" and told me that they were actually off to a "rave."

She said this when we were talking on Skype. Tess was in a good mood that evening, and the mention of this "rave" seemed to evoke happy memories. She started doing some odd movements with her hands, making the shapes of squares in the air, while saying, "Big box, little box, big box, little box." At least two minutes were wasted in this activity, and when I asked her to explain her strange actions she said, "Ah, never mind."

Another of these old pictures was easier to place, even with the little knowledge I had then: a close-up of Tess with very short hair, not longer than a centimeter. This must have been shortly after the head-shaving incident at art school mentioned in her autobiography. Even then, though, she looked good; the sharp contours of her face and her dark, wide-apart eyes were able to carry the odd style, and she was smiling up at the camera confidently. You would never have guessed from the picture—from any of the photos on Facebook— that she was anything other than happy.

After that initial look at Facebook, I tried to proceed in a systematic way. First, I asked her for a list of her immediate family and most important friends. Then I made up a spreadsheet and listed the relations—her mother, Marion; her father, Jonathan; and half brother, William. William was the product of Marion's first marriage to another Englishman whom she had left when William was young, and married Jonathan, who was fourteen years her senior. Tess was born the following year. William—he was never "Will"—was married to a woman called Isobel and had two children, six-year-old Poppy and five-year-old Luke.

Under columns titled *age, occupation, home life, personality traits*, etc., I first noted what I knew of them from the information Tess had provided. Then I did a search through Tess's e-mails for each person, bringing up their messages and Tess's responses, and added what I gleaned from them to columns titled *additional information, e-mail frequency, writing style*, and so on. Tess had had her Gmail account for six years and her Hotmail for even longer, so there was a lot to wade through. I then moved on to her three closest friends, Simon, Justine, and Shona.

For each person, I asked Tess to send me at least one, preferably two, photographs. Of course, most of the significant people were on Facebook, where I could find reams of photographs, but some were not, including her parents. Besides, I reasoned that the pictures posted on Facebook were often carefully selected to show the subjects at their best, whereas those taken casually were more likely to be truthful and reveal something of their character. As well as storing these on my computer, I printed one photo for each significant person and stuck the pictures above my desk, labeled with their name and basic details. The space above my desk started to resemble a board for a murder inquiry in a police detective series.

Tess sent me a group shot of her family. It was taken at William and Isobel's holiday home in the South of France, on the occasion of Jonathan's seventieth birthday; even Tess could remember that. The family had gone out for the weekend, along with Jonathan's best friend, a man Tess called Uncle Frank, although he was not a real uncle. "He used to be a top rozzer; then he got done for taking backhanders" was how she described him, which I eventually ascertained to mean that he was a former police chief inspector who had been forced into early retirement after questions arose about his integrity.

The photo showed them all—except Tess, who was behind the camera—seated around a table outside, at the end of a meal. Marion, her mother, was in the middle of the group. She looked quite similar to Tess, with the same dark hair and skin, but even sitting down you could tell that she was shorter—five feet, three inches, compared with Tess's five-seven—and skinnier. Tess told me she was anorexic. She had on a white shirt with the collar turned up and open to reveal a necklace made of giant green stones, under which you could still see her chest bones jutting out like a grille. Tess told me that Marion saw her jewelry as her "signature style," whatever that means, and, after being frequently complimented on it by friends, had started a small business importing it from Chile and selling it online. Her hair was in a high bun, like a bread roll on top of her head, and her lips were bright red. Everyone had their glasses raised to the camera, but whereas the others were half-empty, Marion's glass was full, and her smile seemed tight and unnatural.

Beside her was Jonathan. This was shortly before his dementia had been diagnosed. Tess told me that on the trip he had forgotten where the bathroom was, despite having been to the house many times before, and had struggled to find the word for cheese, but they all presumed it was just the usual softening of old age. His hair was as white as Gandalf's, short and neat across his head, and he was grinning broadly, his cheeks pink and shiny. He reminded me somewhat of Richard Briers, whom my mum always said she'd like to be married to.

Next to Marion was William, who was dark like Marion and Tess but had a more ordinary face, doughy and unsculpted. He wore a pair of thin frameless glasses and, like Marion, gave a controlled smile. Next to him, his wife, Isobel, had shoulder-length blond hair and a face so regular and unmemorable it could have been computer generated. Luke, who was similarly fair, was on her lap, with the slightly darker-haired Poppy in the next chair. Both were very pretty and clean, like children on TV. Isobel's Facebook pictures showed the family engaged in a variety of activities: in one they were on a boat; in another, walking through the snow with their big yellow dog, the children wearing matching red all-in-one outfits.

Tess didn't get on with Isobel. She described her sister-in-law as an "uptight WASP bitch"—the acronym, I learned, means White Anglo-Saxon Protestant, but can be applied in a derogatory way— who had a limit of two glasses of wine a week and made her children wear safety helmets when they played in the communal gardens of their Holland Park house. Since marrying William, Isobel had given up her job and assumed control of renting out their properties. When Tess had asked to use the France house for her thirty-fifth birthday party, Isobel had made a big deal out of giving her "family rates," which turned out to be only ten percent off the regular price. She pretended to be jealous of Tess's "wild life": "I wish I had the time and energy," she'd say.

Tess was particularly annoyed that William and Isobel had recently gotten into collecting contemporary art, favoring what Tess described as "bogus conceptual crap"—the opposite of the kind of paintings Tess did and therefore, she thought, a snub. Isobel would pretend to be interested in Tess's opinion on current artists: "Whom do you rate at the moment, Tess?" Tess would reply, "Dürer," or "Otto Dix," who are, apparently, old artists, and not what Isobel meant.

Relations were also strained with William, Tess informed me, and a read-through of their e-mail exchanges confirmed this. When corresponding with him, Tess dispensed with her customary kisses, while he signed off his messages to her with Best Wishes. In one exchange Tess complained to him about their mother and he defended Marion, saying She has always done her utmost for her children. Tess replied with an angry diatribe about how he was always Marion's favorite, the golden boy, and he couldn't possibly understand, and how the fact that Marion professed to be so bohemian and unconventional yet reveled in William's success in the city revealed just what a "phony" she was. William hadn't replied to that—or if he had, Tess had deleted it. She claimed she couldn't remember.

Tess only ever really saw her brother and sister-in-law on family occasions, and there was no record of any "chatty" online relationship, so I didn't see them as a big challenge for my future work. But I was worried about Marion. However badly she and Tess got on, it seemed highly unlikely, if not impossible, that she would not want to speak to Tess on the phone at some point. I mean, on the rare occasions I used to go out when Mum was alive, she would call me several times an hour.

When I had raised my concerns during our meeting, Adrian had assured me that she, Marion, relied on e-mail more than the phone to keep in touch, because she was quite deaf.

Tess was equally dismissive of my worries.

Oh, she'll just be pleased I'm out of the way, she wrote. We hardly speak anyway.

This seemed odd to me, but as I combed through the e-mails between Tess and Marion I could see that it was indeed an unusual, difficult relationship. There were lots of them in sporadic bursts, and most were short and factual—what each of them was up to, how Jonathan was. But Tess's accounts of her life were often far from the truth. She would often tell her mother that everything was fine and she was in what she called a "good place," but an e-mail sent to a friend on the same day would paint a very different picture, describing an afternoon spent crying in the bath until the water got cold and her legs cramped, or going out to a bar by herself and getting drunk and blacking out until she came to on a sofa in the flat of a man she had never met before.

Every six months or so there would be a long, heated, and bitter exchange between them in which Tess would be scathing, telling Marion what a bad parent she was (I've internalized your craziness; you make me feel like I have no right to exist), how she was just a trophy wife, and, more recently, accusing her of resenting Jonathan for getting Alzheimer's and leaving her to care for him. There were also references I didn't understand: spiteful tones at dinner, ruined Christmases, and the like. When you came to get me from the flat that time after the hospital, I didn't want you to, because I knew you'd use it against me FOREVER as proof of what a great mother you are, Tess wrote.

Jonathan was less of a concern. There were only thirty-two e-mails between Tess and her father, spread over seven years, all affectionate but formal, mostly concerning money: He had given her several loans over the years, which, as far as I could tell, had not been paid back. Tess told me that they didn't chat over e-mail very much before he got Alzheimer's, and now he couldn't. Don't worry, she wrote, in a few months he won't even remember he's got a daughter.

I started a series of time-line charts to plot events in Tess's life. One was for major events, which I defined as the things her parents would be aware of: job changes, flat moves, her grandfather's death, her brother's wedding and the births of his children. Another was for those things it was likely her family did not know about: random encounters with men, arguments with friends, drug taking, and so forth. For each event I had a column listing the people who, as far as I was aware, knew about it, what exactly they knew, and what their thoughts on it were, as far as I could gather.

There was so much information to deal with that I found that just recording things on my laptop wasn't enough. Ideally I'd have an extra screen to work from, but I couldn't afford to buy one, so I ended up hand-writing a chart on a big piece of paper with linking arrows, which I pinned up on my wall next to the photos.

As you can imagine, all this took a lot of time. Tess's life had been chaotic, and, as quickly became clear, she told different versions of events to different people. Add to that the fact that she was vague on names and locations, and you will appreciate the difficulty.

There were many things that didn't make sense or add up. Some were fairly major facts—in one month, for instance, she claimed to two different people to live in both Shoreditch and Bethnal Green, although there was no record of her moving. There were minor references that could be solved by Google—Farrow and Ball, the Groucho Club, that house Virginia Woolf lived in—but others that could not. For instance, in one e-mail she described a woman as having National Theatre hair; in another, she told her friend Simon how much she liked the way boys take their jumpers off.

In other cases the facts themselves were clear, but I couldn't understand her reaction to them. For instance, an exchange on August 17, 2005, between Tess and a friend called Zanthi. They were having an argument because Zanthi had apparently been staying at Tess's flat for a weekend and had thrown away some dead flowers that Tess had been saving because of their beauty. Tess seemed to think that Zanthi's not realizing this was indicative of a lack of under-standing of Tess's character and what she called the poetry of life, and declared that Zanthi could no longer be her friend. Odd behavior in itself, but then, two weeks later, the two were e-mailing merrily as if nothing had ever happened.

When I asked Tess about these things, more often than not she couldn't remember the details, or even that they took place at all. I told you, she wrote. My brain is fucked. Once, she elaborated: I'll tell you what it's like. You know those grabby mechanical hands in amusement arcades, which you use to try and pick up some shitty teddy bear? It's like me feebly trying to latch on to a memory or an idea. And if I do manage to grab it, it's just cheap tat.

Furthermore, there were lots of blank periods to fill in, the times when she wasn't communicating with anyone at all, when—as I know now—she was seriously depressed and couldn't even summon the energy to wipe the hair off her face, let alone write an e-mail.

Alongside all this, I was making a note of the nonpersonal e-mails Tess received. There were receipts for theater and cinema tickets and Amazon purchases, all of which I cataloged in a file about her tastes. She did a lot of online shopping, and the things she bought tended to be either bafflingly expensive—a single pair of knickers that cost two hundred thirty pounds—or cheap, like a twenty-pence "vintage coaster" from eBay. There were days when she spent vast amounts of money, thousands of pounds, on things it didn't seem like she could possibly need, or in bewildering bulk. One receipt, I remember, was for twenty white tea towels, each costing twelve pounds.

With each of these, I recorded the date and details of the transaction in a separate spreadsheet. How could she afford a hundred-twenty-pound pot of moisturizer when she was working as an artist's model, earning sixty pounds a week? I would then cross-reference her online bank statements to see whether she had taken out a loan or gone overdrawn.

My initial trawl through her in-box left me with a lengthy list of questions to ask Tess. The large holes in her autobiography took first priority. Her replies were more often than not unsatisfactory. I would ask a perfectly simple question, such as what TV shows she watched when she was thirteen, and she either wouldn't reply for days, or she'd get angry and say she couldn't remember or name a program that, when I checked, turned out to have been first transmitted when she was fifteen.

I tried hard to remain professional in our e-mails, but sometimes firmness was required. I would remind her of the seriousness of the undertaking and my requirements for the job. In reply, she'd write, Oh, God, don't have a go at me; I can't fucking remember! Or, if she was in a sadder, more reflective mood she'd apologize repeatedly, saying what a terrible person she was and that she didn't deserve my help.

After a few weeks, I became quite frustrated. I was still doing my testing work, but increasingly I found myself sidelining the reports and instead just waiting for her e-mails. Tess kept going on about how quickly she wanted it all to be done, how desperate she was to "check out"—that was the phrase we used. But it had become apparent that if we kept going at this current rate, with her taking days to respond to an e-mail and then not even answering my questions properly, it would be months before we were anywhere near ready.

So, I had an idea. We had agreed not to meet in person, but there seemed to be no reason we couldn't talk. It would speed things up considerably, and, if we used Skype, it wouldn't cost anything. I considered asking Adrian first, but decided the matter wasn't worth bothering him about. However, I recalled how, on the Heath, he had stressed the importance of "limited emotional engagement" between Tess and myself, and so decided it would be best if we left the cameras off when we spoke.

I messaged Tess to suggest this, and she agreed. We arranged a time for me to call, at eleven p.m. one evening.

I composed a list of questions that had arisen so far:

1. In an e-mail dated 12/27/08, William wrote, "Thank you for ruining lunch." What did you do to ruin lunch? And why is he thanking you?

2. Did you ever meet up with "Pete the Provider" on Valentine's Day 2006 in Wenceslas Square, as promised in an e-mail sent 10/02/05?

3. Was the nickname "Sugartits" widely used, or just by Steven Gateman?

4. What is your father's prognosis for Alzheimer's?

5. In one e-mail regarding a date with a man called Jamie in May 2009, you wrote, "He was intellectually beneath me."

Yet you only got one A level yourself, in art. What kind of qualifications did he get?

6. There are no e-mails or trace of you between February and April 2008. Where were you, and what were you doing during that time?

7. At various points you claim that "You're Nobody till Someone Loves You" by Dinah Washington, "Natural Woman" by Aretha Franklin, and "I Want You Back" by the Jackson 5 are all your "favorite song ever." Which one is it?

8. In an e-mail to Shona regarding a dinner party you attended the night before, you write that you hated your host for claiming she liked "to cook to relax." This seems like an inoffensive statement to me. Can you explain?

9. In an e-mail to your mother dated 06/03/07 you say she was a terrible mother when you were a child, yet in your psychologist "autobiography" you say you had a relatively normal, happy childhood. Which was it?

10. You registered once at the site adultfriendfinder.com in February 2005. What was the nature and frequency of your usage of the site?

11. On 05/16/08, you wrote to Mira Stollbach that you "couldn't wait" to attend her wedding that summer, but then in an e-mail to Justine on June second of that same year, you wrote that you "hate fucking weddings." Can you explain?

12. In that same exchange with Justine, in reply to her wondering whether she should stay with the man she was going out with despite finding him unsatisfactory in several areas, you advise her not to "settle." Justine replies, "That's easy for you to say." Why is that?

13. Your sign-offs are inconsistent, even in correspondence

with the same person. Sometimes you will end with one "kiss," sometimes two, sometimes many, and sometimes none. What are the rules governing your sign-offs? Do they change according to the level of affection you feel for that person at that particular moment?

14. In an e-mail to jo@samaritans.org on 09/17/10 you wrote that you didn't think you were going to make it through the night. Did you attempt suicide that evening?

I was oddly nervous before speaking to Tess for the first time. You have to understand that by that point I had spent three weeks completely immersed in her life, reading her e-mails, examining photographs of her and her friends, trying to catalog the chaos of her past. Looking back, even at that early stage I probably knew more about her than anyone else alive, because she gave such different accounts of herself to different people. But because everything had been done electronically, it was almost like she wasn't a real person.

I decided it would be best if I recorded our conversation and transcribed it afterward, rather than try to note down information as Tess spoke. That way I could give her my full attention; I've never been good at doing two things at the same time. I read once that it was illegal to record someone without their knowledge, but decided not to inform Tess that I was taping our conversation, in case she made an irrational fuss and further held things up.

It was eleven p.m. on a Tuesday. I had my list of questions ready. Tess's laptop rang eight times before she answered, and her "Hello?" was wary. When I introduced myself, she sounded surprised, even though the call had been scheduled. Then she laughed and said, "Oh, fuck, sorry. I was expecting you to be Sylvie."

I hadn't heard mention of Sylvie before, so immediately, before we'd even begun, I had to deviate off my planned list of questions and ask her about this new character. As we spoke, I searched Tess's Facebook friends and found Sylvie: She had a long, sad face and thick dark red hair that, when pulled over one shoulder, looked like a fox's tail.

I didn't think I had any preconceptions about what Tess would sound like. But I suppose I must have, because I remember being surprised by her tone of voice. It was deep and clear and quite posh, not at all anguished.

After she had told me something about Sylvie—a teacher who hated her job, was married to an Italian man twenty years older than herself, and was contemplating an affair with someone at work—I started on my list of questions. I was pleased to find that my Skype suggestion was vindicated. It was far more efficient than e-mail. When Tess went off on tangents, I could direct her back onto the topic.

That first session lasted twenty minutes before Tess became tired and lost focus. We arranged to Skype again the next evening at the same time, and she was more vocal that night. Too vocal, in fact: She went off on tangents all the time, hardly editing her thoughts. I asked her about her job at Threads, a vintage clothes shop in Bethnal Green that she managed for four months, and she segued into a long account of a festival she went to where everyone dressed up in vintage clothes and slid down a helter-skelter, which led to a story about how her mother had saved lots of her designer clothes from when she was younger, but had been very disappointed when Tess couldn't fit into them: "You've inherited your father's shoulders."

The third occasion we spoke, she was in an upset state. She had been to the matinee of a play that afternoon and a woman sitting in the row in front had been rude to her. She couldn't stop talking about it. Ranting, I'd say. When she was in a certain mood these sorts of small things bothered her greatly; even when I thought I'd steered her off the subject she'd return to it repeatedly. Any perceived act of thoughtlessness or rudeness would do it (although, ironically, Tess could be very thoughtless and rude herself). For instance, she hated it when people walked past her on the tube platform to get a good spot next to where the doors would open. "I hate the sound of their clackety heels as they look after number one," she said. She got offended if, when she was waiting at a pedestrian crossing, other people would join her and press the button—did they not think she would have pressed it? That she was stupid?

Transcribing the tapes afterward, I was listening to one of these tiresome deviations when she mentioned some detail that I hadn't known: Jonathan had once lived in Singapore. It occurred to me then that actually, even though these ramblings of hers were not directly answering my questions, and my natural tendency was to filter out everything she said except the facts, they might be quite useful—not only in the accidental details they might provide, but because they revealed something of her character.

In other words, I realized that the digressions might be as important to note as the actual facts I was gathering. If I was going to "be" Tess, I needed to record all aspects of her character.

In our next session, Tess's mood changed yet again. This time she was reflective and, for the first time, asked me questions about myself. She asked me how old I was, where I lived, and why I was doing this for her. I wasn't very comfortable talking about myself, conscious that every minute we spent on me would mean less time for her to answer questions. But I replied, telling her that I was doing it because I believed in self-ownership and her right to control her own death. She asked me what I thought about Adrian and I replied that he was a great man, and that Red Pill had opened up my mind to new ways of thinking. To that, she said something that surprised me.

"Yes," she said, "I really must look at it one day."

I had presumed, you see, that she knew Adrian from the site. Of course, in retrospect, I can see she would not have lasted a minute on Red Pill, with her fuzzy, illogical thinking, but it hadn't occurred to me that she had met him elsewhere, in a different context.

"So how do you know Adrian, if not from the site?" I asked.

Her answer was typically vague: "Oh, I can't remember exactly. Some party or something."

I couldn't imagine Adrian at the kind of parties Tess went to, and pressed for further details, but she claimed she couldn't remember.

Then, because the site had come up and our conversation seemed to have taken a more intimate turn, I asked her something that was not on the list of questions, but that I had been thinking about since we had started the project. Tess talked a lot about how these dark and manic moods were part of her, how she was flawed, how there was, to use her favorite quote, "no hope of a cure, ever, for being me." It had gotten me thinking: How did she know that these extreme states were her "true" character? Maybe they were something that altered the "real" her, like being possessed by an outside force.

When I put this to Tess, she replied that she was sure that it was the "real" her. I pointed out that surely she couldn't be *sure*—she could only take a position. Her tone changed then, becoming harder.

"I thought you were here to help me, not try to talk me out of it."

So then I had to explain that I was indeed here to help, and had no intention of talking her out of it. I was just interested in debating the point. It was clear she hadn't really done any philosophy before, so I told her that was what I liked to do, examine things from all angles.

At that, she relaxed again and then said another thing that threw me. She said that her "husband" thought it was something that possessed her, and that he called her moods "the beast."

I was momentarily lost for words, and then asked her to confirm that she had just revealed that she was married. She sounded surprised, and said, "Oh, have I not mentioned it?" as if it were a trifling matter.

It turned out that she had been married briefly, "in my early twenties." I pushed her for an exact date, and it took her a while to remember that it happened when she was twenty-four. It was to an Australian man called Lee, whom she had met in a queue at a bank in Delhi and married in London five weeks later. Within a year they had split up and Lee had gone back to Australia. "Some time later" they had gotten a divorce. Tess said it was a "moment of madness," and seemed to think it was hardly worth remarking on. She added that they didn't speak at all now and it was highly unlikely he would be in contact.

"I told you," she said. "I've done lots of silly things."

The odd thing was, although she had married Lee, she didn't even count him among what she called her "great loves." The top spot went to a man called Tivo, a deejay whom she had been with for a year when she was twenty-seven. A picture showed quite a short, dark man wearing a trilby hat; Tess was sitting on his lap and did indeed look happy, gazing up at him with adoration.

"He just got me," she said. "We got each other."

I asked her to elaborate.

"Oh, you know," she said.

"No, I don't."

"It's like, when we were together things made sense. He understood everything I said, even things I didn't fully understand myself. I could tell him anything, and he would go with it. But he also knew when to tell me to shut up and stop being silly."

It ended when she had slept with someone else—"the biggest mistake of my life"—and he had found out.

The person she had been out with the longest was Matt, whom she was with between the ages of nineteen and twenty-three. He was a "nice boy," Tess said, but as if this were a bad thing. Marion thought she should have married him—he was now a very successful hotelier, she kept on reminding Tess—and that she had blown her chances.

Tivo aside, Tess didn't have a very high opinion of men. She thought they were weak and simple, and used to leave them for what seemed to me to be innocuous transgressions. When I asked about Charlie, whom she had gone out with for six months in 2004, all she said was that, on a trip to Rome, he had asked for his suitcase to be wrapped in plastic at the airport. This, it seemed, was enough for him to be discarded.

Tess's marriage was not the only surprise. It turned out she had had a very short-lived TV career cohosting a late-night "magazine show" on Channel 4 in 1997 called *Gassing*, in which she interviewed what she called "Z-list fuckwits." It was only a pilot show, and the series never got made.

It was not only most of her experiences that were foreign to me, but her attitudes too. She frequently bemoaned getting older, fear-ing the loss of her looks and "becoming invisible." When I pointed out that it was irrational and pointless to fear something that was inevitable and happened to everyone, she laughed dryly and said, "Just you wait."

Other times, I could understand her attitude, but not her reasons behind it. Like me, she disliked traveling on the tube, but while I found the crowds and shoving and hectoring announcements uncomfortable, her explanation was baffling: She "empathized" too much with her fellow passengers.

"I look at these people and imagine whole scenes from their life. Like, let's say there's a man wearing overalls, obviously a manual worker. I'll think of him down at the pub, on his fifth pint of the day, saying, 'Well, it's just a job, innit?' Or if there's a girl with red hair, I'll imagine the office sleazebag at the Christmas party saying, 'So, Lucy, there's something we've all been wondering—do the cuffs match the collar?'" Once, she described seeing an old man in a flat cap taking a packet of bourbon biscuits out of his shopping bag and looking at them before replacing them in the bag: a sight, she said, that reduced her to tears. "He was just looking forward to his tea. Such simple pleasures. I think I'm too sensitive for this world. Do you know what I mean?"

I didn't, but there was the odd occasion when I understood both her attitude and what lay behind it. For instance, one night she told me about how the previous evening she was at a friend's house for dinner and had been seated next to a boring woman. "She spent literally half an hour telling us all the countries she had ever been to—including, get this, the airports she had just stopped over in, as if they counted."

I told her that Tash Emmerson had done that at school, and that

I found it equally annoying. She even had the countries listed on her Facebook page.

"Fucking hell," said Tess. "Unfriend her immediately. Why are you friends with these people?"

I explained that I didn't like Tash or ever see her, but that everyone at school had everyone else as their Facebook friends, because they wanted to have as high a number as possible.

"Yeah, maybe for those silly bitches," she said, "but you're cooler than that, aren't you? Just ignore the lot of them."

I told her that if I unfriended everyone who wasn't my real friend, then I would have only Rashida left. I decided not to mention that I didn't even see her anymore.

"So what?" she said. "Who gives a fuck? Strike out. Be cool."

I appreciated what she was saying; I was a freethinker, after all. But I had a vision of my profile: Friends [1].

"I can't," I said.

"God, I'm so glad the Internet didn't exist when I was younger," said Tess.

At these rare times when she was concentrating on me, rather than talking about herself, I was keenly aware that we were wasting time, and I made efforts to remain professional and steer the conversation back to her after a few minutes. But I admit that I quite enjoyed it when she decided to pay attention to me; she had a way of making me feel that she was really interested, that she really cared.

One night, she decided that she was going to give me some advice. "I don't have a daughter; you're the next-best thing," she said. "I've been thinking about this all day."

I started to protest, but she continued.

"First," she said, "you're not as crap as you think you are."

"I don't think I'm crap!" I said.

She shushed me and carried on with her list. "Wait until a man has been divorced a year before you think about going near him. It's okay to dislike your family. You'll spend your life chasing the feeling of your first line of coke. It's worth spending money on a good haircut."

I told her that none of the above applied to me; nor could I envisage their ever doing so—and added that, although I appreciated her concern, her energy would be better spent remembering where she was between February and May 2008.

She laughed. "Ah, you're so young; there's still time. Just you wait." Then she sighed, and her mood shifted, as it did. "But then, before you know it, you'll be old. Life is horrifically short, you know."

I said, without thinking, "Well, especially for you." There was a long silence at that, and I felt I had said the wrong thing. I stared at the little black Skype box on the screen until I thought of something to say: "It always seems to be Thursday."

I said it because I wanted Tess to feel she wasn't alone, that I understood, but it also happened to be true. The days seemed to slip away with no resistance: It always seemed to be three p.m., and then it always seemed to be Thursday again, and another week, another month, gone forever.

Other times, as I've said, our conversations were unsuccessful from the start. If she was in the wrong mood, I could barely get a scrap of information out of her. She would give short, brusque answers, say "I don't know" to everything, and generally act like a child. She'd whine, "Oh, when will this all be over! I just want it to be *over*. You said we'd be finished by now!" I'd have to remind her that I had said nothing of the sort; there had been no completion date set at that stage. Sometimes I'd have to be quite sharp.

She could also be spiteful. There was one particular night when I was trying to establish some detail—I think it was whether her friend Katy Wilkins was the same person as a "Catatonic Katie" she mentioned in another e-mail—when she turned on me. She said, "Don't you have anything better to do with your life than this? I mean, really? What do you *do*?"

She kept badgering me, until she suddenly stopped and gave a big sigh, as if she was bored. "Never mind. I suppose it's in my interests that you're a sad sack," she said.

I'm not proud to say that I let my professionalism slip.

"Well, maybe I won't do this anymore," I said. "You're right; I've got better things to do." And I terminated the call. I was shaking, so upset that when she tried to ring me back, I ignored the call. I let her call back four more times.

When I finally accepted the call, she began to apologize and then said, "Wait." The next thing I knew, she had turned her camera on. Suddenly there she was, in the little Skype screen, looking straight at me. I think I might have even given a yelp, so surprised was I at her actually being there. It was rather like seeing a ghost, not that I believe in ghosts. She was wearing a white vest, bright against her skin, and her fringe was pinned back from her face. She looked very young. Her face was close to the camera and she was frowning, that little line clearly visible between her eyebrows.

"Darling," she said. "Please forgive me."

She apologized for "lashing out"; it had been a bad day, she said. Then: "I need you. You know that. I really need you."

She put her hand up and touched the camera lightly, like she was blessing me.

From then on, without discussing it, she left her camera on when we spoke. I still left mine off. I had seen many photos of her, of course, but it was quite different observing her as a live, breathing person. Generally, the view was on her face from below; her usual pose was reclining on a bed with her computer on her lap. On the wall behind her I could see the corner of a poster of what looked like a giant spider. I asked Tess to move the camera to show me the whole thing; she did, and told me it was a picture by an artist called Louise Bourgeois. I noted this, and during our next session asked her to pan the camera around her room so I could see more fully how she had decorated it.

Her room was absolutely crammed full of stuff, junk, really, which made me feel queasy to look at—dusty peacock feathers, stacks of magazines, clothes in heaps on the floor reminding me of the piles dumped overnight outside the Cats Protection League shop in Kentish Town. On top of a chest of drawers, jars lay on their sides or with their lids off, and around her window was a string of Christmas tree lights. There were some unusual objects too, which I asked her the background to: a huge white shell the size of a pillow, which she had bought at an antique shop in Islington; a painted wooden sun that took up half a wall, which she said she had made for a play. A small gold Buddha sat on her bedside table, and even through the camera I could see the incense ash coating it.

Seeing her possessions like that made me think: What would Tess do with all of this stuff when she checked out? I knew that such a query was edging toward forbidden territory—although there had been no official agreement as such, Tess had conspicuously avoided discussing the practical details of her suicide—so I asked rather tentatively, "Do you have a plan for your things?"

She looked confused for a moment. Then she understood.

"Oh, no," she said. "Not yet. I haven't thought about it."

I told her that I used a storage place that was a good value, if she wanted the number. She nodded vaguely, so I e-mailed it to her afterward.

The camera was useful, because I could pick up better on her mood when I saw her facial expression, although, I must say, when she was "down" it was often quite obvious by her voice. It would go thick and heavy, as if she were sedated. And there were little visual things to pick up on. For instance, I saw that she was left-handed and that, in addition to the faint line between her eyebrows, she had one on either side of her mouth, as delicate as fallen eyelashes. One night I noticed a small red mark above her lip. I asked her about it and she said it was a cold sore. I might not have known that she got cold sores if I hadn't actually seen her—and I made a note to give her one at various points in the future. Tess could make even a cold sore look good, like a beauty spot.

She also tended to smoke when she talked to me. I presumed they were cigarettes, but one day I watched her crumbling something into the tobacco and realized it was cannabis. I asked her to confirm it was drugs, and she laughed.

"Are you shocked, Mary Whitehouse?"

After ascertaining the meaning of this reference—Mary Whitehouse was, Tess explained, "a famously disapproving old bag with a mouth like a cat's arse"—I explained that I didn't disapprove at all, and that she was totally within her rights to do whatever she wanted with her body. But, I added, wanting to make my position clear, "If it affected someone else—if you had a small child in the room, for instance—I could not condone your actions. But, as you are, feel free to carry on."

"Why, thank you," said Tess. "You're very kind." She seemed amused by this exchange and smiled as she licked the paper of her cigarette.

"How much does it cost?" I asked.

"I don't know," she said. "A girl never has to buy her own drugs, right?"

"Well, *you* might not have to," I said, "but I'm sure *some* girls do. It's likely that someone would give you drugs for free only if they liked you and wanted you to like them, but not everyone is 'sexy' like you. You've done this before—when you use the phrase 'a girl,' you actually mean 'a girl like me.'"

It was something I'd been wanting to say for a while, and I was gratified to see Tess look slightly taken aback. She took a long suck on the cigarette, and said, "Maybe you're right." It seemed to pique her curiosity, and she started one of her barrages of questions about my childhood and parents, etc. I told her about Mum and the MS, and she became animated.

"Like Dad. God, isn't it shit? How did you cope?"

I told her that I imagined Alzheimer's was worse than MS, for one reason: Mum was always compos mentis and remained herself up to the end, whereas her dad, Jonathan, had effectively lost his identity. When I thought of Jonathan I had the image of a tin of Quality Street, like the ones we used to get at Christmas, but inside was just full of empty wrappers. I didn't say that to Tess, though; I just said that it must have been very hard watching helplessly as her father's memories leaked away, until he had forgotten he even had a daughter.

Tess nodded.

"Yeah," she said. "He basically died years ago."

And then, stubbing out her cigarette in a little shell ashtray by her bed, she said, "I'm glad I'm not going to get old."

Gradually, the spreadsheets were filling up. There was now a pleasing rhythm to my work: At night we would have our conversa-tions; then the following day I would transcribe the tapes, catalog the facts, and make a note of any extraneous but useful details that had emerged, such as unusual words she used or aspects of her char-acter Tess inadvertently revealed.

The more information I harvested, the more my confidence grew, but there remained an area of concern: phone calls. Despite the reassurances of Adrian and Tess to the contrary, it seemed likely that there would be times in the future when a call from Tess would be desirable, even if not strictly necessary: festive occasions, for instance, or in the event of an accident.

Then, one day, as I listened to our taped recordings, something occurred to me. There seemed to be no reason we shouldn't record generic messages, which I could then play over the phone, onto the recipient's voice mail at times when I knew they would not be able to pick up.

I put the idea to Tess that evening, and she agreed. "No time like the present!" I said. It took a while, and I had to keep asking her to repeat because her tone wasn't right, but eventually we had several different recordings. One was for the occasion of a birthday, one for Christmas, and then there were three general ones, varia-tions on "Hello, it's me; sorry to miss you." For her friends, Tess's tone was slangy—"Hey, babe"—while messages for her family were more formal. I got Tess to make me a list of when her closest fam-ily and friends were most likely to let their phones go to voice mail; her mother, for instance, went to her book group every Wednes-day evening—what she called her "me time"—while those friends with children would be busy collecting them from school during the midafternoon.

I also decided that we should take photos of Tess for me to later superimpose on scenes of wherever it was she was going, to post on Facebook. One evening I asked her to show me the clothes in her wardrobe, and she positioned the laptop on the side of the bed and pulled them out, one by one, holding them up against her. Once we had agreed on certain outfits, suitable for different seasons and weather conditions, she put them on, not bothering to move away from the camera, so I saw her strip down to her knickers.

As she got changed, I examined her body. It was so different from mine. Her lack of flesh meant I could see parts of her skeleton I had never seen on myself: the knobbles on her spine and her rib cage as she bent down, her hip bones as she lifted her arms to pull on a top. It was as if she had only a fine sheet draped over her frame, whereas mine was buried under a duvet.

Once she was dressed, I directed her how to use the self-timer on her camera to take photos of herself wearing various outfits against a blank wall in her room, in a variety of poses. She then e-mailed them over for me to check.

Tess seemed to enjoy the session, happily rummaging through her stuff, holding things up for my opinion, exclaiming with delight as she chanced upon a favorite jacket she thought she'd lost. I don't have any interest in clothes and didn't know what she was talking about most of the time—vintage Ossie, my old Dries top—but I quite enjoyed it too. It pleased me to see her happy. I remember thinking about that photo on Facebook of her and her friends getting ready to go out, when she was my age, and wondering whether what I was experiencing with Tess was something similar to that. "Girlie fun."

I felt close to Tess, then, and it was a nice feeling. Not long after, however, something happened that jolted our relationship back to the professional and made me feel that I hardly knew her at all. One morning, as usual, I logged on to her Facebook account and saw that she had sent out party invites to her entire friends list. She must have done it sometime after we had Skyped the previous evening.

Tess's Farewell Fiesta, the invite read. Join me for a glass or five before I set sail for pastures new. The date was the following Friday, and the venue a pub in Bethnal Green. Already, eighteen people had accepted the invite, and her wall was filled with messages from bemused friends: Wait, you're leaving? Where? When? What's all this? Why didn't I know about this?

I immediately e-mailed Tess asking why she hadn't consulted me before such a major move, but she didn't reply all day, and I had to wait for that evening's Skype session to hear her explanation.

"Oh, yeah," she said, with an infuriatingly breezy manner, "I thought I should have a bit of a send-off."

"Why didn't you tell me?"

She shrugged, looking off camera.

"It was a spur-of-the-moment thing. Anyway, you know now, don't you?"

"But you can't have a leaving party yet! We haven't worked out where you're going, or when or . . ." I heard my voice rise, and paused to calm down. "What are you going to tell everybody?"

"Oh, I'll think of something," she said, turning back to me with a touch of irritation in her voice. "I'll say I'm moving abroad. Stop being such a fusspot."

"*I'll* think of something, you mean," I replied, almost under my breath, but Tess gave the camera a quick, narrow-eyed glance and I knew she had heard.

"Oh, and I've told everyone I'm leaving in a month," she added, and smiled sweetly.

As you can imagine, this rather took me aback. No dates for

"checkout" had been discussed up until now, and I had foreseen the information-gathering process continuing for at least another two months. I had seen no evidence on e-mail or Facebook to support this new claim from Tess, and it crossed my mind that she had just thought up the deadline on the spot in order to fluster me. But, whatever the case, once she had said it she refused to budge, insisting we had to wrap everything up within four weeks.

"In that case," I said, "we need to start planning your future."

"What do you mean?"

"Your new life," I said, doing my utmost to remain measured. "Where you want to live, what you want to do, everything. We've got to work it all out."

"I don't care," she said, with an impatient sigh. "I'm not going to be there, am I?"

That was true, of course, and by that point I probably did have enough knowledge of her to make an informed decision about the kind of place she might go and the job she might take, and so on. But I felt both annoyed and hurt by her offhand manner.

"I mean, that's what you're here for, isn't it?" she added, to rub salt into the wound.

I brought the conversation to an end on quite bad terms, but I soon rallied. I had to be professional; I was here to do a job. I sat down and tried to be rational and think of good places for Tess to go. It took quite a bit of Internet research before I found the answer.

Obviously, the main criterion was that it was a long way away. In my initial meeting with Adrian he had mentioned Australia as a possible location, but that didn't seem right. Even leaving aside the substantial new fact that her ex-husband, Lee, was Australian, I knew that the major cities in the country were popular destinations for travel. And even if Tess lived outside one of the main cities, I thought that if one of her family members or friends had already taken a twenty-four-hour plane journey out to Sydney, say, it was likely they would make the small extra effort to go and see her.

Besides, for it to seem authentic there had to be a reason for Tess choosing the place she ended up in. She was, she told me, "very sensitive to environment" and had to be "around beauty," and it would be unlike her to just go anywhere. There would have to be something there that was obviously attractive to her.

So, in summary, it had to be a place that was difficult to get to, had enough "charms" for Tess to want to settle there, yet not somewhere where people might think, *Oh, I've always wanted to go there and here's my chance.*

Furthermore, it would make sense for Tess to move to a place that was entirely different from where she was now, in Bethnal Green. And, I realized, it would make sense for her to move to somewhere "spiritual."

This "spirituality" was a side of Tess I found hard to deal with. She eagerly embraced mystical fads, becoming obsessed with homeopathy and crystals, earnestly telling me about "cupping" and ley lines. To be frank, it offended me, and I challenged her on it a couple of times—"Where is the proof?"—but she stubbornly insisted that it made her feel better.

So, with that in mind, I found some "New Age" Web sites, and lurked on a few forums. I noted what they were chatting about, and when someone mentioned a place, I looked it up. And that was how I came to hear of Sointula.

Sointula is on an island off the coast of Vancouver, a former hippie colony that had been founded as a "socialist utopia" in the 1970s.

It's become more of a normal place, a fishing colony, although it still retains some of that spirit and is something of a destination for the "spiritually inclined." From the pictures it looks quite nice, with empty beaches and simple, low-level buildings. There is a sufficient population to provide employment, but it is quiet enough for it to convincingly be a refuge for a "damaged" person like Tess.

Most crucially, it's very difficult to get to. You have to fly to Vancouver, get another flight to Port Hardy, a half-hour taxi ride to another port, and then a ferry. There was no way that her parents could make that trip, with Jonathan in his current state. It would, I hoped, put off even the hardiest of her traveling friends—even Sharmi, who had been to Papua New Guinea. Besides, of course, Tess would be making it expressly clear that she didn't want anyone to come and see her, that she wanted to start afresh.

Once I had decided on Sointula, I spent a day sketching out Tess's life there. I looked up estate agents and found her a flat to live in. It was a nice little place, on the ground floor of a detached clapboard house, with a part share of the garden. The photographs showed airy, bright rooms, with windows from floor to ceiling hung with checked curtains, and white wooden floors. The flat was furnished very simply, with the bare minimum of furniture—a neat little sofa, a round four-seater table—yet managed to look cozy.

For a brief moment, looking at the flat, I felt a pang that I would like to live there myself. It was, I recall, a Friday night, and outside the window Albion Street was extremely noisy; the smell of onions was seeping up into the flat, and there was the sound of breaking glass and drunken laughter from the pub.

The estate agent's Web site said that the Sointula flat was on the ground floor of a house lived in by the landlady. She, I decided, was a widow called Mrs. Peterson, who looked just like Mum.

After finding Tess's flat—or apartment, I should say—I began searching for a job for her. As mentioned, she had had a checkered employment history, and it would be perfectly plausible for her to work in a lowly capacity, for instance as a waitress in one of the island's restaurants. But I wasn't happy with that. This was her "new life," and I wanted something better for her. Besides, I thought there was a possibility that if there was an emergency at home, and someone wanted to get in touch with her urgently, it wouldn't take them long to discover the names of the few restaurants on the island and call them directly to speak to her.

So I went through the other options. Sointula had a clothes shop called Moira's and a small library. I considered the library, but then, as I was poring over my Tess files looking for inspiration, I was reminded of her brief spell at art school, and it came to me: Tess could be a private art tutor for the child of one of the island's families.

I admit I was rather pleased with this. It meant that Tess could plausibly have her phone turned off for a lot of the time and therefore be unreachable. The role of Tess's mobile in her new life had been a matter of some concern to me, not because I ever intended to pick it up and answer as her—that thought only came later—but because I realized that phone ring tones are different abroad, and anyone ringing Tess's phone would be able to tell that it was still in the U.K. A good reason for it not to be switched on was a pleasing solution.

House and job decided, I put together a package for Tess, with pictures of the island and details of the flat, as if I were selling it to her. She e-mailed back uncharacteristically quickly, her tone once again shifted from grumpiness to appreciation. She said she loved the idea of Sointula, the flat looked gorgeous, and that it was a stroke of genius to think of tutoring.

It's so fab, I almost want to go there myself! she wrote. Darling, you're a star.

I did like it when she was nice to me.

*It seemed to be Massage Day* at the commune today. When I did my rounds, a portion of the residents were lying on their fronts like corpses while others sat astride them, actually on their bottoms, squeezing their brown flesh in silent concentration. I'd never seen a proper massage before—sometimes I would do Mum, but only ever her hands or feet—and I found the sight quite embarrassing. It was also inconvenient, as I had to get up close to look at the squashed features of those being pummeled, in order to check whether I recognized them or not.

Eventually I ascertained that they were all "old" people to whom I had already shown Tess's picture, and there were no new arrivals until midafternoon, when three young Frenchmen turned up in a puttering orange van. When I approached them they said that they hadn't been here last summer and that this was their first time at the commune, but I showed them Tess's photo anyway. *"Non, sorry,"* they said, and one of them added to the other, *"Mais, très belle,"* which I understood from my French GCSE. He had terrible acne, little red volcanoes carpeting all available space on his face and creeping down his neck to meet the hair on his bare chest. I imagined it spreading down his body like slow-moving lava, until eventually only the soles of his feet were left untouched. It was hard not to flinch, and I wondered whether he minded that no one would ever say of him that he was *très belle*.

Seeing him also reminded me that I hadn't checked my own appearance since I arrived, so when I got back to the cave I borrowed Annie's mirror. My reflection was a bit of a shock: Despite my spending most of the daylight hours under the tree, my skin was as pink as strawberry Angel Delight. It must have been from my excursion into town yesterday. Annie, who was watching, insisted on smearing my cheeks and nose with something called aloo vera, which she claims has "healing properties," although without the Internet I can't check that assertion.

"Silly billy," she said. "Skin like yours, you should be on the factor fifty. Didn't your mom ever tell you to wear sunblock?"

I informed her that there was no need for such a thing in Kentish Town, especially if you rarely left your house.

||||||||||||

I realize that I haven't mentioned Adrian's role during the preparation stage. That's because he was hardly involved at all, not nearly as much as I presumed he'd be. I had expected to report back to him on the progress of my information gathering, Tess's state of mind, and so on, and kept comprehensive notes, but days and then weeks passed and he never asked for them.

A fortnight into the project, with still no word from him, I began to consider that perhaps he expected *me* to get in touch—that this was a kind of initiative test. So I prepared a progress report and was all ready to e-mail it to him when I realized that I didn't know where to send it. He had said that day on the Heath that we shouldn't refer to the case on Red Pill, even in personal messages, explaining that a number of the members were skilled hackers, and such was their devotion to the site, they might take it upon themselves to hack into his mailbox in order to get insight into his thought processes. However, he had given me no alternate e-mail address or phone number.

I remembered what he said when we met on Hampstead Heath—"You are, I presume, on Facebook?"—which implied that he would be on there too, but his name drew a blank. So I had no option but to send him a carefully phrased PM on Red Pill:

Adrian,

I was just wondering whether there was any information you wanted from me, apropos the ongoing project.

Leila

His reply came seven and a half hours later:

I have complete faith in you; I'm sure you have it under control. PM not good idea.

As I say, I was surprised he wasn't taking a more "hands-on" approach to the project, but pleased that he trusted me to execute it well without supervision. And something did change after I got in touch: From then on, each Wednesday, he would send me a PM—not mentioning the project, but containing a solitary, unaccompanied, inspiring quote, as if to buoy me from afar. *Great men are like eagles and build their nest on some lofty solitude,* or *All men live life; few have an idea about it.*

Of course, I also "saw" him every day, on the forums on Red Pill. As we had agreed I continued to maintain a presence on the site, every day logging on and contributing something to whatever discussion was the most high profile. But my heart wasn't in it, absorbed as I was in the project, and I felt removed from what was going on there, all the arguing about abstract notions.

It felt odd seeing Adrian's public face, yet having this secret with him, knowing things about him personally that the others didn't. For instance, during a discussion about a podcast Adrian had posted on sibling rivalry, he referred to his "sister." However, I knew, because he had told me on the Heath that day, that he was an only child, like me. I understood that he was using this "sister" for the sake of his argument, but the others on the site would naturally presume that he really did have one. The idea that I alone among the members knew different was, I admit, exciting as well as unnerving, but I felt that now was not the time for encouraging heightened feelings. I had to keep my head straight and my reasoning clear for the project.

There was also a more prosaic reason for not fully engaging with the site: In those final weeks of preparation, my time was becoming increasingly scarce. The Tess work alone could easily fill every waking hour, but I would not start to receive my eighty-eight-pound-a-week salary until "checkout" and so, up till then, was also having to keep up with my testing work for Damian.

For the next month, I barely left the flat. I sat at my computer, in the shadow of the restaurant sign, for eighteen hours a day, sometimes twenty. And I must admit that as April 14 approached, I started to feel agitated in a way that isn't normally in my nature. The realization struck that to fully know the ins and outs of Tess's life would be a never-ending task, like trying to fill in a hole and realizing that it has no bottom.

Sometimes, during those last days, I felt like this didn't matter. I wouldn't actually need that much information to imitate Tess: People were mostly interested only in themselves and didn't attend much to others, even their close friends. Then the next moment, I'd feel like I was totally unprepared and would be caught out immediately. I veered between these two feelings, as if a volume switch were being turned first far too low and then deafeningly high.

The time line of Tess's life was gradually getting filled in, but my new fixation was finding out her opinion on things. In some cases this was packaged up with the information she provided. For instance, when she told me that her friend Susie had recently left her job in advertising to go back to university, it was clear from her comment—"Good girl"—that she approved of the move. But with many other subjects she hadn't made her views clear one way or another, and I had been so intent on processing the facts that I had neglected to ask for them.

I started another long list of questions I needed to put to her. Our Skype sessions lengthened. Whom did she vote for in the last election? What was her favorite flower? Did she take sugar in her tea? Unlike before, Tess didn't get impatient with my questioning. She was in an odd state during those final two weeks, polite yet distant and preoccupied.

Except, that is, that one evening, when she cried.

|||||||||||

"I'm so fucking scared," she'd said. Now I recall other parts of the conversation. I remember summarizing what Socrates had to say on the matter of death: *"Death is either an eternal, dreamless sleep where the dead do not perceive anything, or death is when the soul gets relocated to another place."* Therefore, I explained to her, there was nothing to fear.

When she continued to cry, I quoted Marcus Aurelius: *"It is one of the noblest functions of reason to know whether it is time to walk out of the world or not."*

It was as if she hadn't heard me.

"It's just . . . the void . . . do you understand?"

She sniffed, wiped her eyes, and said again, more clearly, "Do you understand?"

She wanted me to switch on my camera, and I'd had to remind her that Adrian had advised against it.

"Fuck Adrian," she'd said.

"I don't think it's a good idea."

Then, in that unfamiliar, small voice: "I can't do it."

"Of course you can," I told her.

What else could I say?

|||||||||||

The police asked me, "Did she ever express any doubts in her decision? Did her resolve ever falter?" I shook my head.

All I can say is, she was upset and I was comforting her, in the same way Mum comforted me when I said I wouldn't be able to cope without her. "Of course you will," she told me. "You're my brilliant, strong girl. You'll be more than fine." I didn't see it as contradicting her desire to go through with the act. Fear seemed part of it. And it wasn't as if suicide were a spur-of-the-moment decision for her. Tess repeatedly stated that she had been longing to do it for years. If, during one of our conversations, she had said decisively that she did not want to go through with it, then of course I would have been entirely supportive of that decision. Of course I would.

The conversation highlighted the fact that, however much I knew about her, there was something she was holding back from me. As I say, we never agreed to avoid the topic of her suicide—the practical aspects, I mean—but there was an implicit understanding that this was something that was not going to be discussed. It was, I suppose, the one private thing she had left.

However, I was conscious, during those last weeks, that while I was finalizing the details of my plan, she was, in parallel and in secret, doing the same with hers.

Then, two days before the fourteenth, we were on the phone and I was asking her to double-check the spellings of some university friends' names. When she had done so, she went silent. Then she looked at me and tapped on the camera.

"Do you have everything you need?"

She said it in the empty tone of a bank cashier.

I remember looking up at the chart above my desk, which by then was more than two meters long. I had taped extra pieces of paper to it, and it was dense with writing. I had a large quantity of material on my computer too, of course, but this visual chart provided prompts and keywords. I knew that I could go on forever, fixing another sheet and another until this chart of Tess's life filled every surface of my flat, flowing out of the front door onto Albion Street and through the Rotherhithe Tunnel and beyond, but there had to be a point to stop.

So I said, "Yes. I think so."

The intense sadness I felt at that point was, oddly, even worse than how it was toward the end with Mum; I suppose because Tess's suffering wasn't visible, and she looked so much younger and healthier. It seemed impossible that she wasn't going to be in the world any longer, that someone I had been so intimate with was going to disappear.

But, of course, I couldn't say that. So I said nothing. And then, suddenly, there we were, at our final exchange. Her last look into the camera, that salute, her thanking me, my stupid thanking of her, then staring, drinking in the sight of her, her nose, her cheekbones, her mouth, until she looked up, leaned forward, and turned off the camera.

||||||||||

Checkout, April 14, was in effect a "normal" day. I couldn't start the job, because "Tess" would be spending all day traveling to Canada, so I had to wait until the following day to send the first e-mails and texts announcing her safe arrival in Sointula. And not just the following morning, either; because of the time difference, I couldn't begin work as Tess until five p.m. U.K. time on the fifteenth, which was nine a.m. in Sointula.

But, of course, it was not a normal day. That morning I found it impossible to do anything except lie on the sofa, my eyes open but not really seeing anything. It was as if I had been deactivated. I wasn't even hungry. All I could think about was what Tess was doing; yet I had no idea how she was doing it. My mind was whirring, but with no cogs to grasp on to, it produced instead a slide show of imaginary scenes: Tess on her hands and knees, crawling into a tiny cave in a remote mountain range, her pockets bulging with a jar of pills and a bottle of vodka. With her final swallow, she curled up and closed her eyes, rays from the setting sun creeping into the cave and casting a glow over her face. Tess emerging at the top of the tallest building in London, the wind whipping her hair as she took a final look at the silent city below before gracefully leaping off, headfirst, like a swimmer. Tess, at night, breaking into a zoo and lowering her hand slowly into a tank of deadly scorpions. When the sting came, she barely winced before crumpling to the floor.

Of course, I knew that the cave scenario was the only one likely to bear even the slightest resemblance to reality, it being imperative that the method used left her body undiscovered. I also knew, only too well, that death was not a romantic business. Nonetheless, those were the images my mind chose to dwell on.

I lay there in this disabled state for hours, and then suddenly, with no notice, my bowels turned over and I had the most terrible diarrhea, so severe I was left panting on the lavatory.

Halfway through the morning the door buzzer rang, a startling occurrence even on ordinary days, and I was so tense I let out a yelp. It was the postman, with a registered letter for me. Inside, folded within a sheet of newspaper, was eighty-eight pounds in cash: four twenty-pound notes, one five, and three pound coins Sellotaped onto a blank card. Under the coins someone had drawn a mouth, to make them form the eyes and nose of a smiley face. It seemed an unlikely thing for Adrian to have done, so I could only imagine that this first payment had come directly from Tess. None of the subsequent payments had a smile.

Receiving the money galvanized me somewhat—Project Tess was now officially my occupation—so I went to my desk and sent an e-mail to Damian: I am writing to terminate my employment with immediate effect. I then tried to distract myself by playing Warcraft, but for once I couldn't get into it. It seemed pointless, ordering around a bunch of pixels. So instead I turned to Tess's e-mail and Facebook accounts. Although "Tess" couldn't send out any messages, e-mails were still coming in for her, and there was nothing to stop me from reading them and formulating her replies, ready to be sent out the next day.

I logged on to her Facebook. By now, Tess's passwords were second nature; it was my own I hesitated over. We had decided on the wording of her final status update together, and she had posted it the evening before: Finally, I'm off! A new life awaits. I love you all. There were twenty-three messages underneath, all variations on good luck! and you'll be missed! She had five new e-mails that day, excluding spam: four wishing her all the best on her travels and one from a woman called Marnie who obviously didn't know she was leaving, inviting her to a fortieth birthday party in Clapham later that month: dress code: mutton dressed as lamb.

I didn't check my Red Pill messages until later that day, when I found a PM from Adrian. It contained nothing but a quote from Aristotle: *Moral excellence comes about as a result of habit. We become just by doing just acts, temperate by doing temperate acts, brave by doing brave acts.*

Now, as I've said, I have some idea about what happened that day, from the police trace on Tess's passport. She traveled to Portsmouth and from there boarded the night ferry to Bilbao. She arrived in Spain at lunchtime the following day, and her passport was checked at the port. From then on, nobody knows where she went or what she did. She disappeared.

I've looked up the boat she would have traveled on, the *Pride of Bilbao*. There are some videos on YouTube by people who have been on the crossing, and I've watched them all. It looks awful. The cabins are as basic as hospital waiting rooms. The passengers seem to be either very old, sitting silently over cups of tea in the lounge, or young, squawking, single-sex groups of idiots slopping plastic glasses of beer over one another. There are many rows of arcade machines and a gift shop selling cheap cuddly toys and packets of Minstrels. It is not Tess's kind of place at all.

The most obvious explanation for the unlikely choice of transport is that she had planned to jump off the boat in the middle of the night but then, when it came to it, had lost her nerve. I thought of her alone on the deck in the darkness, leaning against the rails and looking down, unable to see the sea but hearing it churning away, ready to receive her.

But if she had intended to kill herself then—why didn't she?

I've often thought about Tess on that ferry, lying in her tiny, plastic cabin, on that flat pillow, listening to the whoops of drunken yobs in the corridor outside. One of the videos shows dolphins swimming up alongside the boat. I hope she saw some of them, at least.

As I say, when she got to Spain, the trail goes cold.

But back to checkout day. Eventually, I couldn't bear watching the hours tick by, my head whirring with unproductive thoughts, and in the midafternoon I did something I hadn't done before: took one of Mum's sleeping pills and knocked myself out.

I woke, groggily, at lunchtime on the fifteenth and, eventually, it was five p.m. and time to start. I logged on to Tess's e-mail and sent my prepared messages to her mother and her friends Simon and Justine. The main body of each e-mail was the same: that I had arrived; it had been an endless journey; I'd glimpsed a seal on the ferry crossing over, the island was beautiful, and I'd taken a room at a guesthouse a street away from the sea. For Simon and Justine I added that there was a man playing the ukulele on the pier when the boat pulled in like a welcoming committee, as if he knew I was coming, and that the guesthouse was charmingly batty, with pink gingham curtains and concrete animals in the garden.

Next, I updated her Facebook. This I was more nervous about, as unlike e-mails it was "live." The update read: Finally landed! Knackered but happy. Saw my first seal! I misspelled the word *knackered*, without the "k," as I thought Tess would.

Almost immediately, people started responding with cheery messages of excitement and goodwill. I had decided that I wouldn't reply immediately, because after going on Facebook to post the update, I—Tess—had gone to bed to sleep off the jet lag.

This may sound odd, but from the start Tess's new life in Sointula felt *real*. It wasn't that I was being imaginative; rather, I had done so much research on her and the island that every detail was fleshed out. I remember that after logging off Facebook that first day I lay down on the floor and closed my eyes. The sounds of Albion Street fell away, and I was Tess lying on her guesthouse bed, jet-lagged and drowsy, thousands of miles from anyone who knew her. She hadn't closed the curtains fully and the late-afternoon sun lit up a slice of the room, warming the dust in the air. I heard the shriek of gulls from the sea and the occasional car driving slowly past outside.

I knew exactly how the rest of her day would proceed. She would wake from a fitful sleep, pull on her denim shorts, even though the weather wasn't quite warm enough for them, and wander down to the island's main road, a few blocks away. She'd go into the grocery store and stand in front of rows of strange Canadian foods and think to herself that soon the foreign brands of bread and soup were going to become familiar and unremarkable. I imagined her walking through the streets, looking through the windows of the clapboard houses, seeing a FOR RENT sign painted on a piece of driftwood outside one of them and wondering whether that could be her new home.

Of course, I already knew which flat she was going to rent—I had it all planned and researched—and it wasn't that one. But it was as if the Tess in my mind didn't know that yet. I was imagining it as if Tess were still alive, and this was real, as if she were a character who really was setting off on this adventure, this "voyage into the unknown." As if she didn't know that I was responsible for her fate.

Those first few weeks of Tess's new life in Sointula were the busiest, in terms of the volume of correspondence, but also the most straightforward. All the e-mails she sent and received were along the same lines: impressions of the island, exclamation mark–ridden expressions of excitement at seeing an albatross, and, for not-so-close friends who hadn't already heard them, earnest explanations of why she was embarking on this new life, and that the name Sointula meant "place of harmony" in Finnish. I had spent so long preparing every detail of her new setup, I didn't have to create anything. It was just a case of rationing out the information, like taking an exam I knew all the answers to.

Of course, there were a few messages that didn't fit that template.

For instance, ten days in, Tess received an e-mail from a woman called Jennifer, who wasn't on Facebook and clearly didn't know Tess had gone to Sointula, saying she had seen Tess the previous day at the Alhambra, a sight in Granada, Spain. I was going to come over and say hi but Ned was having a major meltdown, she wrote. And by the time I sorted him out, you were gone. PS—Love your new hair! I considered replying to say it was a case of mistaken identity, but had no notes on this Jennifer, and it wasn't clear whether Ned was her child or husband, so I left it.

For those first few weeks in Sointula, Tess relaxed and explored the island. She discovered charming features such as the public sauna and the cooperative shop, where volunteers worked for two hours a week in return for discounted groceries. The island had a single ATM machine and a bar run by an ancient old man who had introduced himself as she walked past (not that she would be drinking alcohol in the bar; she was going to be teetotal in her new life). *Quaint* was a word she used a lot. She bought a secondhand bicycle for thirty dollars. Over breakfast of buckwheat pancakes, her landlady told her that a killer whale had been spotted near the coast the day before Tess arrived. She adored the peace and the slow pace of life: I feel like I can breathe for the first time in years, she wrote. She had no doubts she had made the right decision in coming here.

On the fourth day, I changed her profile picture to a new photo of her standing on Sointula beach. This I created by carefully cutting out a picture of Tess in shorts from the photo shoot in her bedroom and superimposing it onto a shot of Sointula beach I found on Flickr.

After six days Tess found her flat, and moved in a week later. I wrote a flowery description of her new home: how it was tiny but sweet, and she could see a sliver of the sea from the kitchen window. She even found the half bath *quaint*.

There was one thing I did not find easy that first week. On the fifth day, I left a prerecorded message for Tess's mother. Tess had assured me that Marion was without fail out at her book group on Wednesday evenings and no one else answered the home phone, but as a precaution I withheld my number. All went according to plan. Marion didn't pick up, the call went to voice mail, and I started my recording at exactly the right time. But hearing Tess's voice—"Hey, it's me; just wanted to let you know that I'm safe and well"—had an unexpected effect on me, bringing back up the thoughts I had suppressed since checkout day. Somewhere, she was lying dead. How did she do it? Where was the body? Had anyone found her? The images that flooded my head were no longer sentimental: The sun's warmth had long ago deserted the cave, and Tess's tiny, curled-up body was cold and stiff. How lonely it must be to be dead, I thought irrationally.

I tried not to indulge such thoughts, however, as those first few weeks were a busy time. I immersed myself in building up Tess's life, imagining what she was going to wear that day, and have for her lunch, and the next thing she was going to buy for her new flat. It was like having an avatar, but much better.

There were rules, however—or, rather, one major rule: Whatever "Tess" did, it had to be something that the real Tess would have done. I had to remain true to her character, even with regard to tiny things that wouldn't be noticed by people back home.

For example: Through my research I discovered that there was a small antiques business in Sointula, off the main street. It was run by a woman from the front room of her house and open by appointment only. I could easily not have mentioned this place in any e-mails—I had no interest in antiques, and none of her family or friends would have been any the wiser. But I knew the odds were that Tess would discover it. She liked walking, and because the island was so small it was likely that she would have passed down the street and noticed the sign in the window of the woman's house and called to make an appointment to see the woman's goods. So I had her do that, and devoted a long e-mail to Justine about what she found there. Her prize acquisition was a pewter soap dish shaped like a scallop shell. I had spotted it on the shop's Web site and decided it would take pride of place beside her bath.

By the same token, I found that I had to know everything about what Tess would be doing or wearing, rather than just the bit I needed to know for the purposes of Facebook and e-mail. It felt important to know every detail of her day, even if it wasn't going to be used.

I've always been like this. When we thought I might be going to college, Mum said I should wear a suit for the interview, so we went to buy one from Evans in Brent Cross. The suit jacket we found had a bright pink lining, but only at the collar and the cuffs, so when it was on it looked like it was fully lined, but when you took it off you could see the unfinished nylon underneath. I didn't like that at all, and asked Mum if we could get one that had lining all the way through, even though it was twenty pounds more expensive. She said it didn't matter, because I wouldn't take the jacket off during the interview, but the thing was that I would *know* that the lining didn't go all the way through. It was one of the only times I can remember really disagreeing with her.

Given the time difference in Sointula, I could be Tess only in the evening and at night, and I quickly got into a routine of working from five p.m. to eight a.m., sleeping during the day and waking again at three p.m. to prepare for the next day's work. I was once told that, before they go onstage, theater actors are given half an hour alone in the dressing rooms so they can "inhabit" their character. But that's only for a two-hour play, and all their lines are scripted. For me, the moment it struck nine a.m. in Sointula, I was onstage as Tess and remained so for the next sixteen hours. I had to improvise on my feet, and the story could go in any direction.

Of course, I wasn't actually sending and receiving messages every moment of the day, but even when not actually online, I was still working. I had to plan my responses, check details, research anecdotes I was planning to use later. I also had to plot her next moves, which required a lot of thought. I found a site for fiction writers that suggested compiling a "backstory" for your characters, to help bring them to life, and so I resolved to do this for each new person who entered Tess's life. I found it hard going until one day I realized that I could just borrow bits from the people I knew. So Jack, the elderly man Tess got chatting to outside the sauna, had lost his wife of thirty-seven years to ovarian cancer, drank a large glass of Baileys Irish cream each day at five p.m., and had a secret online gambling habit—just like Mr. Kingly, Mum's manager at Bluston's. The mother of Tess's pupil, Natalie, was modeled on our neighbor Ashley, who lived two doors down on Leverton Street. She bred guinea pigs, and we could hear their squeaking from our garden.

I also had to practice writing like her. We had very different styles—she rarely wrote in complete sentences, for instance— and even the simplest, most everyday word had to be checked to ensure it sounded authentic. I had to concentrate on the most brief, straightforward e-mails and status updates. She tended to address her recipient emphatically, using exclamation marks and sometimes capital letters—NINA!!—and often a nickname: Sugarplum, Pauly,

Big J. On top of her erratic spelling and grammar she used unfamiliar slang—that's mint; did you get arseholed last night? Sometimes, even an extensive Google search couldn't shed light on a phrase and I would have to take an educated guess. I still don't know whether calling someone a "nelly" is a compliment or not.

Throughout the precheckout stage I had been practicing writing as Tess, under her supervision. Because I had access to her e-mail and Facebook accounts, and looked at them more regularly throughout the day than she did, I would often be the first to see when a message came through for her or when someone wrote on her wall. So we had this system set up where I would write a response to the message as Tess and save it in her drafts folder. Then, when she signed in to her account, she would look at my efforts and critique them over Skype that evening, as if she were my teacher.

"Don't use *yo* as a greeting for Misha Jennings," she'd say. "I only say that to Daniel Woolly; it's this little thing we have. For Misha, I usually use *babe* at the beginning, but sign off *la di da*. It's a reference to the film *Annie Hall*."

Or "Just because I wrote to Alex that Steve's party was A.W.E.S.O.M.E. doesn't mean that you should put full stops in every adjective I use. I just do that occasionally for fun; it's not a habit."

There were many little things to learn—codes, in-jokes, habits—and although I noted everything in my files, I still didn't feel confident enough to write as her without cross-referencing and double-checking. And, of course, there were still the mysteries that had never been resolved: In 2008, for instance, she made several references to someone she called "the Zetty," but try as I might I couldn't discover who this person was, or why she gave them an unnecessary definite article.

Then there were the photos. I had to find appropriate backgrounds on Flickr that could pass for Sointula without being too distinctive, and that had been taken at the right time of year and showed the current weather for the island and that also suited the poses Tess would adopt in them.

For that first month, then, I left the flat only to stock up on food. Tesco Extra was open twenty-four hours a day, and so once a week I would take a break from work and go in the dead of night, at four a.m., when it would be only me, shelf stackers plugged into earphones, and a solitary cashier too drained to attempt chitchat. Thus, my contact with the "real" world was minimized to the point that I could effectively ignore its existence.

My own life, such as it was, I put to one side. I still checked my Facebook and e-mail each day, the former out of habit and the latter in case there was a message from Adrian. Aside from the weekly quotes he sent me through Red Pill, I hadn't heard from him since checkout—and, actually, for some time before that. His Red Pill address was the only one I had for him, my only means of contact, but he had made it clear that we shouldn't discuss the subject on there for fear of eavesdropping hackers. I knew he could find my regular e-mail from my registration details on the site, and so presumed we would communicate about the project on that.

So far I hadn't needed his help, and I suspected that he was leaving me alone in order to demonstrate his trust in me. However, it would be good, I thought, if there were a line of communication open, if and when I should require it; after all, on the Heath that day he had stated that if I took on the job he would be there for me every step of the way, always on hand for advice and support.

There was nothing until, one evening, sixteen days into the project, I checked my e-mail expecting nothing more than the usual spam to find a message advising me that I had a Facebook friend request.

This was not a common event. It had been several months since I'd received one, and that had been a case of mistaken identity, from a man I didn't know who addressed me as babz and said I had been looking fine the night before.

This new request was similarly from someone I didn't recognize: a woman called Ava Root. It was a distinctive name that I was sure I would have remembered had I come across it before, and I was about to consign her to spam when I saw there was a message attached to the request: Hey, there, how's it going?

It was an innocuous statement, but there was something about that Hey, there that struck a chord, and it was only a moment before I recalled that it was a phrase Adrian used at the start of each of his podcasts. It was, essentially, his catchphrase, and he would say the words differently each time—sometimes with a flourish, like a game-show host, at other times quickly and quietly, giving them hardly any emphasis at all.

I hadn't considered that he might contact me through Facebook, but that was only because I hadn't found him, Adrian Dervish, when I had searched for him before. It hadn't crossed my mind that he might set up a fake account to communicate with me, even though it now made sense: After all, why would any hackers be interested in messages between me and my old friend Ava?

My instincts were confirmed when I accepted the friend request and looked at Ava Root's profile. It was blank, devoid of any information save her name, and I was her only friend. Even the choice of

"Ava Root," it now occurred to me, signaled that Adrian was behind it: The name had the same number of letters as, and sounded similar to, that of his heroine, Ayn Rand.

I was pleased and relieved he had finally initiated contact—even though, as I say, I felt I was handling the situation adequately on my own and had no specific questions or issues to bring up. I replied to his message with a brief summary of the progress of the project so far, using suitably elliptical terms just to be on the safe side. If someone somehow happened to chance upon the message, they wouldn't have a clue what I was going on about. The subject's journey to her destination went smoothly; she is settling in well and exploring the island. Mother: seven e-mail exchanges so far and one request for a phone call, deferred by the subject—that sort of thing. At the end, I added: Just to confirm, we are now communicating through this channel, rather than RP?

A reply came a day later: Good work. Yes, communicate through here.

Then the following week came a less welcome intrusion from the wider world. Dozing on the sofa one afternoon, I was rudely awakened by the door buzzer. I couldn't account for the caller: It was Thursday, and I had already received my money for that week. I answered the door to an Indian man in a stained white shirt, who explained that he was from the restaurant below.

"There is a problem with water," he said.

I didn't know what he was talking about, so at his urging I put my bathrobe on over my pajamas and followed him down to the restaurant. It was the first time I had been inside. As it was only three p.m. and they hadn't yet opened, there were no customers, the tables bare except for paper tablecloths. Christmas lights were gaffer-taped to the walls, and there was a stale, yeasty smell in the air.

The man gesticulated toward the bar area, where another waiter was mopping the counter with wads of paper towels. There was a leak coming from my flat, he said—and, indeed, I could see a large damp patch on the ceiling, which would have been beneath my bathroom. He explained that the water had gotten into the wiring and electronic equipment of the bar and now neither the phone nor the card-reader machine worked, without which they could not operate their business. It was clear they expected me to do something about it.

I will spare you the details of what transpired, but in a nutshell: One of the waiters called a plumber, who revealed that the pipes under my bathroom were leaking. He would need to rip up the floor to fix them. Plus, the waiter told me, I would need to pay for the damage to the restaurant. All in all, it would cost in the region of six hundred pounds.

"You'll be able to get it back on insurance," said the plumber, an overly cheery man with a bumpy, shaved head.

The problem was I didn't have any insurance. I hadn't thought to get any when we bought the flat. I didn't have any savings, either. The money I got for my Tess work was just enough to cover day-to-day living expenses; it hadn't occurred to me that I might need extra for a contingency. I Googled how to get cash quick and was directed to a number of companies offering private loans. I called the first number and a man agreed to lend me six hundred pounds at an absurdly high interest rate.

It was clear that, in order to pay off this loan, I would need some extra income. I e-mailed Damian asking for my job back and received a curt reply saying that there was no work available for me and, by the way, he had found the manner of my resignation rude and unprofessional. So I searched online for another software testing job I could do from the flat. But the few jobs on offer were all office based; besides, they all seemed to require a degree, which I didn't have, as well as references, which I doubted Damian would give me. I suppose I didn't appreciate that; dull as it was working for Testers 4 U, it was unusual to be allowed to work from home and choose your own hours.

Getting another, "normal" job was not an option. For a start, I simply didn't have the time. My work with Tess took up most of the night, and I had to sleep during the day. But even if time were not an issue, previous experiences had proven that I wasn't suited to working with other people. First, in the summer after my A levels, I had tried volunteering at the Cats Protection League charity shop on Kentish Town Road. One of the other volunteers was an obese man who smoked, and the smell when he came back into the shop after a cigarette, the nicotine mixed with musty old clothes, was so repulsive I couldn't last longer than a morning.

Then there was the week at Caffè Nero. I was given a hairnet and assigned to the pastries section. A customer would give their coffee order to my colleague on the till, a boy called Ashim, who would ask whether they wanted any pastries, and if they said yes, I had to pick up the specified item with a pair of tongs and put it in a bag or on a plate, depending on whether it was for takeaway or eat-in. Sellotaped below the view of the customers was a laminated sheet showing photos of all the different products.

After an hour I was about to tell the supervisor I wasn't prepared to continue in such a role when she got in there first, telling me off for eating the bits of pastry that had flaked off the croissants—even though, as I pointed out, the flakes were a waste product that couldn't be sold. She changed me to washing-up duties, which was better, because I could have my back to the customers, but before long she found fault with me there too. To alleviate the tedium I had decided to hum, seeing whether I could hold the same note continuously for the time each item took to be washed up, and apparently it was disturbing the customers. I was determined to keep humming, though, and lowered the volume of the hum by degrees until she stopped coming over to complain.

During our fifteen-minute breaks I sat in a back room on a box of paper towels, listening to the *boom-boom-boom* music coming from Ashim's headphones as he texted his friends, and watching Lucy, the barista, shaking the makeup samples she had just stolen from Superdrug out of the sleeves of her jacket.

When I left, it wasn't in a big, dramatic rage; I didn't rip off my hairnet and storm out. One lunchtime, I went out to get my crisps and just didn't go back. It was a Friday and I was owed that week's pay, but I didn't ask for it. Mum understood about my leaving. I think she was pleased to have me back with her.

Tess once used coffee shops to illustrate how her varying moods affected her behavior. "It's like, when I'm on a high I'll haggle with the till guy at Starbucks, try to get fifty pence off my double espresso," she had explained. "Just for fun, to prove my charm. And when I'm low, I'll feel like I'm not even worthy of accepting my change."

Anyway, to get back to my point: It wasn't possible for me to get a normal job. So that was when I thought about getting a lodger.

I probably needn't add that the idea of someone else living in the flat was not an enticing one. It wasn't the fact that I would have to move out of my bedroom and both work and sleep in the front room; I didn't mind that. But I didn't relish the thought of having to make idle chitchat and cater to a stranger's demands. Everything was the way I liked it in the flat, but I acknowledged that the way I lived might not be to everyone's taste, and that they might desire furniture and curtains and more than two teaspoons. It would also mean being much more careful about my Tess work. As mentioned, up until then I had openly displayed my notes on the wall above my desk. I would have to get a lock for my door for when I was out, and perhaps pin my large *Lord of the Rings* poster up over the notes, for added security, when I was at home.

Nonetheless, a lodger seemed the most logical option—indeed, my only real option. I decided that the best thing to do was advertise the room for a low rent, the minimum I needed to pay off my loan, and make it clear that, in return, the lodger would have to accept certain rules.

I posted an ad in the "Room to Rent" section on Gumtree.com.

Small bedroom in shared flat in Rotherhithe. It's essential you have a quiet nature and spend a lot of time out. When you're in, we "keep out of each other's hair." Curry fans will be well catered for. £60 a week.

Within ten minutes of the ad going up I received seven replies. By the end of the day, there were more than a hundred. I didn't realize that cheap accommodation was in such demand in London. I composed a random short list of candidates from every tenth e-mail I received and invited them to come and view the flat. I arranged the meetings for three p.m., so that the onion smell from the restaurant would be at its peak, in order to avoid any later fuss when they discovered this factor. And indeed, some made their excuses within minutes. For others, the sticking point was the single bed.

Most, though, were not so fussy, even trying to think of positive things to say about the flat. "Very minimalistic!" one middle-aged man said, and proceeded to tell me at great, unwanted length about how he too was in a "transitional phase" of his life. He asked whether it was all right if his four-year-old daughter came to stay every other weekend. I informed him that it was not. One girl from Poland tried to engage me in conversation, asking me what kind of music I liked and so forth, until I realized that she was in effect auditioning *me* to see whether we were going to get on. I had to make it clear to her that I had no need of a friend. I just wanted someone who would pay the rent and be out the majority of the time.

Often I cut short the interviews myself, when it clearly wasn't going to work. One applicant, an old man who was bald except for a band of hair around his head, like the ring of Saturn, and reeked of body odor, informed me that he was "into big girls." Another, a young African man, had a Bible in the pocket of his corduroy jacket, which meant he had to be excluded, although he otherwise fit the criteria; he barely said a word and just nodded and smiled.

The majority of applicants were foreign, students from Africa or Eastern Europe. I couldn't decide whether it would be better to have someone foreign, because their English would be more limited, or worse, because they would invariably be learning the language while they were over here and might want to practice on me. After some thought, I decided that foreign would be better; it would also work to my advantage for the person to be unfamiliar with British customs and habits, so they were more likely to accept mine.

It is rather ironic, then, that I ended up with Jonty, who is not only English—well, Welsh—but possibly the most talkative person I have ever come across. But I didn't know that when I agreed to his moving in. He gave a misleading first impression. During our interview he was uncharacteristically quiet; later I discovered that he was so hungover he was afraid he would be sick if he opened his mouth. His appearance was striking, but not unpleasant: short and square, with disproportionately broad shoulders under his duffel coat and spiky, dark blond hair. Although he said he was twenty-five, his face looked much younger.

He nodded yes when I asked him whether he would be out of the flat a lot, and nodded again when I explained that my work required a lot of concentration, and that I had to work at night and then sleep all day, so if he was looking for a "mate," then he was in the wrong place. He shook his head when I asked whether he had many possessions. He seemed to genuinely like the flat, which was odd. He didn't mind that it was a single bed—"I never get lucky anyway," was one of the few things he said—and expressed no surprise at the lack of curtains and other furniture. So I decided on the spot that he would do. I was tired of seeing all these people; it was taking up a lot of time that I should have been devoting to Tess, and I had run out of money.

On the day he moved in, with a single sports bag—a lack of possessions was the one promise he kept—he was, to my dismay, much chattier. He knocked on my door and barely waited for a reply before entering, as if a conversation in my bedroom had been part of a prearranged schedule. Thank goodness I had had the foresight to cover up my Tess notes with a poster. He sat on the sofa, which was now my bed, and told me all about himself: originally from Cardiff, where he had had a successful career working in sales at American Express but had decided to give it up and come to London to be an actor. He told me a long anecdote about his "moment of revelation," when he had been persuading a woman to get another credit card and suddenly realized he had to do something more worthwhile with his life: "Follow my dreams, all that bollocks." He had enrolled with a drama school in King's Cross and given himself a year to make it, which was how long his savings would last.

Jonty didn't seem to be able to do anything without informing me about it. On his first evening in the flat he knocked on my door to announce he was going to "explore the neighborhood." I told him, through the door, that that wouldn't take long, that there was nothing to see in Rotherhithe. I heard him come in a few hours later, but when I left my room to go to the loo his door opened and he started babbling about his evening. "You didn't tell me we were so close to the river!" he said—I didn't know that we were—and went on about this "amazing" pub in the next street called the Queen Bee that was, I quote, "full of these crazy old dudes, seriously old-school." One of them had bought him a pickled egg from a jar beside the bar. I knew it would lead to further exhausting conversation if I told him I hadn't "explored" farther than Tesco Extra.

That's the thing about Jonty: Any response you give, even a "Really?" is like throwing a log on a fire. So, when he'd come back home with all these stories of his adventures around London—finding a shop that sold taxidermied animals in Islington, swimming in an open-air pool in Brockwell Park—I nodded but didn't respond. Even though he claimed not to know anyone in London, he seemed to make friends very quickly. One night, only a few weeks after he arrived, his new colleagues from drama school put him in a dustbin and rolled him down Primrose Hill. Apparently, this was a gesture of affection.

Luckily, his desire to "suck the marrow out of London" did mean that he was out most nights, but I still had to take precautions, because I never knew when he would be coming back. I hid my Tess time line behind three large *Lord of the Rings* posters and got a lock for my door. I also took up the carpet from the corridor, so that I would be able to hear him approaching on the bare boards. He would return in the middle of the night, when I would be up doing Tess work. When I heard his footsteps I would freeze and stop typing. I'd listen to his footsteps pause outside my door, and then retreat back to his room.

Nevertheless, the day-to-day practicalities of communal living were a challenge. Luckily my Tess schedule meant I could use the kitchen at night, when he was asleep, but once or twice he was still up and, when he heard me in there, came through in his tracksuit bottoms for a "chat." He would sometimes get a takeaway from the restaurant below, and the waiters would bring it up to the flat; the first time the doorbell rang, I nearly fell off my chair. He quickly got to know all of them, and I would hear him on the street outside, chatting to them as they smoked. He would tell them about his auditions and ask them about themselves, as if they were his friends.

Even when he was absent, his presence was felt. He liked to cook himself elaborate meals using strange ingredients from ethnic supermarkets, and I would often find a streak of his latest dish down the side of a kitchen cabinet and a jar of strong-smelling sauce in the fridge with its lid half off. In the bathroom, globules of his shaving foam, flecked with hair, hardened in the sink.

After not really having any contact with men before, suddenly I had two. Because it wasn't long after Jonty arrived that I had my first e-mail from Connor.

This was six and a half weeks after Tess had checked out. In Sointula, all was going smoothly. Tess had moved into her flat and had started her job teaching art to Natalie, who was being homeschooled by her parents. Tess attended yoga lessons three times a week and, much to her surprise, had developed an interest in fishing. She had also made some new friends, and that day, the day Connor e-mailed, I had decided that she was going to take a day trip to the mainland with her new friend Leonora, an older woman who ran a *quaint* café on the island.

Her Facebook update for that day was an elliptical one: Wanted a pineapple, got some feet. Tess was fond of those sorts of mysterious updates, and so I made sure to include one every so often, even though I didn't like them—partly because I disapproved in principle, but also because they invariably elicited curious responses from her friends to which Tess then had to respond.

What happened was that the previous evening, Tess and Leonora had been having tea at Leonora's house. Tess had admired a pineapple-shaped ice bucket in the front room, and asked where Leonora had gotten it. Leonora replied that she had bought it from a shop on the mainland that sold inexpensive "quirky" furniture and household items. Tess, whose flat was still quite unfurnished, was keen to have a look, and they decided they would take a trip to the mainland the following day.

The two of them caught the nine twenty a.m. ferry, landing at ten thirty a.m. They took a bus to Main Street, where the shop was located. There were no more pineapple-shaped ice buckets, but Tess spotted some bookends that she liked, stone casts of a pair of men's feet. I know they sound gross, she wrote in an e-mail to Justine later that day, but honestly, they're kind of cool. You look at them and think—where have those feet been? She also bought a red silk throw for her bed, eighty inches by forty inches in size.

There was also a light blue armchair that she liked the look of; however, she wasn't sure whether it would fit into her flat, so she asked the shopkeeper to hold it for her so that she could go home and measure the spot where it would go. She would phone later that afternoon if she wanted it. Then she and Leonora browsed some of the other shops on the street. Tess considered buying a jumper with rainbow stripes, but stopped herself. This place is so fucking folksy, she told Justine. I've got to resist turning into an old hippie with chin hair and Cornish pasty shoes.

They had lunch in a café called the Rosewood, where Tess had a quinoa salad. Although it was tough, she was persevering with the veganism: She found that it made her calmer and her digestion better, and she could swear that the whites of her eyes were brighter. She also felt it "morally right." When Tess mentioned turning vegan in an e-mail to Justine, Justine pointed out the contradiction between this antimeat stance and her newly discovered interest in fishing. And since when was I consistent? Tess replied. I was quite proud of that.

Anyway, in the Rosewood café the two women talked about Leonora's new boyfriend, a local man called Roger who ran whale-watching trips and was kind and attractive, but had suspected "commitment issues." Tess confided in Leonora about her brief marriage to the Australian. Tess liked Leonora, although she was quite earnest and probably not the sort of person she'd have been friends with back in London. That's the thing about this place. Broadens your horizons, makes you consider things you wouldn't normally.

After lunch, the two women took the two thirty p.m. ferry back to Sointula, where Tess spent the rest of the afternoon reading a Russian novel called *Anna Karenina*, which she had always meant to read and was finding very affecting. At seven forty p.m. she watched a black-and-white film called *His Girl Friday* on CBC Canada and ate some brown rice with a tofu-and-cabbage stir-fry, before going to bed at ten thirty p.m.

When Connor's e-mail came through, though, none of this had happened yet. It was twelve fifty-eight p.m. Sointula time and Tess was offline, in the middle of lunch at the Rosewood café. I was at my computer preparing the account of her trip for her to send to Justine when she got home. I checked her e-mails, as I did several times an hour, and saw one from a sender I didn't recognize, Connor Devine. The subject line contained just one word: So . . .

The e-mail continued: . . . Remember your theory about Benny? I've decided that you were right. He was definitely fucking both of them.

That was it. No sign-off or anything. A line at the bottom indicated that the e-mail had been sent from a BlackBerry.

As you can imagine, I was perplexed. Both the sender and the subject to which he was referring were unknown to me, yet the e-mail was written in a very informal and immediate style, as if he and Tess were in the middle of a conversation. I searched for the name in both of Tess's e-mail accounts and there was no record of Connor Devine, nor in the notes from our Skype sessions. I knew he wasn't one of her Facebook friends, but I checked to see whether he was friends with any of her friends. The name was a surprisingly common one—there were thirty-eight of them listed in London alone—but none of them had any links with anyone Tess knew. I searched in my Tess files for "Benny," but nothing came up on that name either. I did a Google search, but, as I say, there were many results for Connor Devine, and I could find no obvious link to Tess with anyone of that name.

This wasn't the first time Tess had received an e-mail from a sender unknown to me. A few weeks previously there had been a Facebook message from a woman called Chandra Stanley, but it had been a standard, Hi, how are you, wow, how's Canada? and I could give a standard response. This one, though, was difficult. The sender's tone was "larky" and the contents clearly referred to a private joke between the two of them.

I decided to ignore the e-mail, thinking that it must have been sent by mistake. But then, the next afternoon, I heard again from Connor Devine:

Fancy some bone marrow at St. John? Sans parsley?

Parsley was one of Tess's dislikes, so it seemed likely that the sender knew her, and that the first e-mail hadn't been a mistake. The name "St. John" also rang a bell. Eight years previously, Tess had had a short-lived relationship with a chef called Toby who had worked at a restaurant called St. John in East London. It was a disgusting-sounding place that served up bits of animals that shouldn't be eaten, for large amounts of money. Toby weighed twenty-three stone, Tess had told me one evening, and she had slept with him because she had never been with a fat man and wanted to see what it was like. Apparently, grabbing handfuls of his flesh "was like ascending a climbing wall," and his skin gave off a sweet, yeasty smell, similar to that of digestive biscuits. She liked him because he was "so pathetically grateful," but the novelty soon wore off.

Curious, I went through my notes for that time in her life, when she was living with Catatonic Katie and managing the vintage clothes shop in Spitalfields. She had had relationships with various men, but there was no mention of this Connor. Neither did he have any association with the restaurant, that I could find.

Also, I discovered, the restaurant had been open since 1994, and a dish containing bone marrow was mentioned in a newspaper review in that same year, so, really, the time frame was hardly narrowed at all: Connor and Tess could have eaten there at any point in the past seventeen years.

The message did reveal one thing, of course: Connor Devine almost certainly did not know Tess was in Canada. I decided to reply:

Sounds great, but not quite worth a 10,000-mile round trip.

He replied with a single:

?

I sent a brief e-mail explaining that I—Tess—had moved to Canada, keeping to the larky, casual tone that had been established. I had several versions of this "introductory" e-mail that I used, depending on the recipient. They ranged from the casual, Fancied a change; I'm loving it! for not very close friends, to a more in-depth and intimate account referencing her depression for those whom she trusted and who already had some context. To be safe, with Connor I went for the first option, because I didn't know how much he knew of Tess's problems.

Good thing I did, because it was clear from his reply that he had no idea about Tess's depression, or the extent of it, anyhow. His reply expressed surprise, and again, using what I could only presume were private references, he bombarded her with questions, sending each in a separate e-mail so Tess's in-box was constantly active: How are you going to survive without a good whiskey sour? Where are you going to buy your stockings? I can't really see you knitting your own beret. . . .

And then in the fifth of such single-line e-mails, there was the biggest clue I'd had so far. And what about Joan? he wrote. Did you smuggle her over in your hand luggage?

Joan was Tess's cat between the years 2000 and 2003, named after an actress called Joan Crawford. She disappeared one day, an incident that sparked a fortnight-long slump. So from this reference I established that Connor had not had a proper conversation with Tess for at least eight years.

A few e-mails later, I was granted my second useful piece of information, which further narrowed down the time frame. When I mentioned that you could reach Sointula only by ferry, he wrote: Ah, well, we know how much you like ferries . . . or does there have to be a major disaster involved?

This, I thought, was likely to be a reference to an incident in 2001, on the day of the September 11 attacks in New York. Tess had been traveling with a friend, Juliet, to a Greek island called Patras, and they had been on a ferry from Italy when they heard the news of the planes from another passenger. It was a twelve-hour crossing, and that night Tess had sex with a stranger she met on board, an eighteen-year-old public-school boy called Rollo with curly blond hair "like a Botticelli angel" and a conditional place at Oxford. They did it on deck, with their fellow passengers sleeping all around them.

So Connor must have known Tess after 2001, but stopped communications with her in 2003, before the cat disappeared. However, I was still none the wiser on who he was or the nature of their relationship. And, indeed, why he was contacting her again after all this time. From the beginning, the tone of his e-mails had an intimacy that wasn't commensurate with his and Tess's relationship in recent years—which was, as I say, nonexistent. He wrote as if they had never lost contact and were in the middle of a fascinating conversation. There was a sort of . . . what's the word? A presumption. He was also quite forthright with Tess, in a way that most people weren't. I think lots of her friends were a bit scared of her—or at least indulged the silly or mad things she said.

And he was extremely curious, asking questions that sent me rummaging through my more obscure Tess files. Do you still think the pop band a-ha are highly underrated? Did Shauna end up running that guesthouse in Sri Lanka? Or he would send me a joke, and ask me to finish it off, or a silly clip from YouTube. He was by far the most frequent e-mailer Tess had, and I found I was spending much of my time thinking about what I was going to write to him.

At first, I took the tactic of ignoring his questions and instead asking some of my own, to try to gather some more information. Initially his replies were flippant and uninformative; he seemed incapable of giving a straight answer. For instance, I asked him what he was doing now and he replied, Still overpaid, still battling against rotters, which was unhelpful. After a few of these bantering exchanges, I decided that I was going to take a risk and ask him to give me direct replies to my questions.

K dude—one of Tess's e-mail habits was to drop the "O" from "OK"—come on, give it to me straight. I haven't seen you in forever.

Just tell me what's happening with you. Stating requests so explicitly may have not been the way Tess interacted with him, but I figured that I could get away with it, as so much time had elapsed since they had last communicated.

The strategy worked. The next e-mail from Connor was much longer, and, although not wholly free of flippancy, provided a certain number of facts. He was working as a lawyer for a large firm based in Temple, specializing in property law, and lived in Kensal Rise. He had been married but split up with his wife, Chrissie, the previous year. They had two children of whom they shared custody, a five-year-old girl called Maya and a two-year-old boy called Ben. He didn't say how long he had been married, but it couldn't have been longer than seven years, even if he had met Chrissie just after he and Tess lost touch.

It was a short, factual e-mail, but later, at eleven thirty p.m. U.K. time, he sent another one, with the heading Continued:

You're wondering why I've gotten back in touch with you. Here goes. You know that when I was with you, it was the happiest time of my life. Yes, scoff away; I know it wasn't very long. But honestly, I look back on those months like they were this holiday in another life, the life I imagined I would have when I was a teenager. Full of bravado and daring and risk taking, the feeling that anything was possible. You were beholden to nothing. We talked about big issues, important stuff, about how best to live. You inspired me. You encouraged me to take my photography seriously, to not sell out, to live boldly.

I'm not trying to guilt-trip you; I just want to be honest. You make me want to be honest. I was absolutely devastated when you ended it. Beyond gutted. I pretended that it wasn't such a big deal, that I knew we weren't suited, that I agreed with whatever bullshit rationale you used—"We don't make each other the best possible versions of ourselves," or whatever. But you did make me the best "me." I honestly think I knew then that you were it, my chance for the life I wanted, and that I'd blown it (I still don't know how exactly), and that the rest of my life would be a compromise.

Chrissie was a mistake. I met her maybe a month after you; it was this dinner party set up by my mate Dennis, meant to cheer me up because I was still in bits about you. These friends of mine were nice people, but they were quite dull, you know. Lawyers. And Chrissie was like them too—sweet and nice and pretty and unchallenging and perfectly happy with the status quo. She had no ambitions beyond the ordinary. And I don't know whether I was just exhausted and wanted some security, or if I thought in a bizarre way that it would be getting back at you (not that you would have given a shit). I thought, "Okay, then, I'll do it. I can be this. I'll settle, I'll give in. Maybe they're right, and I'm wrong, and a steady, settled life is the key to happiness. Arranged marriages report the greatest levels of happiness," etc., etc.

It's amazing how easy it is to fall into these things, really. It's like, when you get to your mid-thirties, especially if you're a guy, the moment you stop struggling you find yourself being carried down this path toward marriage and babies and a family car. I started seeing Chrissie, and there we were, going for walks along the South Bank, taking a bottle of Wolf Blass to dinner parties, having minibreaks in two-hundred-pound-a-night fishermen's cottages in Whitstable, being taken aside by her friends at parties and told that I'd better be serious about her, because you can't mess around with women in their thirties, you know . . . and how she'd make such a good mother, being such a nurturing person . . . being taken to meet her uptight parents in Gloucester, her revealing her teenage eating disorder, blah, blah, blah. And then it was a year later and that meant it was time to move in together. So we did that. Then the trips to Habitat and the box sets. The group Sunday lunches in gastro pubs, the predictable opinions lifted from the *Guardian*, the Jamie Oliver Flavour Shaker.

I just surrendered to all of it, took the path of least resistance. I know that you have no respect for that sort of behavior, and it goes against everything you believe in. So I'm taking a big risk in telling you this, because the last thing I want is for you to think less of me.

I should say that I wasn't unhappy all the time. There were periods when I was content, when I thought, "Maybe this is what it's about." Especially when Maya and Ben came along. They're gorgeous, really; you'd love them. I tried so hard for their sake, but Chrissie and I just grew farther and farther apart, and in the end it was unbearable. When I came back home from work, she wasn't the person I wanted to talk to. I didn't want to tell her about the little thoughts I had, the things I saw in the street that made me smile or feel sad. I just knew she wouldn't understand; she didn't "do" complicated or murky; she didn't question. She saw the world in black-and-white and wasn't interested in the gray areas. And eventually I realized that the only thing that matters is finding someone whom you properly connect with, who understands you. Otherwise, what's the point?

And so I left. It was not a decision I took lightly. I agonized over it for months and months. Went to a shrink. Talked to my friends. They all tried to talk me out of it. But I had to do it, for my sanity.

I wouldn't say that you were the reason I did it. After all, I hadn't spoken to you for years. But I did think about you a lot, about what you stood for, and I think that's what gave me the strength to do it. You were—are—the only person I know who has the courage not to live her life by convention.

P.S. I know that you won't know how to reply to this, so please don't. I don't expect anything from you; I just wanted to tell you.

The next morning, he was back to his cheery, inconsequential one-line e-mails, as if nothing had happened. That afternoon, however, he asked me to send him a photograph. I pointed out that there was one on my Facebook page and asked him to friend me; to my surprise, he replied saying he didn't "do" Facebook:

It's rubbish. Old-school e-mail's the way forward.

I duly sent him a picture of Tess leaning against the rail at Sointula harbor—my most successful attempt at Photoshop. Fuck me, he replied, you're even more gorgeous than you were nine years ago. How did you manage that? But of course, without his friending me on Facebook, I couldn't see what he looked like—which, by that point, I was rather curious about. I looked him up anyway, in case by not "doing" it he meant that he didn't like it, not that he wasn't on it at all. As I said, there were dozens of Connor Devines from London listed, and of course I didn't know which one of them he was—if, indeed, he was any of them. And several of the profiles didn't have photographs—or had those ones where you couldn't see the person's face, just their silhouette or the back of their head—so it was also possible he was one of them.

Obviously I couldn't risk asking him which profile was his, in case it was one of the ones with a picture; nor could I risk sending a request to all the likely Connor Devines, in case several of them accepted. The information would show up on my profile, and would look suspicious.

I wrote back asking whether he could send me a photograph— Come on, you've seen me; fair's fair—and got an attachment within half an hour.

The picture showed a man in close-up, apparently in a park. He was wearing sunglasses but also had a scarf tied in a loop around his neck, so I surmised it might have been spring or autumn, when the sun was shining but the temperature still chilly. He had short dark hair with a little tufty bit at the front, like that cartoon character—I can't remember his name, and without access to Google I can't find out—and his ears stuck out. His eyebrows were thick and he had lots of dark stubble. He was smiling straight at the camera, but I couldn't see his eyes behind the glasses. If he was Tess's age, then he would be almost forty.

I am finding it quite hard to write about Connor in an objective manner, not colored by emotion or hindsight, but I am trying. At the time, what I remember feeling on reading his confessional e-mail was surprise that a relationship could mean so much to one person, and so little to the other. Here was Connor saying that the time he had with Tess was the most exciting period of his life, yet I had asked Tess over and over again to tell me about every person she had had a relationship with, however brief and insignificant, and she had never mentioned him. I don't think that she held back for any reason; after all, she told me about lots of terrible things she had done, and she didn't seem to mind what I thought of her. She must have totally forgotten about it.

On Skype one evening she had said something along those lines: "It's so weird, isn't it, how you can have a one-night stand with some-one and never forget them, and then go out with someone for, like, six months, and they leave no trace on you. The moment it's over, you forget about it. Don't you think?"

"Mmmm," I had said.

Obviously Tess and I were very different people. But I felt that if I had done any of these things that Connor said he and Tess had done together—dancing on the tables at a Spanish bar in Soho, gate-crashing an awards ceremony for gas fitters at a fancy hotel, going to Paris just for lunch—or if someone told me that I was the most extraordinary person they had ever met, I would have remembered them.

||||||||||

Something else happened at the commune today. I wasn't going to mention it, but I confess I still feel rather shaken, and perhaps it'll help to write it down.

I woke this morning with the usual film of grease over my skin and my hair stiff and sticky. My customary cleansing with wet wipes felt unequal to the job, and I felt a great desire for a proper wash with water. I remembered Annie saying yesterday that she and the children had gone down to the river to bathe, and so I asked her how to get there. She immediately offered to come with me, but I demurred; judging from her casual display of her bosoms, I sus-pected that she would expect us all to take our clothes off.

The directions she gave me sounded needlessly complicated. After all, I thought, as long as I kept walking downhill, I couldn't go far wrong. I set off down a little rocky path lined with scrubby plants at the south end of the site, and before long the sounds of the commune, the bongos and the barking, faded. The sun was high and scorching. I had forgotten to wear my hat and quickly found myself weakened by the heat. Sharp bushes nipped my ankles. I started walking straight down, but the ground was uneven and I kept finding myself going uphill again. The sun was really beating down on my head; my hair felt heavy as a helmet and my limbs like swollen pieces of meat attached to my body. I began to feel disoriented, so I headed for the shade of some trees. I got some relief from the sun, but the problem then was that I couldn't see where I was going, because of the trees. By now the noise of the commune had entirely receded, replaced by the fierce chirrup of insects and, under that, what I imagined was the distant rush of water. It was then, in the woods, that I had the oddest sensation. I felt suddenly, intensely lonely—more so than I had ever felt in my life, even after Mum died. In fact it was an entirely different feeling—more fear than emptiness.

I'm finding it hard to describe.

I remember Tess once saying that sometimes when she was depressed she felt like she was just a sum of her parts, her upbringing and influences—that there was nothing intrinsically, uniquely "her." At the time I didn't know what she meant. But at that moment, I understood. And then I had this sudden, overwhelming realization that one day I wouldn't exist. I felt like screaming, but even screaming as loud as humanly possible wouldn't have been enough to express how I felt. And after this thought that was too huge and formless and awful to grasp, I started to think about tiny, specific things: that after my death someone else would move into my flat and set up their computer by the window; they would still be selling tents in Tesco Extra; another set of old men would be eating pickled eggs at the Queen Bee pub. People and things would continue to exist in a world where I did not, and no one would ever think of me.

And, if that was the case, then what was the point of existing in the first place? I could just expire here, under this tree. I imagined my body in time lapse, decomposing and sinking into the soil until, within a matter of seconds, there was no trace of me left.

Maybe, I thought, this was the exact spot where Tess died—it wasn't impossible. She could already be down there, in the ground; I could join her, our molecules blending together in the soil. The thought was not unappealing.

I must stress that I wasn't feeling that I wanted to die, exactly— more that not being alive might not be such a terrible thing. After all, Tess was not alive; Mum was not alive.

I don't know exactly how long I was there in the forest. At some point, what I suppose was a survival instinct kicked in, and I started walking toward the sunlight and out of the forest and uphill and eventually the sounds of the commune grew louder and I arrived back at the tent. Annie was cooking dinner and cheerily asked me how my swim went.

"Did you manage to find any water? There's just a trickle left. Sad, isn't it? I don't know how the poor animals are coping. If it doesn't rain soon it'll dry up completely. Do you want some dinner?"

All I could do was shake my head.

*The commune was almost deserted* when I woke today. Annie told me that on Sundays there's a market in the nearby town, where everyone goes to try to sell tourists the tatty rubbish they've been making all week. Only she didn't use that phrase; she said "handicrafts." She hadn't gone herself because the baby was poorly. The site was eerily quiet, and it felt as if we were the only ones left behind: the same feeling I used to get when I stayed at home with Mum instead of going to school.

I probably should have gone to the market; it would have been a good place to show around Tess's photo. But I didn't. Partly because of the effort involved in the heat, but also because I am starting to think that this whole exercise is pointless. Even if I do manage to find someone who positively identifies Tess, who says they saw her here last summer and could back up their claim with sufficient evidence, what then? In order to fully complete my mission, I would still have to find her body, and how can I do that? I can hardly search the entire mountain, especially not in these temperatures. And even if she did spend her last days in the commune, who's to say she didn't travel elsewhere to carry out the act, and her body is lying in another forest or up another mountain or in a lake, twenty or eighty or two hundred miles away?

Instead of going to the market I lay watching Annie make her stools. In the shade of the van's canopy she was sanding the slices of wood, Milo helping out. The repetitive motion of the sander over the surface of the wood was rather hypnotic, and the work looked satisfying and not too onerous, so after a little while I asked her if I could have a go. As we worked, I told Annie about how I sometimes used to help Mum paint her miniatures, which was really the opposite of what we were doing—all about tiny little strokes rather than big sweeping gestures—but was similarly relaxing.

At one point, Milo started talking about his school, how he was looking forward to going back but found the maths lessons hard. Except he said "math," without the "s." I was very good at maths, so I asked him what it was he found difficult, and we talked about it for a while.

"It's good; you talk to him like he's an adult," Annie said. "Most people don't do that."

A little while later, when we had each finished the slice of wood we were working on, she said to Milo, "I think it's time to cut your hair, little legs."

She got out some tiny scissors and started hacking away at his curls. I watched, and the thought of feeling air on my neck was such an enticing one that I asked her whether she would cut mine too.

"Certainly," she said, and finishing with Milo she came and sat behind me with the scissors.

"Just a trim today, madam?"

"No," I said, "up to here," and indicated just below my ears.

"Are you sure?" she said. "It looks like you've been growing it for years."

She was right; I had. I nodded. Annie cut slowly and carefully, and it was half an hour later when she came around to inspect me from the front, head tilted in a critical manner.

"Okay, I think that's as neat as I can make it. I think you look rather like . . . Who was that old movie star? The one with the dark bob?"

She offered to get a mirror so I could see what I looked like, but I said no, I didn't need to. I felt a stone lighter and kept stroking my newly exposed neck, a part of my body that hadn't seen the daylight for decades.

||||||||||

The problem with having all this time and no Internet is that unhelpful thoughts float into one's head. I don't just mean what happened yesterday in the forest; smaller matters too.

This afternoon, after the haircut, I was in my usual position under Annie's canopy when, out of nowhere, I remembered something Tess once said about Adrian. It was after that time she told me I was sad and pathetic, and she was trying to make it up to me, being nice and saying how lucky she was to have me and how perfect I was for the job. "Adrian isn't stupid," she said. "He did his research well."

I didn't really think much of it at the time, but today, lying on my mattress, that memory linked up with another one, like the way that bubbles used to rise up and merge in my Lava lamp. It was about my meeting with Adrian by the hospital. I was thinking again what a coincidence it was that, out of all the places in London, he asked to meet somewhere so familiar to me, and the revelation that his wife had also had MS. And then it occurred to me that perhaps it wasn't really a coincidence after all.

You see, two years ago, when Mum could still use her hands, I suggested to her that she should get involved with the forum on an MS Web site. This was after I had started contributing to the caregivers' section and I thought it might be good for her to communicate with others in the same predicament. She was quite active on the forum for about six months, until it became uncomfortable to type, and on it she mentioned appointments at the Royal Free. I posted on the site's "In Memoriam" board when she died: nothing fancy, just the bare facts of her death, along with a note that she was the best mother who ever lived.

The site was public, so Adrian could, in theory, have found it, if he had Googled me. The thought came to me that perhaps the reason he asked to meet at the Royal Free was because of the connection with Mum. To remind me of her illness and the general misery of the artificial prolonging of her life, in order to increase the likelihood of my being sympathetic to the idea of someone wanting to take control of her own death.

Of course, I reasoned, the location could have been pure coincidence, as I'd previously assumed. But even if it wasn't—if he had indeed done his research—did it matter? You could say it didn't reflect negatively on Adrian, that, in fact, it demonstrated his commitment to Tess and the cause, since he wanted to do all he could to ensure that I would help her. And I was almost certain it hadn't affected the outcome of the meeting, either. I had considered the proposition with independent thought. Even if he had put the idea to me in, say, a wine bar, I think I would have agreed to take on the job. So the fact that he might have been more calculating than he appeared did not actually alter the course of events, did it?

I was also thinking today about the horoscope moment with Connor. How it changed things, and whether it would have happened if I hadn't found the original e-mails between him and Tess.

Through what Connor had said, I had built up a picture of what had happened between them. They had had a short relationship sometime between 2001 and 2003; she had ended it, and he had been devastated. But it still bothered me that I couldn't find any evidence of the relationship in Tess's files. I felt I needed it in front of me. Every time Connor gave me a new clue in an e-mail, I would follow it up, searching through my notes.

The breakthrough came two weeks after Connor first got in touch. He made a passing jokey comment about being a former Renegade Master, and the odd phrase rang a bell. I did a search in Tess's file and found it in a folder named "Unimportant men": short-lived e-mail correspondence, mostly from her old Hotmail account, with men whom Tess either couldn't remember or claimed were of no importance. "Just some bloke. Not worth spending any time over, honestly."

Renegademaster72@yahoo.com was the address. There weren't that many e-mails between them, eighteen in all, which was explained by the fact that the affair took place mostly over the summer. At that time Tess did not have a desk job and was painting backdrops for festivals, so they'd have been mainly texting instead. And this was before Facebook, of course.

So, now I had more details of their relationship. They had met at the party in Brixton—Did you get a nosebleed going south of the river? he had written in his first e-mail—and he had been crazy about her, it was clear. Even though his e-mails were not "love letters" as such, and he was trying to be casual, you could tell how much thought had gone into even the briefest of messages, how carefully selected the jokes and links he sent her were, and how quickly he responded to her e-mails.

Tess's e-mails to him were much more dashed off, as was her style, but at first she responded in kind to Connor's larkiness. She would come back with a joke or link of her own and would make an effort to be flirtatious.

As the weeks went on, however, you could trace the drain of interest, the same pattern as in so many of her other relationships. She started to make less of an effort, to take a few days to reply, to not acknowledge his jokes. It made him look a bit foolish.

This was illustrated by one rather bizarre exchange. On Monday, June 17, 2002, at ten thirteen a.m., Connor had written a one-line e-mail to Tess: I want to lick your armpits.

Tess had replied, I haven't shaved them for five days.

Connor wrote back: All the better. I want every bit of you I can get. Any toenail clippings going spare? xxxx

Tess had not replied to that for fifteen hours, and then when she did it was just an Ugh. No kisses.

Another difference was that before, in their early flirting days, their habit was not to give each other a straight answer to questions— everything had to be at a sort of "angle" to the point, witty or whimsical. As Tess's interest ebbed, however, she became more and more to the point. And she was, I thought, quite unfair to him.

For example: At the beginning, Connor had tried to organize

things for them to do when they saw each other, until Tess had told him in no uncertain terms that she disliked plans, preferring to be "spontaneous" (which is rather ironic, considering our project). But then, in one e-mail he wrote of his excitement at seeing her that evening and added, in a fanciful and high-spirited manner, The world is our oyster, Heddy. Shall we get smashed in Claridge's? Hop on a train to Brighton? In other words, he was doing exactly what she wanted: being adventurous and spontaneous. But she wouldn't play along. Her brief reply stated that she didn't know how she was going to feel that evening.

Toward the end, in late July 2002, she wasn't even bothering to reply to his messages, and it was clear that he sensed something was wrong: Was something worrying you last night? You were a bit quiet.

In reply, she wrote: We need to have a chat.

That was the last in their exchange.

Reading the e-mails, I felt that Tess had not behaved very nicely toward Connor, and felt a little sorry for him. And it was perhaps that which led to what happened with the horoscopes.

As I've mentioned before, I had one strict rule with my Tess work: Whatever I did or said as Tess had to be something that *she* would do or say, to the best of my knowledge of her character. And, as I've also mentioned before, part of her character was a belief in all sorts of mumbo jumbo. Sometimes it was just a phase she went through, like homeopathy and Reiki—even, for seven months, Christianity, after she attended something called the Alpha course at a church in West London. But she retained a constant, infuriating faith in horoscopes. Not so much the daily predictions in newspapers—although she did read those—but the notion that our personality traits are somehow predestined by the stars.

Often when we were talking, I'd ask her to describe someone and she'd say something like "Oh, you know, he was just a typical Leo," as if: (a) I knew what "a typical Leo" was; and (b) that meant anything at all. I tried once to challenge her on it and explain why it was nonsense, and that I thought that this assignment of character traits was an abdication of responsibility for a person's own actions. She didn't take it well. She was in a low mood that day and told me I could fuck right off.

So, one day, three weeks after we began corresponding, Connor told me about a conversation he had had the evening before at a drinks party for a colleague who was leaving his law practice. He was talking to the wife of another colleague who was, I quote, three sheets to the wind—which means drunk—and she told him a long story about how her eldest daughter had wanted to marry her boyfriend and, because she was an amateur astrologer, she decided she would do the couple's "chart." Apparently the man's sign was a bad match for the daughter's, and she had advised her daughter not to marry. The daughter had told her not to be so stupid and had gone ahead anyway and, lo and behold, the couple were divorced within six months.

In reply, I wrote: What a silly cow.

Connor's reply: Has the leopard changed its spots? I thought you loved that stuff. You were always telling me that I was, if I remember rightly, "unspontaneous and stodgy," because I was a Taurean.

At that point, I could have gotten away with it. I could have fudged it and said what I meant by the remark was that the woman didn't know what she was doing, and those signs were actually perfectly compatible, or something along those lines. But I didn't.

Well, I've seen the light, I wrote back.

After a moment's hesitation I pressed send, feeling a surge of anxiety mixed with excitement. By knowingly making Tess do something that she would probably not have done in real life, I had broken the one big rule I had for my job. It felt rather like going back in a time machine and interfering with the past—except, of course, it was the present.

When Connor's reply came seven minutes later, however, my worries evaporated.

Aw, Heddy, he wrote—that was his nickname for Tess; I never found out where it came from—that makes me happy. Don't get cross, but that was always something I had to bite my tongue over with you. I always thought it was a load of old bollocks. Welcome to the rational world!

Seeing the word *rational* gave me a thrill; it seemed further confirmation of the rightness of my decision. I wrote back, as Tess would, Oi, don't push it!

But it was as if I had broken a seal. From then on I began to put more of myself into the correspondence.

I don't want to overstate this. It wasn't that I suddenly abandoned Tess and started responding as myself. I didn't do anything that would alert suspicion. At that stage, there was just the occasional moment when, if it was fitting, I would respond to him more as myself than as Tess. It was only minor things, and, as I say, it was mostly what I left out: her irrationality, her "mysticism." I replied promptly to his e-mails, rather than leaving them for hours or days, like she did. I answered his questions. I didn't go on and on about feelings and dreams.

Sometimes, I had to improvise when Connor asked me a question I didn't have the answer to. For instance, he was initially quite keen on reminiscing about the past when he and Tess were together. Do you remember that man with the kitten on Dean Street? And I would say, Of course, even though it was quite likely that Tess didn't.

Occasionally he'd ask trickier questions, such as, Did you really mean what you said about those Hampton Court photos? And I would have no idea what he was talking about, and whether the original comment had been bad or good. In those instances I would deflect the question.

He also had a tendency to tell stories or make observations about his children, and use these as a springboard to ask me questions about my childhood. For instance, he told a story about how his daughter, Maya, had asked him whether he had liked being five years old, and how he couldn't remember anything about being that age, and then he'd ask me what my memories of being five were.

Unless I definitely knew Tess's answer to this, I would answer as myself, adapting details when necessary. For instance, I substituted Kentish Town High Street for Dulwich, where Tess had lived with her family from the ages of three to eleven. It was quite interesting to consider my past like that. I hadn't done so before. I didn't even talk about those things with Mum. She and I talked a lot, but mostly about little things, arrangements or school or what was on the TV. We didn't really discuss past events—because we had both been there, I suppose, and there was no need.

The time difference helped me a lot here. By the time Tess woke up in Sointula it was four thirty p.m. in London, and there would be at least three or four e-mails sent by Connor during the day. She would then respond to them promptly. But, of course, since I could see Connor's e-mails as soon as he sent them, I had time to do any research and formulate my replies before "Tess" woke up and I pressed send. I found myself sleeping less and less during the day, unable to resist checking Tess's in-box.

I was concerned at first that I would say something that contradicted what Connor knew about Tess. But it quickly became apparent that he had little knowledge of her background. Either they had never discussed it, or he had forgotten. For instance, he thought she had a sister rather than a brother and had grown up in Greenwich, not Dulwich. After that, I felt I had license to be freer, since: (a) it was clear that he did not know Tess that well; (b) even if he had asked her the same questions nine years ago, it was unlikely he would remember the answers; and (c) Tess was known to be mutable and change her story and have a bad memory herself.

And, after all, they had last seen each other nine years ago. Naturally, she would have changed over such a period. I think that essentially we're not the same people as we were nine years ago: All our cells have been renewed, let alone our attitudes and experiences of the world. Locke's socks, it's called. It's a discussion I've had with people on Red Pill, and I actually brought it up with Connor one evening, when we were talking about what age children's memories start forming. He seemed very interested in what I had to say on the matter and responded in an intelligent, considered way.

That was the thing, you see. Connor and I had much more in common than he and Tess ever did. We were like-minded. As a lawyer, he had to keep a level head, examine things in forensic detail, identify weaknesses, follow arguments to their logical conclusion. He couldn't let himself be clouded by emotion. And once I became a little less Tess-like and a little more myself, I found that the tone of his e-mails changed. It was like he relaxed and didn't feel that he had to work so hard. As if he had taken off a tight suit and put on some tracksuit bottoms. His tone became more straightforward and intimate.

Only occasionally did I remember the age difference between us, such as when Connor made references to TV programs and songs from the eighties—*Bagpuss*, for instance, or Spandau Ballet—which I would have to Google. But then, I had to Google the references of my own generation, so I was used to that.

In contrast to the other e-mails Tess sent and received, which were mostly exchanges of information, ours hardly ever had practical, boring things in them. Instead, we wrote about thoughts and observations. Often, the e-mails would be just a few lines long, like we were having a conversation next to each other. They could be silly or profound. In one he described how that morning on the way to work he had seen a tramp cry on the street near London Bridge, and how awful that made him feel. Or he might send me a poem he had made up when bored in court that morning. There once was a QC from Hull / Who had a tendency to mull. . . .

Sometimes, when he knew I was online, he'd switch over to IM and fire a series of one-line questions at me, on seemingly random topics: Twix or Snickers? Is it okay to have no interest in contemporary dance? Because I had no time to process his messages and prepare my answers, those sessions were rather challenging, but the speed required was exhilarating too. I had never had that kind of exchange with anyone, and enjoyed using those new muscles.

The thing I found most interesting about it all was that there was no wrong answer. Connor seemed to find everything I said funny or wise, as if he were clicking "Like" next to every response.

I should point out that I wasn't neglecting other aspects of Tess's life as a result of such frequent contact with Connor. I answered the e-mails that came in, updated Facebook. I played prerecorded messages to the voice mails of her mum every few weeks and her friend Susie on her birthday. I spent three hours researching contemporary sculpture in order to form an educated but sarcastic opinion about a new artist Isobel was considering investing in. I continued to spend a large chunk of time each day working out her plot lines and revising areas of her life I wasn't so good on.

After Connor, the correspondent I spent most time on was Tess's friend Shona. Shona was an old school friend of Tess's, married with a fifteen-month-old baby called Rufus. She had thin blond hair and a sharp nose, and her profile picture showed her gazing down at Rufus in the manner of an old religious painting. To look at her profile, you'd think she was loving being a mother, but her messages to Tess told a different story. She was, she wrote, in mourning for the old me. She said there was a conspiracy that being a mother was fulfilling, and that if she could go back to her single life, when she could walk out the door whenever she liked, she would do so at the drop of a hat. Tess's taking off to Sointula had started to obsess her—you're living my fantasy—and for the first few weeks she wrote almost daily, complaining about being stuck indoors with the baby and asking for details about what Tess was up to. It seemed to me that she was torturing herself, like someone starving asking for a vivid description of a meal. So, for Shona, I had to not only think of new and interesting things to tell her about Sointula, but also console her over her anguish about being a mother, which, as you can appreciate, was not my forte. I discovered a Web site forum for parents and studied their responses. It's always hell for the first few years, I wrote. Soon he'll be his own little person whom you can talk to and then it'll all seem worthwhile.

I was diligently providing progress reports to Adrian, or "Ava," through Facebook. After that initial hey, there contact we had settled into a semiregular exchange of messages. Well, it was regular on my side, not so much on his. Twice a week I would send him an outline of what Tess was up to, a list of what communication she had had with friends and family, and any new plans I had made for her future. His responses were much more haphazard. Sometimes he wouldn't reply at all to these reports, or I'd get one a few days later: Good work! You sound like you've got it all in hand. I knew you were the woman for the job. His messages often had a rushed feel; sometimes his spelling and punctuation were sloppy. He was, I knew, a very busy man, and I didn't resent these irregular and sketchy replies, but I was pleased on the rare occasions when he had obviously had more time to consider his response. In those messages, he would pick up on things I had said and ask further questions, as if he were really interested. For example, if I had mentioned that Tess had gone horseback riding on the weekend, he might ask what color her horse was and whether they had gone over any jumps during the ride.

And then sometimes, he wouldn't seem bothered at all about Tess and instead ask me about how *I* was doing, how I was bearing up, with what felt like real interest and concern. Then I would be reminded of our real-life meeting on the Heath; it was the electronic equivalent of those moments of eye contact when he fixed on my face in a way I'd never had before, even from Mum. I'm fine, I would reply. More than fine. Happy. Yes, I'm enjoying the work very much.

Anyway, as I was saying: All things considered, those first six weeks of Project Tess were not very taxing. It's surprising how little people actually need from someone they don't see. Even Shona's messages started tailing off after a few weeks, and those who were initially keen to talk on Skype, like Simon, gave up after I made a few excuses. No one bothered to ask three times. I probably could have gotten away with just a few status updates each week.

Even so, I admit I was concerned about the amount of time I was spending on Connor. I knew that the more extensively I corresponded with him, the less likely it was that I was doing what Tess would have been doing. After all, Tess had been the one to end their relationship, and she had thought the whole affair so unimportant that she hadn't even mentioned it to me. Furthermore, apart from her first ever boyfriend, Michael "Bootsy" Collingwood, she didn't believe in remaining friends with "old flames," as she called them. *Never go back* was her view. So, it was quite likely that she would not have been receptive to Connor's reestablishing contact. She may have exchanged a few polite messages, but it was doubtful she would have spent as much time e-mailing him as I did.

It was for this reason that I didn't mention Connor in my reports to Adrian; although he was officially a correspondent of Tess's, it was as if he were more part of my life in London than hers in Sointula. And it was by that same token that I decided that it was time to give Tess her own boyfriend.

You see, rather than sitting at home writing to Connor, she would most likely have been out exploring the island and meeting new people. And it seemed to me to be quite possible that during that time she would have met a new man. Tess seemed to meet men everywhere; she was often approached in public by aspirant suitors. Once one came up to her as she was leaving a tube carriage and gave her the book he was reading, called *The Alchemist*, with his phone number written inside. And when she worked in the clothes shop and the art gallery, nearly every day a customer would ask her out; the attention seemed entirely routine and unremarkable to her.

So, it had always been on the agenda for Tess to find a boyfriend, and I had penciled it in for three months after she arrived on the island. In the circumstances, however, I decided to bring the event forward a month. I informed Adrian of the development in my next message. Good idea, about time too! he replied. And who is the lucky gentleman?

I had already roughly sketched out the character of Wes Provost: Canadian, thirty-three years old—Tess liked younger men. His looks I modeled on a builder called Mike, who for one summer worked on the house next door to us in Leverton Street. He had thick, short forearms and oddly red lips, like a girl. After he found out my name, every time he saw me he used to sing, "You knock me off my feet," which Mum said was a line from a famous song called "Layla." I pointed out to Mike that my name and the song title were not spelled the same way, but he kept on singing it.

Mike's van was always getting parking tickets, and I'd hear him get upset when he discovered them. So, when he was up on the scaffolding, I'd watch from the window and, when the traffic warden put one under his windscreen wiper, I'd rush out and take the ticket and push it down the drain in the road before he saw it. I also took some photos of him on my phone, without his seeing, and I did this thing on my computer where I made the pictures into a montage and had the song playing in the background, like a pop video. It was just for me; I didn't post it on YouTube or anything.

At the end of the summer, when Mike was taking the scaffolding down, I told him what I'd done with the parking tickets: There had been five I'd disposed of for him. I suppose it was my way of telling him that I felt the same way about him that he felt about me. I was expecting him to be pleased, but his face went pale and, just for a moment, scrunched up. Then he smiled weakly and said, "Thanks, very good of you." He didn't sing the song the next time he saw me, and left the street without saying good-bye.

Anyway, I only used Mike's looks for Wes; the rest of his character I made up. I was getting better at being imaginative. Wes worked on the whale-watching boats with Roger, Leonora's boyfriend. That's how he and Tess met. He had lived on the mainland in a place called Edmonton before moving to Sointula with his girlfriend four years previously, wanting to be closer to nature. The relationship hadn't worked out and she had left to go back to Edmonton, but Wes had liked the island and stayed put, going into business with Roger. In his spare time he liked listening to sound tracks from musicals and cooking, especially pies. He drank only white wine, because red gave him migraines. On their first date, he and Tess went for a glass of ginger beer at the Waterside Café, and since then had seen each other three times. At first Tess was worried he was "too" good-natured—Everything I do or say is "great"!—but liked him more and more the better she got to know him.

There would need to be a photo. Tess's friend Simon, in particular, would insist on seeing one. Pic needed was his standard response when, in the past, Tess had e-mailed him about a man. I looked in case I had kept any of those photos of Mike, but then remembered I had deleted them that day he left without saying good-bye. Anyway, they depicted him as a scaffolder in London, whereas Wes worked on boats in Canada, so they wouldn't do.

I realized I would have to use a photo of a different man. I thought I'd find a suitable one on Flickr and spent an evening compiling a short list of candidates, but I couldn't shake the worry that because it was in the public sphere, one of Tess's friends might chance across the photo. The risk was small, it's true, but there nonetheless. Much more preferable would be to take a photograph myself, because then I could be in control.

It was then that I thought of Jonty. The chances that anyone Tess knew would bump into him in the street and recognize him were very slight (I checked his Facebook friends, but there was no connection with anyone Tess knew). He was fifteen years younger than them and had only just arrived in London. He moved in entirely different circles from Tess's friends, many of whom were married with children or in long-term relationships and lived in affluent London suburbs. Most of Tess's friends rarely went out, and when they did it was to the cinema or to Pilates classes or to big group lunches in a pub at which, according to the e-mails sent afterward, someone would always leave behind some item of baby clothing or not have paid their share of the bill. When Jonty went out with people from his college, they went to kebab restaurants in Dalston or moved between sports bars in central London according to their happy hours.

Besides, even if by any chance someone did run into him in London and thought he looked familiar, Occam's razor said that they wouldn't think it was Wes, who, after all, was in Sointula. Even if they approached Jonty and asked whether he was Wes, he would of course have no idea what they were talking about. So the very worst that could happen was a message to Tess from one of them saying that they had seen someone who looked quite like her new boyfriend.

With Jonty I'd be freer to pose the picture as I wanted it, to be Photoshopped onto a Sointula background later, and I would have the opportunity to use him again if need be. At twenty-six, he was slightly too young for Wes, but I decided that the photo I'd take would show him with sunglasses on, like Connor's had, which would help to obscure his face. He was not as good-looking as the men Tess usually went out with, but I figured that this was quite appropriate. After all, there would be a much smaller pool of men to choose from on Sointula, and his being ordinary looking was indicative of her new, less shallow approach to life, going for what was inside rather than appearance.

Once I decided to use Jonty, I wanted to get the photos done as soon as possible. But ironically, the one time I actually wanted him to be around, he wasn't, and I had to wait for a day and a half before he returned to the flat. It was a Sunday afternoon, and he told me that a party to celebrate St. George's Day on Friday had, I quote, "turned into a bit of a bender." He and his friends seemed to view even the most obscure occasion as an excuse to get drunk. I waited until he had gotten back in his room and had put on his music before knocking on his door. It was the first time I had approached him since he had moved in, and he looked surprised when he answered.

"Oh, hello!"

I was in turn taken aback, because he was just wearing his underwear. His chest was thick with blond hairs. I averted my eyes and glanced around his room. I hadn't seen it since he had moved in, and he had transformed what was a featureless box into what I can only describe as a disgusting dump. It wasn't like the mess in Tess's room, where you could tell that, despite the disarray, her possessions were of good quality; this was a standard, cheap mess. The walls were papered in photographs of him and his friends and pictures cut from magazines. There was a big poster of a cat wearing sunglasses, and one for a band called the Stone Roses. There was no cover on his duvet, and a couple of big holes in the wall where the plaster had been gouged out.

Jonty saw me looking at the wall and explained that he had tried

to put up a shelf, but it had fallen down because the walls were
so soft.

"I'm going to sort it out," he said. "Sorry, sorry, sorry."

I told him I didn't mind, which I didn't, and then cleared my
throat and said that due to the fact that it was a pleasant day, I had
decided to go for a walk and wondered whether he cared to join me.
He looked even more surprised, and far more delighted than was
warranted by the request.

"Yes, yes," he said. "Let's go to the beach!"

"What beach?"

"The one on the Thames I told you about. It's only five minutes
away."

I couldn't remember him talking about a beach, and thought he
must be mistaken, but I nodded.

"It's quite sunny," I said. "Perhaps you should bring some sunglasses."

"Of course," he said. "Never go anywhere without them."

So far, so good.

On his suggestion, we stopped at Londis to buy a "picnic." I
picked up a bag of crisps and a Ribena, but he bought a whole basket
of things, little tubs of olives and spreads, a baguette, and some cans
of beer. He greeted the man behind the counter as if he knew him.
When we left the shop, he whispered, "Have you noticed that Manu
puts white wine vinegar in the fridge, beside the chardonnay?"

Then he led me down a side street in the direction away from
Tesco, which I hadn't been down before. We passed a pub with a
sign outside reading TONIGHT: LIVE SINGER CLIVE STEVENS.
Quite soon our surroundings became prettier, the road turning from
tarmac into cobbles and the houses from new redbrick into older,

crooked white buildings. Jonty kept up a running commentary about the history of Rotherhithe, which he seemed to have researched.

Within minutes we were at the river. I had no idea it was so near the flat; as mentioned, my knowledge of Rotherhithe was limited to the tube, Tesco Extra, and Albion Street. There was a path running alongside the river, and you could see Tower Bridge and the tall buildings of the city in the distance. It was quite nice.

And Jonty was right—below the footpath was a beach, accessed by a rickety-looking ladder. The beach was small and pebbly, and there was a fair amount of junk washed up, plastic bottles and the like, but it was a beach nonetheless.

I had planned to take Jonty's picture with the sky as background, but then I had a new thought: The beach could stand in for the one in Sointula. That was pebbly too. If I took a close-up of him, cutting out the surroundings, then I would hardly need to use Photoshop at all.

I was pleased by this unforeseen and fortuitous development, but kept my excitement to myself. First, we climbed down the ladder and sat on the stones to have our picnic. It occurred to me that this was my first meal alone with a man, and I had been slightly concerned about what we would talk about. But I needn't have worried. Jonty cheerfully chatted away about the history of the area, about pirates and whaling boats.

"Imagine all the things that have gone on right here, on this beach," he said. "It's mental."

I said that I didn't really think about things like that, and I couldn't see the appeal of history. He reacted to this with exaggerated surprise.

"But aren't you interested in how you fit in?" he said.

"I've never thought about it," I said, but was distracted just then by the memory of something that Tess had once told me: that she had attended a party at a flat overlooking the Thames, got drunk, and climbed down into the mud of the riverbank, ruining her dress. I looked at the flats lining the water, the rows of empty little balconies, and wondered whether it was one of them. I imagined her standing on the railings, her arms outstretched, like that scene in *Titanic*, ignoring the entreaties of her friends to come back inside.

Jonty had started talking about his acting classes, telling me how they had done an exercise in which they had all gone to London Zoo, picked an animal to study, and then had to spend an entire afternoon acting like that animal, in front of everyone. He had chosen to be a monkey.

"I mean, it's pretty obvious, but what else would I be?" he said. He then told a story about how there was this "amazingly fit" girl in his class and word had gotten around that she was going to be a gazelle. On the day of the performance, no fewer than four of the men in the group chose to be lions, and spent the afternoon prowling around after her.

It was a fairly amusing story, and I filed it away to tell Connor that evening. I'd attribute the story to Leonora, who had once been an aspiring actress.

"Are you any good at acting?" I asked.

He laughed. "Not very. I seem unable to be anything but myself, which isn't ideal. But I got a call back for an ad for insurance company. They're after, I quote, 'a gormless bloke.' I can do that. So that's exciting."

I pointed out that it was ironic that he had left the insurance industry for acting and now he might appear in an advert for it.

"I never thought of it like that," he said. "But yeah, maybe I'm a hypocritical twat." He didn't sound too upset by the prospect. "What about you? What do you do in your room all day?"

I had prepared for this question, and told him that I was writing a film script.

"Cor!" he said, eyes wide. "What's it about?"

"A love story," I said.

He gave a big sigh and lay down on the pebbles. It must have hurt his back.

"Don't talk to me about love. I'm totally hopeless. I just get obsessed and then they think I'm a freak. I keep on falling for girls when they just want a bit of fun."

By then I had finished my crisps, but Jonty was still munching French bread—he had a habit of assembling each mouthful so it contained a bit of each topping he had brought, leaning on his elbows to construct a small tower of cheese and ham and spread. I tried to hide my impatience, but the moment he stopped chewing I took out my phone and asked him whether I could take a picture.

He readily agreed—"As long as you send it to me"—and leaned back in a relaxed pose. He had, however, taken his sunglasses off while we were eating, so I suggested he put them back on again.

"Yeah, may as well try to hide the hangover."

As he put them on I casually moved aside the picnic, so the English packaging wasn't visible, and took a picture from above so only the beach was in the background. Then he insisted on taking a photo of me, which I let him do so he didn't think the whole thing was too odd.

Afterward, we walked back to the flat. Jonty seemed sincerely delighted with our little trip. "It's good to hang out," he said. I let him hug me, trying not to show how much I disliked it.

Back in my room, I prepared the picture—I was right; it needed only a tiny bit of Photoshopping—and drafted e-mails to Justine, Shona, and Simon. Okay, so, I've met a bloke. . . . Marion I would also tell, but later, and in more formal language.

Justine wrote back immediately. I don't fucking believe it. Or, rather, I do, but it's SO UNFAIR! I haven't had a sniff for two years, and you score before you've even unpacked your wash bag.

Simon, meanwhile, replied in his usual blunt manner: Fairly cute, but I need to see him without the glasses. Eyes = windows to the soul, and all that.

I didn't take much notice of this at the time. Simon was my least favorite of Tess's friends. While everyone else seemed happy to take what Tess said at face value, Simon seemed to see it as his role to challenge everything, as if he knew Tess better than she did. Obviously, I like people who think about things, and take issue with stupidity, but he didn't do it in an intelligent way; rather, it was his default reaction to everything. He was also very shallow, interested only in socializing with the "cool" people and judging others purely on what they were wearing. He did this even when they were supposed friends of his and Tess's, like Joy, whom he disapproved of for still wearing boot-cut jeans. Describing a night out to Tess, he said that the club wasn't as glamorous as he hoped, full of suburbanites and size eights. He had nine hundred thirty Facebook friends, and his updates were meaningless and annoying, links to songs that he demanded everyone listen to right that second, or just updates of where he was—Vauxhall. Home. Berlin—as if the world were hanging on details of his whereabouts.

But his comment lodged in my head, because it chimed with something that had been bothering me somewhat about Connor: I didn't really know what he looked like. In the only picture I had of him, the one in the park, he too was wearing sunglasses. I didn't think I'd be able to spot him in a crowd. I had, suddenly, an intense desire to see his face.

It then occurred to me that, actually, seeing Connor in the flesh would be a perfectly simple thing to arrange, and not in the least risky. I knew where he worked: at a solicitor's called Asquith and Partners in Temple. I knew vaguely what he looked like. And, from our e-mails, I had a pretty good idea of his daily routine.

My plan, then, was to go past his office at lunchtime, on a day I knew he was there and not in court, and wait for him to come out to get some lunch. I would then be able to get a good look at him. I rationalized it: After all, it could only aid my work for Tess to have a thorough knowledge of one of her correspondents. All the information I could gather on Connor was pertinent to my job.

That evening in our e-mails I asked him what he was doing the next day, whether he was going to be in court. He replied that he was stuck in the office, working on a particularly dull case. He asked me what I was doing, and I told him that I had a double session with Natalie, the girl I was tutoring, because she was preparing for a scholarship exam for an art school in Vancouver.

The next day I woke at noon, having slept through my eleven a.m. alarm, and didn't have time to pick up my washing from the launderette, so I put on the same tracksuit bottoms and T-shirt I had worn the previous day. My outfit didn't really matter, I thought; after all, Connor was not going to know who I was; he might not even notice me. I left the tube at Temple and my Google map directed me off a main road down an old passageway not much wider than myself, at the end of which I emerged into a space that, had I been the kind of person to gasp aloud, might well have made me do so. It had

the appearance of a secret, magical city. The streets were cobbled
and the buildings ancient; there was a beautiful church made from
stone the color of Werther's Originals. There were almost no cars or
signs of contemporary life—it wouldn't have looked out of place in
a Harry Potter film. It was quiet and peaceful, and everyone I saw
seemed to be wearing a dark suit, as if there had been a sign advising a dress code that I missed on the way in. It was hard to believe
that this place was actually in London, and I remember feeling a
moment of regret that Mum had never taken me to places like this,
that we'd spent all of our time in the house.

It took a while to find the offices of Asquith and Partners, which
were housed in a wonky, narrow building. Beside the black door was
a plaque with half a dozen names on it. Connor's wasn't on there,
but I knew that he wasn't yet a partner in the firm, so perhaps that
was why. There was a little park opposite, and I sat down on a bench
to wait.

It was twelve fifty p.m. when I arrived. I presumed that Connor
would be coming out for lunch at some point between one and two
p.m., but of course I couldn't be sure. I had with me a free newspaper that I had picked up on the tube, and so pretended to read that
while I kept an eye on the door.

Inconveniently, the park bench faced away from Connor's office,
so I had to keep twisting around. Although I had of course thoroughly examined his photograph, I was concerned I might miss him,
because men in suits look quite similar. Besides, I didn't know when
that photograph he sent me was taken, and I reasoned that he could
have cut his hair or changed weight since then.

But as it turned out I did recognize him, instantly. It was one
seventeen p.m., and I was half reading a newspaper article about a

teenager who was stabbed to death when the door opened and there he was.

I wasn't prepared for the effect of seeing Connor in the flesh. I felt almost dizzy, my heart pounding; when I stood up, my legs seemed boneless. I think it was the subterfuge of it, as much as anything; I remember something of the same feeling from watching Mike from behind the curtain on Leverton Street.

He was with another, older man, both in suits. They appeared to be in the middle of a conversation and headed up the street together. Connor had his hands in his trouser pockets; the older man produced a cigarette and lit it as they walked.

My legs still feeble, I started to follow them, picking up pace until I was about ten meters behind. I reminded myself that there was no way Connor could know who I was. Obviously, I could mostly just see the back of his head. His hair looked different from the photo; now it was wet looking and slicked back. Occasionally he would turn to say something to the man beside him and I would catch a glimpse of his profile, but from that position it was impossible to get a good look at his eyes.

I wondered whether the other man was his colleague Colin, whom he mentioned often in his e-mails. Colin was, Connor said, a "good bloke" but had a tendency to be pedantic and dull, and Connor enjoyed winding him up. He had never mentioned that Colin smoked, however, and he didn't seem to find this man boring. Indeed, Connor was laughing quite hard at something Colin said. From the glimpses I got when he turned his head, his eyes crinkled up when he smiled.

It sounds odd, I know, but when I saw them laughing together I felt a pang of discontent that he was finding someone else amusing and engaging. He had told me that writing to me was the highlight of his day, and so I suppose I expected to see him looking more miserable than he was. But almost as soon as the thought entered my head, I reprimanded myself for being unreasonable. I should be happy that he was enjoying his working environment and the company of his colleague.

The men walked along the street for a hundred meters or so before turning off into a smaller, cobbled road. They stopped at a café. It must have sold very good sandwiches, because the queue snaked out the door. Connor and the other man joined the back of it. I hesitated, and during my inaction a woman got in behind them. I quickly moved to take a place behind her.

It was actually a good thing that I wasn't directly behind Connor. My heart was still pounding so loudly I felt like everyone in the queue could hear it. There was an odd, hollow feeling in my stomach, not quite the same as being hungry, but close.

Even with the woman between us I was near enough to make out some of the conversation between Connor and his colleague. They seemed to be talking about a footballer who had performed badly the previous evening: "What a joker," Connor said. "I can't believe he missed that penalty." "Schoolboy error," his friend agreed.

At that proximity I could smell a lemony fragrance that seemed to come from Connor, and noticed that he had a patch of thinning hair, the size of a Wagon Wheel. The back of his neck was newly shaved, and I had a bizarre, fleeting urge to touch the skin there. I looked at his ears, which stuck out just like they did in the photograph, and thought of how, if I stepped forward, I could whisper things in them that would give him the shock of his life. Private things that he had told me in e-mails. He had confessed that when he was a teenager he had had a crush on the singer of a pop group, and even now the word *T'Pau* made him shiver. I could have whispered that. I could have told him what he was thinking about in court the day before, during that hearing for the Polish shoplifter, about an article he had read in *GQ* magazine about an explorer in the Antarctic who had to eat emperor penguins to survive.

Of course, I didn't actually say any of those things. The queue inched forward into the shop, where heaps of sandwich fillings lay congealing under a glass counter. I wondered which Connor would choose and decided something fishy; he had told me he was jealous of all the fresh seafood available on Sointula. I couldn't help a quick smile when his turn came and he asked for crab mayonnaise on a white baguette. That he would accompany the sandwich with cheese-and-onion crisps I knew almost as a certainty, as he had confided in me during some of the ironically trivial banter we had exchanged that he was worried he was actually addicted to them, and felt ill if he didn't have a packet a day.

What didn't occur to me, however, was that it would be soon be my turn to be asked for my order by the brisk man behind the counter. I was caught unawares, and said the first thing that came into my mind: "A packet of cheese-and-onion crisps."

It was only when the man asked me for fifty pence in return that it struck me that I hadn't brought any money out with me. However, I remembered there were often some coins in the lining of my coat that had slipped through the holes in the pockets, so I ran my fingers over the material in order to feel whether there were any hiding there. I found some promising hard disks, but then had to work them through the lining to get them out, and ended up ripping the hole a bit bigger to allow easier access.

I was so absorbed in the task that I only faintly registered a loud sigh from the server man, and his, "Yes, mate?" as he went on to take the order from the person behind me. After a minute or so, I had rescued five coins from my coat lining. Laying them out on the glass counter, I saw that they added up to only thirty-eight pence.

By now the man had started serving the people behind me in the queue, leaving the bag of crisps beside the coins on the counter. I was counting the money again when an amazing thing happened: Connor stepped forward. He and his colleague had been standing to one side, waiting for a sandwich to be toasted, and he must have observed my fumbling. He placed a ten-pence piece and a two-pence piece on the counter beside my coins.

"There you go," he said, and gave me a wonderful smile. I stared at him. His eyes were light blue, and they almost disappeared when he smiled. Then the man behind the counter handed his colleague his sandwich in a white paper bag, and Connor turned to leave the shop with him.

I was tempted to follow them back to the office, but I was feeling so churned up I turned the other way and walked down the cobbled street, trying to calm down. I couldn't even eat my crisps. I wandered around for twenty minutes or so. Then I sat down on a curb and logged on to Tess's Gmail account from my phone.

I felt a great need to see an e-mail from Connor. I wanted to see whether he mentioned the encounter he had just had with me in the café. The first time I logged on there was no new e-mail from him, but then, twenty minutes later, there it was. However, all it contained was a link to a clip on YouTube, with the message: I think she looks rather like you. No mention of the incident at lunch. Although mildly disappointed, I concluded that he must practice these small acts of kindness all the time; for him it wasn't even worth mentioning.

When I got home I clicked on the YouTube link. It was a music video of a singer performing a complicated, mesmerizing dance alongside lots of people in brightly colored leotards. "One, two, three, four, tell me that you love me more," she sang. The woman had some similarities to Tess—thin, with dark eyes and a fringe—but she wasn't quite as attractive.

I think I'm prettier, I replied.

Goes without saying, wrote Connor.

It's five twenty a.m., and my battery icon is flashing red. The tent is still zipped up but I can tell it's growing light; the canvas is brightening and the birds are starting their manic chatter. I just saw a shape scurry past, which made me jump, but I presume it's just one of the dogs, or Milo going to the lavatory. I hope. Good night.

*I told Annie about Mum* this evening. I didn't intend to, and what concerns me is less the possible consequences—I don't think she'll tell anyone—but the fact that I let it slip. I think I might have been under the influence of drugs. Not that I took any myself, of course, but everyone around me did, and the air was thick with sweet smoke that it was impossible to avoid inhaling and that may have resulted in a weakening of my faculties.

What happened was this: At around three thirty p.m. I was woken by Annie, who informed me that it was time to start preparations for the Full Moon Feast. I ascertained that whenever there was a full moon, the commune residents cooked and ate a meal together, and everyone was expected to "muck in." I explained to her that I was unaware of this custom and would not be participating, but she said,

"Oh, shuddup, come on," and I ended up getting off my mattress and following her and the children to the main clearing.

Outside the big tepee a temporary kitchen had been set up, with some rusty, rudimentary cooking apparatus and buckets of vegetables on trestle tables. Some of the residents were milling about, chopping and carting things and generally expending more energy than they had done all week. I recognized most of them now from my inquiries: Davide with the tiny shorts; Johanna, the German with silver studs in her eyebrows; Maria, who had thick multicolored knots in her hair with rings around them, like fingers; the Frenchman with the terrible spots. Deirdre, who was one of the few people at the commune who wasn't thin—rather, tall and thickset, like a fridge—appeared to be in charge of proceedings and announced we were making a vegetable stew. I was shown a bucket and assigned to cut up the carrots, along with Annie and Milo and Bandit, a slight Spanish man.

Once I started, I found that I rather enjoyed the chopping. I concentrated on cutting the disks identically, each one approximately a centimeter thick. These I arranged like those chips they have in casinos, ten to a column. The repetitive, methodical nature of the work made my thoughts drift, and I started remembering lunches at Granny Margaret's. Mum and I visited her three times a year, on Boxing Day, Easter Sunday, and her birthday, and she always served tinned carrots. It was the only time I ever ate vegetables. Mum said it was a pretty good deal; after all, most parents made their children eat vegetables every day.

I don't know why we called her Granny Margaret; it wasn't as if I had another grandmother to distinguish her from. She lived in sheltered housing in Kent and always had the heating right up, even at Easter. When Mum started to be intolerant of high temperatures, she refused to turn it down. "We all have our ailments," she said, as if her rheumatism were equivalent to Mum's MS. She had lived in Elm Tree Court for as long as I could remember, since my granddad Geoffrey died in 1994, but she still seemed annoyed to be there. She was always complaining about the staff not doing things right, and the other residents being too old. She also thought everyone was trying to take advantage of her and rip her off—even her own daughter. Mum would bring tins of biscuits and a bottle of Baileys Irish cream, and Granny Margaret would examine them suspiciously, sniffing the bottle and putting on her glasses to read the ingredients, as if hoping to find poison listed on there. Then she'd serve up a horrible meal, like a dry chicken breast, and always with these disgusting, mushy little rounds of carrot.

I could never think of anything to say to her, and she didn't have much interest in me either, even on her birthday, when, on Mum's suggestion, I gave her a DVD compilation I'd made of the best moments of *Bargain Hunt*. The only time she had perked up was in 2007, when we thought I might go to college; when Mum mentioned it, she asked when I would be leaving and questioned Mum about the dimensions of my bedroom and whether this big, ugly wardrobe she had would fit in. On the train back, Mum explained that Granny Margaret thought that after Granddad's heart attack, Mum should have asked her to come and live in Leverton Street, even though she had visited once and knew that we only had two bedrooms. She thought that Mum had made a mistake by not getting married, because then Mum would have a bigger house. She was bit old-fashioned about the fact that my father wasn't around.

The next visit, when she found out we had decided against college, she was even grumpier than usual. When I went for a third biscuit she pulled the tin out of reach, and announced I was too fat. "You overindulge her," she said to Mum, as if I wasn't there. "A big, weird child. You're never going to find someone to take her off your hands." Mum's usual way of dealing with her was to be polite, but that time she got angry and said that she never wanted me to be "taken off her hands," and that if by "overindulgence" she meant letting me be my own person and showing me love, then she would continue to do so, thank you very much.

When it got to the point when Mum was unable to get down to Kent to visit, there was no question of Granny Margaret coming up to London. She didn't even come to the funeral. Instead, she sent me a note to read out at the service:

My daughter, Susan, was a good child who had a range of
hobbies and interests. Although her adult life did not entirely
fulfill the promise of her youth, she endured setbacks with
resilience and made the most of the circumstances in which
she found herself.

Needless to say, I didn't read it out.

I was so immersed in my thoughts that my chopping had slowed right down, to the point where my knife just rested on the carrot. My reverie was broken by Deidre putting her hand on my shoulder.

"Maybe hurry things up a bit, yeah?"

I looked around and saw that everyone else had finished and big metal urns were already steaming away over the fire. I quickened my pace and finished the supply of carrots. While the stew was cooking everyone hung around, sitting on the floor and smoking their tiny cigarettes, which needed to be relit every few minutes. Annie had gone back to the van to change the baby, so I sat down next to the old man with white chest hair and a floppy hat whom I had talked to on my second day. On his other side was a couple whom I couldn't immediately identify in the flickering firelight.

"Hey, how you doing," the man said, and then turned to the couple. "You know, she took a taxi all the way from the airport."

This is apparently how I am known here. The male half of the couple asked, "How much did that cost you?"

When I told him, and he had done the usual sucked-in-breath, hand-waving reaction to the amount, the man said to his female friend, "There was that woman last year who got a taxi to Granada; do you remember?"

I hadn't been paying much attention, but at this I snapped alert, remembering the e-mail Tess received not long after checkout from her friend Jennifer, claiming—mistakenly, I had thought—to have spotted her at the Alhambra in Granada.

"When was this?" I asked.

August, they said.

I showed them Tess's picture, and they conferred and said that yes, it could have been her.

It was the most definite response I had gotten so far to my inquiries. On further questioning the couple said that they had been at the commune for two months the previous summer, and were sure she had been here when they arrived. A few days after they first saw her she had gone to Granada, then returned to the commune, where she stayed for another week or so before leaving. To where, they didn't know. She had camped alone, as I had guessed. I would have thought that she would have kept to herself, but apparently not: She was quite sociable, they said, and had often joined others in the communal area.

I asked what the woman had talked about.

"She didn't speak much," the man said. "She was quiet."

"She said she liked my necklace," the woman said.

"How did she seem?" I asked.

The woman shrugged. "She was shanti," which, it transpired, meant "calm and happy" in hippie-speak. Then she said, "I remember. Her name was Joan."

Because of her accent, I misheard the name as "John."

"But that's a boy's name."

"No, no," she said. "J-O-A-N."

Joan, as you might remember, was the name of Tess's cat, the one who disappeared. It could have been a coincidence, and I tried not to get too excited. Besides, even if this "Joan" was Tess, I was still no closer to finding out what happened to her. Nonetheless, this was by far the most positive identification, and I felt content that my suspicion that she had come to the commune could be proven right.

The couple turned back to talk to each other, and I gazed into the fire. I've always liked fires; I used to make them in the back garden of Leverton Street when I got home from school. Here, potatoes were baking in the embers, and I watched their skins wrinkle and blacken. There were now a lot of people gathered around, waiting for the food, and loud chatter in various languages rose above the ever-present sound of bongos and guitars. One man had brought out a long stick that made a rude noise when he blew into it.

When the stew was finally ready, people massed greedily around the pots, clutching tin plates that they seemed to have provided themselves. No one had mentioned that we had to bring our own plates, and of course I didn't have one, but Annie had brought me one of her spares from the van. I waited until the queue had thinned out and then went up and asked the man serving for a tiny portion of stew and took three pieces of heavy white bread. I sat down beside Annie and Milo and was just about to start eating when Deirdre made this noise, a kind of "ommmm." Everyone else replied, "Ommmmm," and then there was a cry: "Thanks for the food!"

I had intended to eat quickly and go back to my tent, but I found myself remaining seated after I had finished. To my surprise, I found I was quite enjoying myself. As night fell lots of people had put on hoodies, like me, and I felt more similar to them compared to the daytime, when they had their brown flesh on display. I remember looking around at all the people there, hoods up and faces illuminated by firelight as they chatted away to one another, and thinking that they all looked nice. More than that: At that moment I had a sense that they were not just random strange foreign people but that we were all part of a group, like a tribe resting the night before a long trek or battle. The children were running around, feeding bits of stew to the dogs—who, I noticed, quietly spit them out again. The moon was bright and low in the sky, stars twinkling like they were sending me messages in Morse code. Someone kept throwing orange peel onto the fire, which made a lovely smell, and there was another sweet, acrid odor too. Once I started noticing, it seemed like everyone was smoking except me—even Annie accepted a drag of a cigarette, and I saw Bandit showing his admiring neighbor a stick of something strongly scented that looked like green candy floss.

Sitting beside me was an oldish woman called Esme, who had tiny plaits in her gray hair and a completely flat chest. She was engaged in an animated discussion with the man crouched in front of her about the pros and cons of running vehicles on vegetable oil. On my other side, Annie was talking to Synth, a dreadlocked woman around the same age who had also bought her children with her to the commune. I tuned in to their conversation. Annie was telling her about her furniture, and how she wanted to start making it with bamboo. Synth asked her where she was planning to source it.

"China," replied Annie.

"Are you happy with that?" said Synth.

"Well," said Annie, "it's a very sustainable material."

Synth shook her head, and then launched into some speech, most of which was drowned out because the man had started blowing his rude stick again. When he paused for breath, I heard Synth say, ". . . and the pandas?"

Annie laughed.

"Oh, I think there's enough bamboo to go around. Aren't there only about eight pandas left, anyway?"

At this, Synth got even more animated, her long bony hands slicing the air as she spoke.

"They're not helped by China exporting all the bamboo. They need to eat tons of it each day."

Annie's expression was the closest to cross I had seen it, her cheeks flushed red. I leaned forward, raising my voice so Synth could hear.

"What's wrong with letting pandas die out?"

Synth and Annie both turned to look at me.

"What do you mean?" said Synth.

"Extinction is a part of life on earth. And if pandas are inefficient and ill equipped to deal with life, then we should let them die out. Especially if they're an obstacle to more important species. We shouldn't be sentimental. We should only save things that are worth saving."

Now it was Synth's turn to be annoyed.

"That's a ridiculous thing to say, and—"

She was cut off by the arrival of Bianca, the tiny, shaved-headed woman who had accosted me on my second day. She crouched down in front of me and started to speak quietly. I couldn't hear over the crackle of the fire, so I had to lean closer and closer until my cheek was almost next to hers before I could hear that she was still talking about the toilet and why I should use the proper place.

"I can't believe you're still going on about that!" I replied. "I've dealt with enough shit in my life, okay, and I don't want to see yours." And then, to clarify, I added, even more loudly, "I had to wipe my mum's bottom."

I think I was as surprised as Bianca at my outburst. As I say, I believe I had become intoxicated by the drug smoke around me. At the time, though, it felt good to speak like that. Bianca gave me a funny look and moved to speak to Esme, and I turned my attention back to Annie and Synth. Synth was still rabbiting on, and I caught the word *karma*. What this was in connection with I didn't know, but the word triggered something in me and again I felt compelled to intervene.

"Karma doesn't exist," I said.

Again, Annie and Synth looked over. Synth said, this time in a measured voice, "I don't mean to be rude and you're entitled to your opinion, but really, how old are you? What do you know?"

"It's"—I tried to think of the word Tess would use—"bollocks. Bollocks. Life isn't fair. There isn't this kindly force rewarding you for good deeds. My mum was a good person who had never done anything wrong, and she got MS."

Annie put her arm around my shoulders. I didn't shrug her off.

"Oh, you poor thing. That's very tough."

Then Synth started talking again, tapping on Annie's back to get her attention. Annie turned back to her, still keeping her arm around me, and I listened to them resume their conversation without really hearing the words. I looked at the other people around the fire, everyone yapping away, and now it didn't feel like we were all in it together; instead, it seemed to me that no one really cared what anyone else was saying. They pretended to, but really they just wanted to transmit and not receive. What would it take, I thought, for them to be genuinely interested in what I had to say?

I squeezed Annie's knee hard, so that she turned to me. Synth's face contorted with annoyance at the interruption.

"I killed my mum," I said in a low voice.

Annie's arm suddenly felt very heavy across my shoulders.

"What do you mean?" she said quietly.

"I killed her. With morphine."

She was silent. The hiss of the fire was deafening, the other voices miles away. Then I lifted her arm from my shoulder, stood up, and went back to the tent.

Ten minutes later, Annie came back. I heard the sounds of her putting Milo and the baby to bed in the van, and then her footsteps approaching the tent. She knelt down and unzipped the door.

"Do you want to talk?" she said.

"Okay," I replied, and proceeded to tell her everything, from the first time Mum fell over, that Saturday night in 2002, as she was carrying the foot spa full of warm water over from the kitchen. The expressions on people's faces on Kentish Town High Street when we went past, moving out of the way because they thought she was drunk, and how I would run after them and inform them that that wasn't the case. The nappies. The hoist. Her useless, dead-bird hands in her lap.

Annie asked me about that final night. I explained how difficult it was to stockpile the morphine, because the nurses kept a strict eye on it, so I had devised a plan. The nurses had given us a laminated sheet of emoticons, from smiling to miserable, which they called a pain scale. When they arrived in the morning and asked how she had been during the night, I told them that she had indicated she was at the highest level of discomfort on the pain scale, even when she hadn't. They then prescribed an appropriate amount of morphine that would go straight into the drip attached to her arm. Later, when they left, I would unscrew the drip and skim a small amount of morphine off the top, and put it in a bottle in the fridge. The bottle was from a head lice treatment that I had bought from the chemist and washed out, and I told Penny that I had a persistent lice problem, so she wouldn't go near the bottle—a bonus was that she also kept her distance from me.

I kept on skimming off the morphine until I had a fair amount. Then, on a Saturday night—that was important, because the nurses didn't come in on Sundays—I administered the extra morphine slowly, over the course of twenty-four hours. Mum went into a coma and died. On Monday morning, I waited for the nurses to come in and they rang the doctor. The death certificate cited the cause of death as complications arising from MS.

Which, I added to Annie, wasn't strictly untrue.

Annie asked whether Mum had explicitly asked me to give her the morphine.

"No," I said. "By then, she couldn't speak."

"Had she mentioned euthanasia in the past?"

"No," I said. "We didn't talk about things like that."

"So how do you know it's what she wanted?"

I replied that I just knew. I could tell from the look in her eyes.

Annie nodded slowly, her face still and grave, and then gave my arm a squeeze.

"I'd best get back."

She zipped up the tent door and got to her feet, and I listened to the sound of her footsteps and the clunk of the van door as she slid it shut.

||||||||||

I don't want to give the impression that I was neglecting Tess because of my frequent communication with Connor. But, as I say, it didn't take much work to keep her life running smoothly. After the initial flurry of activity upon her arrival in Sointula, she had settled into the new apartment and her job teaching Natalie. Her small group of acquaintances had been established. With practice, writing and reacting as Tess had become much easier, and now I barely had to think before pressing send on messages. The bulk of my work consisted of responding to news about her friends' lives on Facebook.

Most people, it seemed, were self-centered—even with someone as popular as Tess, it was a case of "out of sight, out of mind." After a few weeks, even her closest friends had stopped showing an interest in her life—genuine interest, I mean, rather than a token How's it going? tacked onto an essay of volunteered information about themselves. When I posted the first photo of Tess in Sointula on Facebook, it received sixty-seven "likes"; one I posted a month later got a paltry two.

I felt slightly aggrieved that so much of my careful preparation was going to waste—clearly, no one was going to ask why the Finns chose to settle in Sointula, or what Natalie had drawn that day, or what mark Tess had received in her GCSE history (a B). It did, however, make my job easier, and allowed me to devote more time to Connor.

For me, something had changed after the incident in the sandwich shop. I started to think about him in a different way. And it was not long afterward—five or six days—when he wrote something that made me think that his feelings had also shifted up a gear.

First, I should explain that we had been e-mailing about *The Princess Bride*. Connor had asked what books I had liked as a child, because his daughter, Maya, was starting to learn to read and he was wondering what to buy her. I mentioned *The Princess Bride*, omitting the fact that it still was my favorite book. The next day, at the end of an otherwise innocuous e-mail about a gig he had been to the previous evening, he wrote:

Hey, and remember—kiss me first.

*Kiss me first.* The phrase meant nothing to me, and it was nowhere in Tess's e-mails and files. Google told me that it was the name of an Italian film about lovers who were separated and spent their lives yearning for each other. But the film was released in 2003, after Connor and Tess had broken up.

Besides, Connor had not capitalized the words, which I was sure he would have done if it were a reference to the title of a film. Like me, he was punctilious about such things.

The most likely option, then, was that it was a private joke, a reference to something that one of them had said to the other when they had been together. And, I thought, it couldn't be a coincidence that he had introduced it so soon after our conversation about *The Princess Bride*, and that it had the same number of words and syllables as the phrase "As you wish."

If you're unfamiliar with *The Princess Bride*, "As you wish" is what the hero, Westley, says to Princess Buttercup as code for "I love you."

*As you wish. Kiss me first. I love you.*

I don't normally jump to conclusions, but in this instance the implication seemed clear.

The next step was to consider how I felt about this development. That didn't take long: The fact that Connor loved me made me feel very happy, and my instinct was to respond in kind.

However, I suspected it was irrational, if not impossible, to be "in love" with someone you'd never actually met. I did some research, cross-referencing various definitions of the emotion with my feelings for Connor, and was pleased to discover the existence of what was described as a sort of "prelove" state, called limerence:

> A cognitive and emotional state of being attached to or even obsessed with another person, typically experienced involuntarily and characterized by a strong desire for reciprocation of one's feelings.

This description tallied with my feelings, and I concluded that I was in limerence with Connor.

I decided that the best course of action—what Tess would have done—was not to acknowledge the declaration immediately. So

Connor and I continued e-mailing as normal, and it was not until four days later, at the end of an e-mail describing that day's painting session with Natalie, that I signed off in kind: kiss me first xxx.

His reply: ! xxx.

In his next message, he abbreviated the phrase to kmf. I followed suit, and from then on we both signed off all our e-mails like that, our own private code. Kmf.

So, it was official. I began to apply myself to being in limerence. One of the symptoms I found was a desire to associate myself with the things he liked, to feel closer to him in lieu of his actual presence. Although his e-mails had already provided me with a certain amount of information on his tastes and interests—I was by that point eating three packets of cheese-and-onion crisps a day, and had read up on snowboarding and photography, his two principal hobbies—I was greedy for more. I instigated a whimsical e-mail game in which we both compared our likes and dislikes of nine years ago, when we last saw each other, to now, in order to show how we'd changed. I was rather proud of this idea, since not only would it provide information on him, but also give me an opportunity to establish how Tess had changed since he had last seen her. How she was, in effect, a different person.

Connor sent me his lists first, along with explanatory notes:

2002—

Film: *Scarface*
Book: *Mr. Nice* (Yes, I know. I'm being honest, okay?)
Music: Eminem

2011—

Film: *Lost in Translation*

Book: *The Master and Margarita* (It took me eight years to
   get around to reading it, but you were right; it's amazing.)

Music: the XX

My turn. Selections for the "old" Tess of 2002 was easy: I had
lists of relevant information compiled from our conversations and
receipts for her purchases:

Film: *Three Colors: Blue*

Book: *Norwegian Wood* by Haruki Murakami

Music: Bach's Six Suites for Unaccompanied Cello

For the "new" Tess of 2011, I decided, after some deliberation,
on a combination of her tastes, mine—and Connor's:

Film: *Lord of the Rings: Fellowship of the King*

Book: *Anna Karenina*

Music: the XX (Snap!)

That night, I downloaded the album of our new favorite band,
the XX, and listened to it three times over. As far as music went,
it was quite nice. I also got *Scarface* and *Lost in Translation* and
watched them both. *Scarface* was awful, horribly violent, and I was
glad it was no longer Connor's favorite film. *Lost in Translation* was
better, although nothing really happened and I didn't really understand the point of it. But it was, as far I could see, about two people

who liked each other, which was pleasing. Also in the interests of understanding Connor better, the following afternoon I spent some time in the toiletry aisle at Tesco sniffing the different aftershaves in an attempt to identify the lemony one I smelled on him in the sandwich shop. Eventually a man told me off for opening the packages, but I found one that smelled quite similar, bought it, and put it on my wrist every day.

We continued writing to each other. One of the things that surprised me was how easy it all was. At school, the girls were always talking about "the rules": what to say and how to act to get a boy to like you. "Don't call back. Don't be too keen." But with Connor everything that I said seemed to be the right thing, and seemed to make him like me more.

Then, two weeks after Connor's initial kiss me first, something happened that temporarily diverted my attention from him.

I had, by that point, left three messages on Marion's voice mail—all the variations on "Sorry to miss you; I'm doing fine" that Tess and I had recorded. After the last, she had sent an e-mail:

Darling, you know I have book group on Wednesday; do try to call at some other time. I keep trying your mobile but it's always off. Have you got your landline installed yet? We really must speak.

I felt both annoyed and vindicated. I had, after all, voiced my suspicions to both Tess and Adrian that Marion would not be satisfied with just voice-mail messages and would require greater contact. I didn't, however, feel panicked, as I might have done had this happened in the early stages of the project. It seemed like a minor hiccup, rather than a disaster, and one that could be resolved with ingenuity.

I listened again to one of the taped conversations with Tess, to see whether it was feasible for me to amend my voice to pass as hers. It was not. My voice was much higher, my accent not so "posh," and I discovered I was not a natural mimic; in fact, my attempts were laughable. Even when I spoke very quietly, to replicate the effects of Marion's reduced hearing and added the crackling sound effects of a bad long-distance line, I did not think it would pass.

Listening to the recordings of our late-night conversations put me into an unexpectedly sad and pensive mood, and it was a while before I could refocus on the matter at hand. It then occurred to me that there might be a way of using the recordings. After all, I had hours of Tess's speech recorded, all the raw material one could need, and it was possible there was software that enabled one to form new sentences from individual words and sounds.

Some investigation on Google revealed that such a thing did indeed exist: a voice-changing program with a virtual audio device. The process involved importing Tess's voice into the program, recording my own voice, and then comparing the two, making adjustments using the equalizer and noise reduction. When the two were comparable, my words would be translated into Tess's when I spoke via the computer's microphone.

This was an exciting development, and I put everything else aside for the afternoon. After downloading a pirated version of the software I imported several hours of Tess's speech, which was quite a fiddly job, then did a practice run, slowly reading out the nearest thing I had to hand—a takeaway menu leaflet from the restaurant downstairs—and recording the results on the Dictaphone. It was not a success. The occasional simple word—*rice, naan, prawn*—was passable, but the vast majority did not sound like Tess, and the whole thing had a tinny, electronic quality that could not be explained, when it was put into action, by a long-distance phone line.

Over the following hours I repeated the process over and over again, adjusting the equalizers to find the right combination of pitch, intonation, and timbre. With each recording, I added some lines I thought would be likely to crop up in my phone conversation with Marion: "Succulent lamb in a thick, creamy, spicy sauce." "Yeah, Mum, it was the best decision I ever made." "Chicken cooked in butter and topped with almonds." "How is Dad getting on with the new caregiver?" "That's amazing your necklace was featured in *Harper's Bazaar.*"

Eventually, I had something I thought might sound vaguely convincing as Tess, but by that point it was hard to be objective, and I thought it best to test out the imitation before using it on Marion. First, to make sure I didn't sound like myself, I phoned Rashida. She and I had not spoken for some time, but she was still the person who knew me best, after Mum. I dialed her mobile, having first taken the precaution of shielding my number, and hoped she hadn't changed it since we last spoke. Sure enough, she answered.

"Hi, it's me," I said, through the software.

"Who?"

"Me! You know—me!"

"I'm sorry, but . . ."

"Do you really not recognize me?" I said.

"Is this Kerry?" she said.

"I think I have the wrong number," I said, satisfied, and hung up.

Next came the real test: someone who knew Tess. After careful consideration, I chose a friend of hers, Shell, who had recently announced the birth of her first child on Facebook. As well as there being a legitimate reason for Tess to get in touch, Shell's status updates constantly referred to how busy she was, so I thought she would be happy to have a short chat.

A woman answered, her voice weary.

"Yeah, hi?"

"Shell, it's me!"

"Who?"

"It's me! Congratulations about Ludo."

"Yeah, thanks. Sorry, who is this?"

I didn't want to lead her by giving Tess's name, but I decided a clue was allowed.

"I'm sorry it's taken me so long to get in touch," I said. "It's been a bit crazy, settling down over here." When she didn't reply, I added, "And then there's the time difference and everything."

"Oh, my God," said Shell, finally. "Is that *Tess*?"

I smiled to myself. Shell and I exchanged a few more pleasantries before I pretended my phone was running out of batteries and hung up.

Finally, I felt ready for Marion. Compared to that first time I left a recorded message on her answer phone, I felt calm and confident, even though this was a far-riskier endeavor. I called at six twenty p.m. GMT. My hand was steady as I dialed her home number. She answered in five rings. Her voice was loud and clear like Tess's, but with a trace of an accent.

"Hello?"

"Mum, it's me."

"Tess? Is that you?"

"Sorry, this line's terrible."

"Tess, it's been two months. What's going on over there?"

"Oh, I'm so happy, Mum. This was the best decision I ever took."

"Yes. Well. I'm glad, of course. I got your pictures. Your flat looks quite nice. Did you get that chaise longue in the end?"

"Yes. How's Dad?"

There was a pause. "Not good. He's becoming very distressed. Tess, I don't think I can cope."

"Oh, dear."

"Are you all right? You sound odd."

"Oh, no, I'm so happy."

Another pause. "He asked after you a few times. Where you had gone. Not recently, but at the beginning, when you left. Will you speak to him?"

Before I could say anything, I heard the sound of Marion's footsteps, presumably moving toward Jonathan. This was not in the plan, and I was about to hang up when it occurred to me: Jonathan had advanced Alzheimer's. He couldn't even remember the names of his children, let alone what their voices sound like. I stayed on the line.

I heard Marion saying something in a low voice to Jonathan, and then the sound of him clearing his throat as he took the receiver.

"Dad?"

For some seconds there was no reply, just breathing. Then, "Hello?"

His voice was wary and tremulous, as if this were the first time he had spoken into a phone.

"Dad, it's me. Tess. Your daughter."

Another long pause. Then, "They keep on moving my chair."

"It's Tess."

"I don't care who you are. Would you be so very kind as to tell the cunt to stop moving my chair?"

From a meek beginning the tone of his voice had quickly esca-
lated in volume and fury; the "c" word was spit out. It was clear that
Jonathan's realizing I wasn't his daughter would not be an issue. He
lapsed into silence again, and I heard, in the background, the sound
of someone sobbing.

Just as I was about to hang up, Marion came back on the line. If
it had been her crying, which it surely was, there was no longer any
trace of it in her voice.

"Who are you?" she said to me, loudly and distinctly.

I immediately hung up, my heart thumping so hard it felt like it
would leave a bruise on my chest.

It took some moments—hours, really—before I was in a state to
process what had just occurred. I kept on replaying Marion's "Who
are you?" in my head. Although her tone had been plain and flat, it
went around and around in my head to all sorts of different rhythms
and emphases. *Who* are you? Who are *you*? Who *are* you?

Obviously, the most logical explanation was that the comment
was directed at someone else in the room. Perhaps a new care assis-
tant had just walked through the door, unannounced. Or maybe she
aimed the comment in a nonliteral sense at Jonathan, a rhetorical
question about where the husband she had known had gone. But
if either of those was the case, surely her tone would have been
distant.

After spending some hours thinking it all over, I decided it was
time to ask Adrian for advice.

As mentioned before, I was proud of the fact that I'd never asked
anything of Adrian with regards to Project Tess. I wanted him to
think me capable and strong and that he had made the right decision in choosing me for the job—besides, up until that point it really

had been quite straightforward. Now, however, it was time. I wanted reassurance that this turn of events would not derail the project, and to be told what action to take. I wrote Ava Root a message on Facebook outlining the phone call and requesting a meeting so we could discuss the incident.

He did not reply—for two, then five, then twelve difficult hours. I concluded that I had no choice but to try to reach him on his Red Pill e-mail. Mindful of his ban on openly discussing Project Tess, I simply stated in my message that I needed to see him urgently.

Three hours later, I got a reply: Is this really urgent?

That was odd, I thought, as the fact that it indeed was urgent was pretty much the entirety of my message.

I repeated that it was. He replied, telling me that he would be at a shopping center called Westfield the next day, and I could meet him there at one p.m.

I had thought I was quite familiar with shopping centers, but this place, Westfield, was nothing like the ones I had been to. Stepping off the tube at Shepherd's Bush the next day I joined a mass of people flooding toward a complex so vast and shiny it made Brent Cross look like a shabby corner shop. The scale was hard to grasp: The ceiling seemed a mile high and the shops never ending, constructed out of acres of gleaming glass. It was not just the size of the place that was overwhelming, but also the sheer number of people. They all seemed to be young too. At Brent Cross, there were lots of women like Mum: older ladies in purple rainproof coats walking slowly. Here, everyone seemed to be my age or younger, the girls heavily made-up and—I suppose—fashionably dressed, as if they were going to a party rather than buying a new pair of tights or whatever it was they were here to get. A girl who stopped beside me to answer her phone had eyelashes so weirdly thick and long she could barely keep her eyes open.

I, of course, was not made-up or smartly dressed. I had considered putting on the same outfit I'd worn during that first meeting on the Heath, but had found a smear of melted cheese down the top and, anyway, felt that now that Adrian and I were close friends I didn't need to dress up. So I was wearing my normal uniform of hoodie and tracksuit bottoms.

As I walked through the shopping center looking for Boots (where Adrian had said we should meet), with all these thin girls darting around me, I started to feel an old sensation coming back, one that I hadn't had for a long time: being conscious of the fact that I was different. Not that I cared, but I was aware of it. It was like I was back to being Leila, when in recent months, especially when I had been talking to Connor, I hadn't felt like that: not like someone different exactly, just not like my old self.

I was determined not to let these feelings distract me from the task at hand. After ten minutes of wandering around I asked several people where Boots was, but my inquiry was met only with shrugs, so I had no option but to continue along the gleaming walkway, hoping I'd chance upon it.

And then, about twenty meters ahead of me, I saw a man emerge from a shop. I recognized the shirt first—it was the same blue corduroy one he wore in his podcasts and for our meeting on the Heath. He was carrying a red plastic bag with the words TIE RACK on it.

Adrian walked swiftly, and I worried he would be swallowed up by the crowd, so I stumbled after him, calling his name. At first he didn't hear and continued walking, and it was only when I caught up with him and laid a hand on his shoulder that he turned, an expression of annoyed surprise on his face. When he saw it was me, he rearranged his features into a half smile.

"Hey, there," he said.

"I couldn't find Boots," I said.

"I haven't got long," he said. "Let's find somewhere to sit, shall we?" He started off walking, me behind him. I noticed for the first time that his body was an odd shape: his shoulders narrow and sloping under his shirt, his hips large and almost womanly. He looked as out of place as I did among all the darting, sleek young people. The atrium was noisy with chatter and all the benches were occupied, so we stood instead, a few meters from a stall at which a young man was leaning back in a chair having something done to his face by a woman brandishing a piece of thread. I couldn't work out what was happening, but whatever it was, it seemed a very odd thing to do in a public place.

Adrian didn't seem to notice.

"So. Tess. There's a problem?"

"Yes, I told you," I said. "With Marion, her mother." I explained the situation with the phone call all over again, and as I was speaking noticed that Adrian's gaze didn't rest on me, as it did on the Heath that day, but rather flitted around the atrium and, once, glanced down at the watch on his left wrist. His face, too, looked different: That day I remember his cheeks were pink and glowing, but now his skin appeared ashy and coarse. Even his chinos seemed creased and grubby.

So marked was his change in demeanor, I felt somewhat thrown off course, and when he peered into his plastic bag, as if to check that the contents hadn't escaped, I broke off from my account and asked whether he was okay.

"What?" he said, as if he couldn't believe what I was saying.

I faltered. "Um, is everything all right with you?"

"Yes, of course," he said. "Extremely fine. Now, I do only have a few minutes, I'm afraid. . . ."

I quickly finished describing the phone call, feeling somewhat perturbed at his manner. Perhaps for that reason, I ended my account with a comment aimed at him: ". . . told you so."

Adrian's eyes finally met mine and he said, quite slowly, "What was that?"

"I told you this was going to happen," I said, "at the beginning of the project. I said I was sure that Marion would want to talk to Tess on the phone at some point, and that that would present a problem."

Adrian nodded, looking off over my shoulder toward the woman in her booth.

"If you felt such misgivings about the project," he said, "why did you embark upon it?"

I opened my mouth to reply, but no words emerged.

"Did I not teach you to think independently?" he continued.

"Yes, but . . . ," I said, hearing my voice quaver. "You assured me it was going to be all right. So did Tess."

At this, Adrian gave a short laugh. "Have you brought this up with her too?"

"No, I can't, because she's . . . ," I started to say, before realizing that this was Adrian's idea of a joke.

He looked at his watch again. "I really do have to go. Look, Leila, I trust you to take whatever course of action you think best. You know the situation and the people involved better than anyone, and you're a clever girl."

He held out his hand for me to shake. "I trust you, Leila," he repeated. "And by the way, your contribution to the 'Does luck exist?' debate last week was first-rate."

I hadn't contributed to that thread on the site and opened my mouth to tell him so, but then closed it again.

"So, farewell," he said, and started walking off into the crowd.

After a moment, I called after him. He turned, impatiently.

"Yes?"

"How did you and Tess meet?"

He frowned. "Why do you ask?"

"I'm just curious," I said.

"She came to one of my lectures in New York," he said after a moment. "Summer of—what was it now?—2004, I believe," Adrian said. "The subject was 'Nurture, Not Nature.' I think she found it rather inspirational. She asked a lot of questions during the talk, and then approached me in the foyer afterward. We stayed in touch."

Then he lifted his hand and disappeared into the crowd.

||||||||||

But as I knew full well, Tess had never been to New York. "Embarrassing, isn't it," she had said on Skype one evening. "I kept meaning to go, but then for whatever reason it didn't happen." She told me about a dinner party game her friends played in which everyone had to name something they hadn't done that they thought everyone else would have, and said she always won with not having been to New York.

"I would have been good at that game," I had said.

"Yeah?" she replied.

"Yes," I said. "I've never been kissed."

She laughed, thinking it was a joke.

Anyway. I could only presume that Adrian had made a mistake and confused Tess with someone else. But even taking that element out of the equation, our meeting had not been a success. On the long tube journey home I went over everything that had occurred since that first meeting on the Heath, but just couldn't account for his change in attitude toward me. He had seemed pleased with my progress reports; everything had gone smoothly up until now, and this was the first time I had asked him for help.

The only possible conclusion was that something else was troubling him, unconnected to me or the project, something so all-consuming that it prevented him from focusing. This was, of course, a matter of concern, but I felt that my immediate priority was to address the Marion problem.

It didn't, in fact, take too long to decide on a course of action; after all, my options were limited. Ceasing contact altogether would be unwise—it would only fan her suspicions—yet another phone call was, of course, out of the question. It would have to be an e-mail. The only sensible way of dealing with the "Who are you?" I decided, was to ignore it and instead make a bold "grand gesture" that I knew would please Marion, in the hope that her surprise and delight would replace any lingering suspicion.

This is what I drafted when I got home that day:

Dear Mum,

I'm still feeling a bit shaky after that phone call on Tuesday. Sorry I hung up, I was just really shocked to hear Dad in that state. I had thought that episode in France last summer with the cheese was pretty bad, but had no idea it could get so much worse. It's hard

being so far away and not being able to do anything or help
you out.

I really admire the way you're dealing with this. I know I've
never said that before, and I'm ashamed I haven't. It took coming
here to really see things clearly, and I regret the years we spent
in conflict. It was almost always my fault—that incident at Har-
rods aside!—and I think I knew that at the time, which is why I was
so defensive and angry with you. Anyway, I just want to say that
I think you've been an amazing mother to me and I admire you
greatly as a person too. I can only hope I'll be as strong as
you when I'm your age—and as beautiful too.

I can't remember if I mentioned it, but I'm seeing this great
therapist here, Trish. She's really helping me get to the bottom of
myself—a fascinating process, if sometimes scary. Yesterday I was
telling her all about Dad and you and the phone call, and how bad
I felt about everything, and she suggested I write it all down—this
is it!—and then have a period of time by myself, to reflect and
embark upon the healing process. So I hope you don't mind if we
don't speak for a while. I know I'll be a better person at the end
of it—someone fit to be your daughter.


Tess x


I had barely pressed send when a whole new tricky situation presented itself: this time with Connor.

In an e-mail composed of amusing but inconsequential details
about his day, he asked with a deceptively casual P.S. what my plans
were for the following weekend.

None so far, I replied. Combination of walking on the beach, trying to finish *A Suitable Boy,* and drinking gallons of Rooibos tea with Leonora, I expect.

Him: How about a combination of walking around an exciting new city, four-hour lunches, and drinking espresso martinis with me?

Me: What u on about, sport?

Him: I'm being sent to the Toronto office for a few days. Fortuitous, or what?

At first, I thought I had a failsafe get-out: Aw, lovely thought, but I am S.K.I.N.T. You do realize that Toronto is about two thousand miles from Vancouver, right? Don't think I'll be able to fit in the however many hours of art lessons necessary to earn the plane fare before next Friday.

His reply: I'll pay.

I thought quickly. Fuck, you know what? Just remembered I promised to visit Sheila. This old lady I met on the ferry over. She's disabled and I said I'd go over and spend Sunday with her.

Him: Rearrange?

Me: She's disabled, dude! Stuck at home, no visitors, such a sad, sweet lady.

Him: Well, if she's disabled she'll still be there the next weekend, won't she? She'll understand. Come and run around Toronto with me. A few days of classy debauchery.

Me: I've given up drinking.

Him: Well, we'll have Lucozade then. Wheatgrass milk shakes. Whatever! Come on, Heddy, we can't pass this up. This is our opportunity. It's usually Richard who gets to go, but he's on paternity leave. It's not going to happen again. It's fate; don't you see?

In my reply I decided on a variation on the approach I took with Marion, just a few hours earlier:

Okay, straight up. I can't see you. Please understand. I told you a bit about what's been going on with me, and why I had to leave London. I feel like I'm getting better, but I'm still not there yet. Yes, I associate seeing you with happy times, but it was also a tricky period in my life. I was doing too much gak, being lairy, going mental . . . all these things that I have to avoid now for my life's sake. I think that if I see you they'll all come flooding back, and then that'll be me gone, all the good work undone. I'll be jumping on the ferry to Vancouver every evening to try to score, hanging around horrible skanky little bars, getting into trouble. I'd love to see you, but please believe me when I say it's not a good idea. We can see each other when—if—I come back to London for a visit. Deal?

Connor's reply came a nerve-racking thirty-five minutes later: Okay, deal. But if you don't come back soon I'm going to come over there and find you.

Thx, I replied. We can still write, tho?

Of course, he replied. This is what gets me through the day.

Again, my initial reaction to this incident was a sense of satisfaction at my deft handling of a potentially tricky situation, and pride at my fluent use of Tess's tone and vocabulary. However, it also sowed the seed of an idea, which over the next few hours rapidly grew until it blocked out all other thoughts.

I *could* see Connor again. Not just look at him, like in the sandwich shop, but actually meet and talk to him. And perhaps he and I could start a relationship. A real one.

You see, I felt that things between us had developed to the point where Tess was surplus to requirements and could be cut out of the equation altogether. The fact that it was ostensibly Tess whom Connor was professing his love for—not me, Leila—was not difficult to rationalize. By this point in the proceedings—that last exchange excepted—the content of my e-mails to Connor was largely mine: that is, my own thoughts and feelings, rather than those of "Tess."

And remember the facts. Connor had not seen Tess for nine years, since a time when she, and he, were very different people (I don't blame you for dumping me, he wrote one evening. I was a tosser. The insecurities of youth, and all that). When Connor got in touch with her that first time, he wasn't in love with her; he was, he had said, just catching up with an old friend. It was only through the e-mail exchanges, *my words*, that he fell for her again. It was me who had created that love. *Me*.

There was, however, the physical issue. From their old e-mails, it was clear that Connor had found Tess very attractive. There were many comments along those lines. Hot stuff. Sexy beast. Woman of my dreams. And it's true that she did possess attributes that are apparently considered desirable in women: large eyes, a small chin, and a heart-shaped face.

Yet her features were definitely flawed. As I have mentioned, her eyes were too wide apart, and one was slightly smaller than the other. Although mine were not as large as hers, they were more symmetrical. Furthermore, her eyes were dark and mine blue, which men prefer because it reminds them of babies. She also had short hair, whereas men prefer long. And she was thin with no discernible curves, which are a marker of fertility and thus desired by the opposite sex.

My biggest advantage over Tess, however, was age. I was fifteen years younger than she was. In their e-mails, Tess and her friends often talked about how men like younger women. They made it sound as if that were the deciding factor, the one that negated all others. Bet she's younger, they'd say, talking about an acquaintance's new girlfriend. Twenty-five-year-old bitches. I feel ancient. I had what they seemed to covet more than anything: youth. Moreover, I decided that I looked even younger than twenty-three. I have no lines on my face, except for a very faint crease between my eyebrows from frowning at my computer.

So, in conclusion, I thought there was a strong possibility that, on appearance alone, Connor would find me as attractive as Tess, if not more.

There was one major obstacle, however. If Connor was in love with Tess, that would preclude an active interest in other women. Were we to meet, it was likely that out of loyalty to her he would not engage in the length of conversation necessary to establish our similarities and "connection." He had mentioned several times in his e-mails that he had left social events early because he had found other people lacking, because they're not you.

The obvious thing to do, I concluded, was for Tess to end their relationship prior to my meeting Connor in real life. That way, he would feel free to converse with a "new" woman. The following day, Tess sent Connor an e-mail:

Sweetheart. I've been thinking. This is madness. I'm here; you're there. I think about you all the time, and it's not healthy, dude. Let's release each other! There must be a million women in London who would adore to be with you; I'm depriving them of you. Thirty-something single men are like unicorns. Agreed?

And then, in a moment of inspiration, I added:

In fact, I can think of one girl I should set you up with. You're really similar; I think you'd get on like the proverbial house on fire.

His reply came quickly:

What the fuck are you talking about, Heddy? Don't be ridiculous. There may be a million women out there, but they ain't you. I'm not interested in anyone else. Don't insult me.

As you can imagine, my reaction to this was mixed. Part of me was pleased at the strength of his feelings; another was dismayed. I decided to try again, this time with a firmer approach:

K, I'll be straight with you. You know before, when you asked me whether there was anybody else, and I said no? Not strictly true. There is this guy. It's early days, but I do like him. He is not as great as you, but he's calm and kind and I think he might be good for me. He also has the advantage of not living four thousand miles away. What do you think?

Again, his reply came a moment later:

What do I think? I think that I want to cry, and I think that I want to jump on a plane and come over there and shake you. Come on, who is this guy?

Another e-mail followed almost immediately. It contained just one line:

If you're really serious about this, then I can't keep writing to you.
I'm sorry.

My chest seized up, as if filled with concrete, and my hands fell
limp on the keyboard. It took some moments to collect myself suf-
ficiently to reply, and my fingers were still feeble as I typed:

No, no, don't say that. We can't stop writing. The thing with this
guy is nothing serious; my heart belongs to you; you know that.
Please don't stop writing.

His reply came a whole, agonizing minute later:

I won't.

I closed my eyes and exhaled with relief. Then, when I opened
them, another e-mail was waiting:

P.S. Kiss me first.

Despite this scare, I couldn't shake off my need to see Connor
in the flesh again. After a day in which I could think of little else, I
concluded that there was nothing to be lost in engineering a meeting anyway. Even if it didn't lead to the desired outcome, a face-to-
face encounter would at least replenish my stock of mental images
of him.

I admit, though, that I still held out hope that it would lead to
something more, that the "connection" between us would be strong
enough to override his loyalty to Tess. A key weapon in my arsenal

was that fact that I had extensive knowledge of his likes and dislikes, and so could quickly introduce those topics into our conversation.

Bumping into him was the easy part. I knew that he went out with fellow lawyers most Friday nights, often for someone's leaving drinks. So, the following Friday, as soon as I logged on, I casually asked what he was up to that evening.

Oh, the usual—swilling five-pound pints with gentlemen of the bar.

Who's leaving today?

Justin.

Which one's he? He had told me amusing stories about many of his colleagues.

The part-time bodybuilder who keeps Tupperware boxes of chicken breasts in the fridge.

Aha, yes. Jumbo Justin. And what's the venue for this thrilling event?

Some grim hole in Shoreditch.

Ah, the old stomping ground. I did a quick check in Tess's file from that period. Is the Electricity Showrooms still going?

Haven't you been there since then? Blimey. No, the Leccy closed years ago.

So where do the cool kids go now then?

Well, I wouldn't know about that. But we deeply uncool middle-aged men are going to the Dragon Bar. Know it?

After a hasty Google to check that the Dragon Bar had not opened recently, I wrote, Of course, had several a crap evening there. Have fun!

It was that easy.

That was at six fifteen p.m. GMT, so I had to leave to get down to Shoreditch almost immediately. I had already prepared my outfit—

my long black tasseled skirt and my newest hoodie—and washed my hair in anticipation. I had also dug out some of Mum's makeup: a pot of blusher and some face powder that had broken up in its little box but was still usable. Although I knew that Connor wasn't shallow and believed that it was what was inside that mattered, I wasn't naive: It would do no harm to look my best. Before I left the flat, I wrote Tess a status update saying that she was out all day on the mainland, and put my copy of *The Princess Bride* in my bag.

I had never been to Shoreditch before, although the girls at school used to go all the time. In fact, after seeing Facebook photos of their nights out there, I had sworn I'd never set foot in the place: It looked a vile scene, full of sweaty people in ridiculous clothes, crammed up against one another and grinning inanely. Sometimes the men they had their arms around would be wearing makeup, and the expressions on their faces made it clear they all thought this was something to be immensely proud of.

I emerged from the Old Street tube just before seven p.m., my phone's GPS directed me to a grimy side street, five minutes' walk away. The bar didn't look like much from the outside, but inside it was already quite full with drinkers talking loudly over the music. Contrary to my fears, many of them looked fairly regular—lots in suits—although I did spot one woman who looked like she had put her top on backward, and a man with spiky bleached hair. The few tables were already taken, but I found a stool at the bar, ordered an orange juice, and opened my book, ostensibly reading but keeping an eye on the entrance.

At seven forty p.m., Connor arrived. When I saw him push open the door, I felt that same jolt of adrenaline you get when you're not watching your feet and you miss a step. He was wearing a dark blue suit that was almost identical to the one before, only the pinstripes were a little thicker, and I thought he looked very well, glowing and happy. He was with two other men, including the one who had been at the sandwich shop, and a woman with very neat brown hair and a tight black suit. I watched Connor as he scanned the room. On spotting a group of people, he exclaimed, "Aha!" and pushed through the crowd toward them. There were seven people in the group he joined, all in suits, the men holding pints of beer and the women glasses of white wine. Connor slapped one of the men on the back and said something, at which the man laughed. His colleague, the one from the sandwich shop, went around the group, gesturing at their glasses with raised eyebrows, and then headed off to the bar.

I hadn't predicted that Connor would be in such a large group, and wondered how I would get close enough to speak to him. I gave up the bar stool and pushed through the crowd until I was standing a few meters away, within hearing range. I continued to hold my book up, although it felt unnatural standing reading in a crush. Connor was still talking to the man he had slapped on the back, and I heard the words, "Fucking typical, right?" although I didn't catch what the statement pertained to. The other man was, I deduced, Jumbo Justin. The bulk of his upper arms strained against his pink shirt, and his neck was only a little narrower than his head.

Justin started talking about someone whose name I didn't catch, telling a story about how he, Justin, had once caught him in the office kitchen doing something he shouldn't have. The others all seemed to be familiar with the story and kept laughing, swaying backward and forward slightly on their feet as they did so. Then another man butted in and started talking about going to Latvia. I couldn't hear all the details of the story, so it was hard to keep track, but I noticed that the dynamics of the group seemed to be that they were all just waiting for their turn to tell a story or make a joke. A man wearing similar glasses to those worn by Tess's brother, William, then told a joke, which ended, "Well, that's what she said." This got a big laugh from the group.

Connor laughed and nodded during his colleagues' stories, but I noticed that his eyes were not fixed on the speaker, instead roaming over the crowd, as if he were looking for someone. He also checked his watch regularly. One of the men sidled up to him and asked whether he wanted to go to the toilet with him, as though they were girls at school. "Nah, I'm all right, mate," said Connor. I thought back to what he said about how he found social occasions pointless without Tess. I wanted to go over and touch his arm and tell him, "I'm here."

When everyone had finished their drinks, another man gestured around the group in the same way Connor's colleague had. If they were buying rounds, it soon would be Connor's turn. That would be my chance to get him alone. In preparation, I pressed myself farther into the crowd around the bar so that I would be in a good position to talk to him when the time came. There was no room to read my book in a normal position, so I had to hold it up high and close to my face, peering around its edge in order to monitor proceedings.

As it turned out, three of the others bought rounds before Connor, so I had plenty of time to observe him. He had little wings of hair over his ears and three spots around his hairline, and when he was listening he tilted his head. He stood with one hand in his pocket and the other holding his drink, and had a large leather bag over his shoulder. I had a strong desire to know what was in the bag. I noticed the lines around his eyes and felt jealous of the people who had made him laugh in the past. Isn't that silly?

Eventually, it was Connor's turn to get the drinks. "All right, chaps. Same again?" he said, and started to move toward the bar.

This was my chance. Making sure that my book was held up so he could clearly see the cover, I squeezed through the crowd and accidentally on purpose pressed rather too hard against him.

"Sorry," I said, and then, "Hello."

"Hello," he said, looking down at me. My eyes were level with his mouth and freshly shaved chin, and I could smell the beer on his breath. His right hip pressed against my arm. For an awful moment I thought I wasn't going to be able to speak, because my heart was beating so frantically. Then I swallowed and took a long breath, and focused on the conversation opener I had decided upon the evening before.

"So, do you come here often?"

For some reason, this seemed to amuse Connor. He threw back his head and laughed. It was more a bark, actually.

"I don't think I've ever heard anyone actually say that," he said. Then: "I'm sorry, how rude of me. The answer to your perfectly valid question is, yes, I do come here quite often. How about you?"

"I've never been here before," I said.

He peered closer at me. "Have I seen you somewhere? Are you at Clifford Chance?"

I shook my head.

He shrugged, but in a nice way. He then noticed the barman coming near and waved at him, said "Excuse me" to me, and leaned in to give his order.

"Five Stellas, pint of Guinness, large glass of white wine, and a Diet Coke."

He turned to me.

"Are you okay?"

It seemed an odd question to ask me, as although my insides were churning I was making an effort not to show it.

"Yes, I'm fine."

It was only when he turned back to the waiting barman and said, "Yeah, that's it," that I realized he must have been asking whether I wanted a drink. The barman started pouring the pints and Connor turned back to look at me.

"You know, I'm sure I've seen you before."

As I opened my mouth to say no, his hand moved toward my face and I froze, thinking for a moment that he was about to stroke my cheek. But instead his fingers touched the memory stick on a string around my neck. Since Jonty moved in, I had made a habit of downloading all my files onto it and wearing it whenever I went out, in case he forgot about one of his stews and burned the flat down in my absence. The stick was on the outside of my hoodie, so Connor's fingers did not actually touch my skin, but still I shivered at their proximity. His nails were very clean and evenly cut; Mum would have approved. When he took his hand away, my fingers involuntarily flew to the spot he had just touched. Then I let out a little gasp when it registered exactly what data was contained on the little plastic stick: Tess and him. Him and me.

"Have you come to fix my computer?" he said, and giggled. "The IT geek at work has one of those, but he has it down here." He mimed pulling a curly rubber cord from his belt, accompanying it with an exaggerated *boiiinnng* sound.

"Roger," I said, without thinking. That was the name of the "IT geek" at Asquith and Partners. Connor had told me about him before: how he stuck his lower lip out when he was concentrating and had had to be cautioned for staring at the female staff.

Connor looked at me, confused, and then his face cleared.

"Right, yes. Roger, over and out." He did a sort of salute, oddly similar to the kind Tess used to give me at the end of our Skype calls when she was in a good mood.

"Did you know that 'over and out' is actually an incorrect phrase?" I said. "In voice procedure 'over' means 'over to you,' and 'out' signals the end of the conversation, so it doesn't make sense to use both. It's commonly misused."

Before he could reply, the barman asked Connor to pay for the drinks, which were now lined up ready on the bar. I realized I would have to act fast, and held up my copy of *The Princess Bride*.

"I actually came to find somewhere quiet to read my book," I said. "But I think I chose the wrong place!"

I watched his face carefully as he looked at the cover. His reaction wasn't quite what I expected. He raised his eyebrows and smiled, but he didn't actually say anything, so I was forced to ask, "Have you read it?"

After a moment, he said, "No, I haven't, actually."

This was a surprise: I was counting on the book to be a topic of conversation.

He gave the barman two twenty-pound notes and struggled to pick up all of the glasses.

"Can I help?" I said, and before he answered I picked up two of the pints from the bar. I tried to add a third, but my hands were too small. Connor looked bemused.

"Okay, if you insist."

I followed him back to the group, carefully holding the drinks in front of me so they didn't spill. When he saw me behind Connor, Justin said, "That was fast, mate."

The others laughed as they accepted their pints from Connor and myself. Connor patted me on the shoulder.

"Thanks very much," he said. "You're kind. I hope you find a quiet place to read."

The dark-haired girl was in fits of giggles.

"Okay, then," I said. "Well, good-bye."

I slowly turned and walked to a spot in the corner, where I resumed "reading." I stayed in that position for half an hour, the book shielding my face as I tried to process what had just happened. We had not talked for long, but he had offered to buy me a drink. What would have happened if I had accepted? He said I was kind. Yes, *The Princess Bride* moment was a disappointment, but perhaps he had bought the book for Maya and not gotten around to reading it yet.

By the time I left—the group was still there, but I made an effort not to look around at Connor—I had concluded that, all things considered, the meeting had not been a failure. As soon as I was back in the flat I logged on to Tess's e-mail, curious to know what, if anything, Connor would say about his evening in the Dragon Bar. I had to wait until the following morning to hear from him.

How was the fondue? Did you drop the bread? I hope they don't do kissing forfeits in Canada.

The previous day I had told him that I was spending the evening at a dinner party at Leonora's, where she had promised to make her famous fondue.

You will be proud to hear that not a single crumb dropped from my fork, I wrote. How was Jumbo Justin's jamboree?

Tiresome, he wrote, then proceeded to tell me that it was the custom in their company for those leaving to attend their farewell drinks dressed as a woman, and Justin had honored the tradition, arriving at the bar in a dress. Deeply disturbing, he was. Made John Travolta in *Hairspray* look like Audrey Hepburn. This was odd, I thought, because I had witnessed no such thing: Justin had been wearing a shirt and tie, like all the others.

There was no mention of his encounter with me, but I suppose that wasn't too surprising. He wouldn't tell Tess about meeting another woman.

I concluded that he had embellished his account of the evening, adding the Justin dress anecdote, because he couldn't mention what had really been the notable event of the night—our meeting. It was a minor, understandable lie.

Our e-mails continued, but now vivid visual images of him accompanied our exchanges. I thought of those clean, shiny fingernails tapping on the keys, his black leather bag beside his feet under his desk. The ha-ha with which he sometimes responded to my jokes now came with the memory of his eyes disappearing when he smiled. When he went out for a drink after work, I imagined him ordering a Stella and pulling his wallet from the right hand pocket of his pin-striped trousers and calling the barman "mate."

And it appeared that Connor, too, was yearning for the same sort of visual detail from me. One night, quite late, he sent an e-mail from his Blackberry.

What are you wearing?

Unusually, there was no kiss me first in his sign-off, but I presume he had forgotten because it was late and he was tired.

By then I was feeling confident enough to reply as myself, rather than in the guise of Tess, so I gave him an honest description of my outfit.

Navy-blue tracksuit bottoms. Slippers. A Red Dwarf sweatshirt with the slogan SMOKE ME A KIPPER.

Very funny. Spoilsport, was his perplexing reply.

From the start of our correspondence there had been hours when I had no messages from him, sometimes up to half a day, when he told me he was seeing his children. These hadn't really bothered me at first; besides, I had had lots of other work to do for Tess. Now, though, I was finding these stretches of no contact increasingly difficult; the minutes dragged by, and I was starting to develop a twinge in my right hand from constantly refreshing Tess's e-mail account. I had no details to fix on during these hours; although he had once said he'd send me photos of his children, he never had. I tried to imagine him in his flat in Kensal Green, but, as I had never been inside a flat in Kensal Green, my mind came up blank. I couldn't see farther than his black leather bag in the hall, his striped scarf draped over a banister. Beyond that, there was nothing.

It was during one of these no-contact periods—a Saturday, I remember—that I started to wonder whether, now that I had actually met and spoken to Connor, I could upgrade from being "in limerence" to being "in love." Furthermore, I had become interested in investigating the concept of "soul mates." I thought of what Tess had said about Tivo the deejay, whom she claimed was hers.

*I wanted to tell him everything. He got me. I felt lost without him. The world was colorless when we weren't together.*

At the time I had thought this typically whimsical and over-dramatic of her. Recently, however, I had been remembering her words, because they described exactly the way I felt about Connor. Yet, surely the notion that there was just one person out there for each of us was nonsensical?

I decided to do what I had done in the past when wrestling with an idea: put it to the forum on Red Pill.

In retrospect, I can see that it was perhaps not a wise move, not least because starting a whole thread was out of keeping with my recent pattern of posting. Since I'd started Project Tess, my contributions to the forum had dwindled dramatically: Although I still logged on every day, as requested by Adrian, it was usually just to make a token, banal comment or to agree with what someone else had said, rather than putting in any real effort or thought.

Of course, I hadn't forgotten how oddly Adrian had behaved when I met him at Westfield, but, as I said before, I had come to what seemed like the only rational explanation—that he was distracted by an unconnected personal matter. Besides, it had seemed as if things had gone back to normal between us. After sending Marion the e-mail, I had mentioned it in my next report to "Ava," and he had replied with his usual Good work! Neither of us had mentioned our awkward meeting, and we had exchanged a couple more amicable messages since then.

It certainly didn't cross my mind that he would object to my starting a thread on "soul mates." I thought, if anything, he would be pleased to see me engaging more fully with the site than I had done in recent weeks.

I logged in to find most of the Elite Thinkers already present, in the middle of a discussion about Adrian's latest podcast, which I hadn't listened to. For form's sake I probably should have joined that debate for a while before launching my own thread, but I didn't have the time or patience. So I started a new thread with just a single-line question: Do soul mates exist?

My first response came two minutes later, from lordandmaster.

Shadowfax, are you going soft in your old age? There is no fate. Everything is a choice.

I replied, But isn't it possible, if not probable, that on a planet of seven billion people, there is one who exactly satisfies your needs and desires? Who "gets you"?

I knew, as I pressed send, that that "gets you" was a mistake. Jonas3 weighed in.

"Gets you"? Yes, I recall Socrates using that phrase . . . NOT. No, there is no such thing as soul mates; it's just humans needing certain things from each other to bring up a new set of genes. "Love" is a mere concept to sustain life.

I have two replies to that, I wrote. First, in *The Symposium*, Plato advocates the notion of soul mates, so to imply that no "great thinker" believes in them is erroneous. Second, what if you have no desire for children?

The reply: Plato used the analogy of a person with four legs and arms, split in half by Zeus and scattered around the world, who then roam the world looking for their other half. Do you believe in Zeus too? Even "great thinkers" can make mistakes, Shadowfax.

Before I could reply, someone else joined the discussion. Adrian.

Jonas3 is right, Shadowfax, he wrote. Even Elite Thinkers can make mistakes. I suggest you remind yourself of your moral duties as a rationalist, and don't let yourself get swayed by woolly thoughts like this.

To say I was taken aback by this intervention would be an understatement. I knew, of course, that it was possible that Adrian was monitoring our exchange; after all, it was his site. But he rarely interjected in such a manner. He would answer a question if it was put to him, but on the whole he took the position of a silent presence, overseeing the conversation and adjudicating only if called upon.

My initial reaction to this public rebuke was embarrassment. My wrist had been slapped. As the shame began to fade, however, I started to wonder whether it was possible Adrian had found out about Connor. But how could he have?

I concluded that the most likely explanation for the reprimand was this: He thought that my "soul mate" inquiry wasn't in connection with Project Tess, but referred to something else that had happened in my personal life. A boy I had met. And Adrian was scared that this new interest was going to distract me from my job.

Now that the thought was seeded, I felt annoyance rising. How dare he suggest I was being unprofessional? I had been fulfilling my duties; I had given months of my life to the project, at a degree of risk to myself. And the thought—even unproven, even in theory—that someone might want to stop me from talking to Connor made an unfamiliar, powerful sensation rise up in me: the desire to protect against this happening at all costs and to strike out at the threat.

Adrian's accusation of "woolly thinking" stung too—this from a man who couldn't even remember where he met Tess, who confidently stated it was in New York when I knew that to be untrue.

I'm not trying to justify what I did next, just explain it. I concede it was a childish, impulsive move.

I was still logged on to the forum. No one had added anything after Adrian's rebuke to me—it was as if they were all holding their breath to see what was going to happen. I started typing:

By the way, Adrian, you didn't meet her in New York. She's never been there.

Despite my anger, I was still careful not to say anything that would make any sense to anyone else. I just wanted to give him a jab, to let him know that, when it came to Connor, at least, he couldn't push me around.

My comment was met with more silence from the other members—this time stemming from confusion, I suspected. Riven with adrenaline, I waited to see how Adrian would react to my posting.

The forum stayed exactly as it was for a minute, and then two, then three. After three and a half minutes the lack of any action started to feel odd and unnatural. I thought that perhaps my screen had frozen, so I pressed the refresh key. The next screen that came up was a facsimile of the Red Pill home page, overlaid with a red circle with a line through it and the phrase You do not have permission to access this site.

At a stroke, my anger was replaced by incredulity. He had banished me? As I stared at the screen, trying to process what had just happened, there was a sudden smash of glass from the street outside—a pint glass kicked over outside the pub, most likely—and I flinched violently, as if it had shattered an inch from my face.

As the shock wore off, however, I began to think more reasonably, and before long I had concluded that this turn of events was not so terrible; in fact, it was a blessing in disguise. For some time now, my heart had not been in the site; I wouldn't miss it. And if Adrian was going to be critical and unpleasant, I wouldn't miss him either. As long as I could still have Connor—and Tess—I'd be okay.

*For the next few days* I hardly thought about Adrian at all, because there was so much else going on. The e-mail I had sent Marion had been successful, in that she had heeded my request not to speak on the phone and the *Who are you?* was never mentioned again.

However, the conciliatory nature of my e-mail had also provoked an unexpected outpouring of emotion and reminiscence on her part. In subsequent e-mails came a gush of words, thousands at a time, in which Marion gave her account of the relationship, and to which Tess was clearly expected to respond. She dredged up incidents from the past, many details of which did not tally with my notes, and asked lots of awkward questions—How exactly was I a narcissist? What more could I have done for you as a child? Were you jealous of William? I decided the safest bet was to ignore her questions altogether, replying instead with tales of Sointula life told in a light, chatty manner, in the hope that she would give up asking.

I was also thinking about sex. I had, you see, decided to meet Connor again and make another attempt to further our relationship. I hasten to add that I wasn't planning on having sex with him the next time I saw him. I was just aware that, were my plan to be successful, the matter would have to be addressed at some stage. It started to occupy my mind.

I had thought about sex before—quite a lot, in fact. When I was seventeen, I watched things on the net and saw how it worked. I even attempted to try it once, in the summer of 2006. To meet an appropriate partner, I joined an Internet dating site and spent a long time crafting a profile, which was ridiculous. You had to answer the question *Which six things can't you live without?* For which I wrote, *Oxygen, water, food, heart, lungs,* and then, because I felt I had made my point, *Internet.* I got only one reply, from a forty-six-year-old man with a shaved head who stated he was an animal-rights activist and *an extremist in all aspects of life.* He said I could come over to his flat in New Cross but didn't give a time or an address, and then he stopped replying to my e-mails.

So I abandoned that route, and instead got talking to a fellow player, Necromancer3000, in the game I was involved with before World of Warcraft. His real name was Marcus. He said we could meet at a pub in Edgware, where he lived, so I told Mum I was going to a party with people from school and got on the northern line to meet him. On the tube I realized that I didn't know what he looked like, but it didn't matter, because he stood out among the crowd in the pub garden: It was summer, and he was the only person in the pub garden wearing a long black overcoat. He was my age, and so tall that even when I craned my neck my eyes reached only his Adam's apple, and so skinny that no trace of his body was visible under his black T-shirt and jeans. He had long dark hair, quite similar to mine, and a series of leather bands on his thin, hairy wrist.

We sat at a table, surrounded by young people drunkenly laughing and vomiting cigarette smoke. Marcus talked about his job at the Virgin media help desk, and his Web site, Cui Bono, which was dedicated to exposing the Bilderberg Group. He seemed nervous and angry at the same time, and kept on looking at the silly, laughing girls in their flimsy clothes and calling them "sheeple." I didn't want to talk; I just wanted to go back to his house and get on with it. But then we got into a silly argument about eating meat—I told him it was a morally indefensible position—and after forty minutes he decided to go home without inviting me to join him. And that was the end of that.

So it was not as if I had never considered the prospect before. The difference was that in the past I could contemplate having sex with strangers, but not with people I cared about.

Also, there was the question of what one actually did. As I say, I had seen things on the net and was aware of the basic idea, the thrusting and the rolling. But as I may have mentioned, Tess was a very sexually active person, and from the things she said it seemed that there was more to it than that. There were many references to the act in her e-mails, and she talked about it without embarrassment, in the same way she enthused about certain books or whatever New Age fad she was interested in that month. Some of the messages exchanged between her and her boyfriends— Connor included—were really rather explicit. I won't go into details, but it was clear that she went beyond what I suspected was "normal" practice.

In 2002, for instance, she wrote to her friend Jen about how, the previous evening, she had gotten dressed up like a Romanian whore and gone to a hotel bar. Her boyfriend at the time, Raj, had then come over and chatted her up as if they didn't know each other. She pretended to be a prostitute and kept in character all evening.

In the e-mails between Tess and Connor back when they were seeing each other, the references were not so intimidating, but there was still some cause for thought. For instance, he would request that when they saw each other that evening, she do what you did to me last time. Of course, I didn't have a clue what these things were, and that would be a problem if they were expected by Connor.

It also appeared that they engaged in "sexting," and used a webcam on at least one occasion. You looked fucking hot last night, Connor wrote, on a day my records showed that Tess was away in Copenhagen visiting a friend. I couldn't help but think of Tess as I had seen her on Skype, lying back on her bed in her white vest, with those thin legs that she kept repositioning, not caring that I could see her knickers. She would lean her head back against the wall behind her bed and look down into the camera, as if I was there on the bed with her, and I imagined her doing the same to Connor. I wondered whether I should practice, to try to gain the same physical ease about myself she had. If only she were here to give me some guidance, I thought.

This may sound odd, considering everything, but sometimes I felt very sorry that Tess was no longer around. It wasn't just at moments like this when I wanted to know something only she could tell me, but at unexpected times—like when I was in Tesco and reminded how many plain, ordinary people were still living. It was as if a rare bird had been shot, rather than one of an endless supply of pigeons.

Anyway, in lieu of Tess's advice about sex, I had no choice but to turn to Google, something I almost immediately regretted. There was a vast amount of material on there, but none of it seemed to answer my very simple questions. I was reminded of a customer who once came into Caffè Nero and shouted at Lucy when she ran him through the list of options for his drink. *I just want a plain, ordinary coffee!* he had said. *Is that too much to ask?*

So there was that to think about. I had also decided to change my appearance somewhat, in the form of new clothes. As you might imagine, the prospect of a third meeting with Connor had thrown up a dilemma. Considering that he had thought he recognized me after giving me twelve pence in a sandwich shop, he would almost certainly remember offering to buy me a drink in the Dragon Bar, touching my memory stick, etc. Should I, then, disguise myself so he didn't spot me, or go looking as I did before and risk his feeling disconcerted at the "coincidence" of our bumping into each other again?

I decided on a compromise. There was little point in disguising myself as an entirely different person, since, if our meeting was a success and our relationship developed, it would be impossible to keep up the deception. However, I decided it would be a good idea to change my "look" and wear clothes more like the ones Tess would have worn, my thinking being that the more I looked like her, the more Connor would be able to imagine me as her replacement.

So went the reasoning, but the practicalities were less straight-forward. The few clothes I had bought in the past had either been from the Internet, like my Red Dwarf hoodie, or from Evans in Brent Cross, or, when Mum was alive, from Bluston's, using her staff discount. Bluston's was aimed at the more mature women, its curved window displaying items such as beige raincoats and twinsets that Mum said were old-fashioned even for her generation, but when we went in the ladies would all cluck around me, saying they would get the "trendy" clothes out. When these emerged from the long wooden drawers they were not noticeably different from the others on display, but I didn't mind: Clothes were clothes, after all, and I liked being in the shop, which was dark and cool and smelled of new cotton.

But none of these would do for "Tess": her clothes were small and tight and fashionable. I remembered the girls at school talking about Topshop on Oxford Street—they seemed to go every weekend—so, one afternoon, I headed there.

It was not a successful experience. The shop was confusingly vast—I felt like I had at Westfield—and the music as deafening as that in a bar. The automatic doors kept opening and admitting wave after wave of identical-looking young women, streaming in like Orcs going into battle. We were then sucked down an escalator lined with mirrors—in unison, the girls turned to inspect their reflections—and disgorged into a huge underground pit. There the girls immediately dispersed and started plucking at clothes, dismissing them in milliseconds according to some private criteria. They were as focused and ruthless as the Terminator, pushing aside obstacles in their path—me—to get to the rails. The pumping music forbade standing still, insisting on a continuous forward velocity. The shop seemed limitless and clothes were everywhere, but in no discernible pattern. I stopped a woman wearing an earpiece and asked her where the skirts were, and she waved her hand around the store as if to say, *Everywhere.*

Eventually I found some skirts, but they were horrible: short and made from orange leather with holes punched in them and costing eighty pounds. Also, they didn't have size fourteen. So I escaped back up the escalator and out to freedom. I've never been so pleased to be on Oxford Street.

I ended up getting my new outfit from Tesco Extra. The clothing department had plenty of items my size, and I chose a short blue clingy skirt and a thin pink jumper. Back home I tried them on. I had never worn tight clothes before, and the feel of them was quite alien on my skin. I didn't look very much like Tess. Still, I thought, I looked more like her than I had previously.

My plan to meet Connor followed exactly the same lines as before. The next afternoon, Wednesday, at five p.m. GMT, we exchanged our customary "Good morning" / "Good evening" e-mails. I told him I had been woken early by the sound of seals mating on the beach; Arf arf, he replied. I asked him what he was up to that evening, and he said he was attending the birthday party of his friend Toby. I extracted the information that they were going to a place called the French House in the West End.

All was going according to plan. I got dressed and prepared to leave the flat. I had almost safely reached the door when Jonty came out of his room. He looked at me with confusion, and then whistled.

"Hot date?" he said, in what I think was an attempt at an American accent.

I nodded, and then shook my head. "Yes. I mean, no. Not a date." I thought quickly. "I've got a meeting with someone."

"Ooh, very fancy. What about?"

"My script."

"You've finished?" said Jonty, eyes widening with what appeared to be sincere delight. "You are the darkest of dark horses. Good luck. Let's celebrate later."

I nodded again and hurriedly made my way to the tube.

And it was there, sitting in the tube carriage heading toward Green Park, just before six p.m., that I saw the paper. It was one of the free ones, tucked behind one of the seats beside me, and I unfolded it to see a fuzzy picture of Adrian on the front, which I recognized as the head shot he used on Red Pill. Above the picture, the headline read: INTERNET SUICIDE CULT EXPOSED.

My hands involuntarily released the paper; I remember it making a surprisingly loud sound as it hit the floor. I heard raspy breaths and realized they were coming from me, my rib cage feeling as if it were doubling in size with each inhalation. The man sitting opposite looked up at me from his phone and I closed my eyes for what could have been seconds or minutes. When I opened them, the man had been replaced by a woman, who was reading a copy of the newspaper. She was holding it up, so I had a full view of the front page; Adrian smiled warmly at me. I looked down the train and it seemed that every person on there was reading the same paper, the carriage populated by a hundred Adrians.

Eventually, I managed to lean down and pick up the paper, in what I hoped was a casual manner. The story ran across both the first and the third pages, although there wasn't much to it, very few facts. All it really said was that a Red Pill member—no mention of whom—had told police that Adrian had asked him to virtually "take over" the life of someone who wanted to kill himself. "Sinister Internet guru Adrian Dervish has been encouraging vulnerable people to commit suicide and then brainwashing his followers to impersonate them online," I think was the wording. This unnamed member had gone along with the plan for a while but had then gotten cold feet and told his parents, who had gone to the newspapers. The police were now looking for Adrian.

I sat on the tube, the paper on my lap, as people filed on and off the carriage. The seats beside me were occupied and then empty and then occupied again. I was dimly conscious of legs pressing against mine, elbows pushing onto the shared armrest. The train went past Green Park, my stop, and carried on to Stanmore, where it terminated. The doors opened but I remained in the carriage, and then eventually got out and sat on a bench on the platform.

The first thing that struck me on reading the piece was not the wider implications in terms of Tess and my own involvement, but the fact that I wasn't the only one Adrian had enlisted. The paper didn't say how many there were, but hinted darkly at a "squad" of "computer whiz kids."

It was true that Adrian had never actually said there weren't others doing it. Nonetheless, I thought back to that day on Hampstead Heath, how special he had made me feel. It had been—I thought it had been—our own secret project. He said he had picked me because I was an extraordinary person, uniquely capable of understanding both the ethical and practical dimensions of the undertaking. Although it sounds irrational, I felt betrayed.

My head fogged with emotion and unhelpful thoughts. It was only after a few moments that I started processing properly. If the police were after Adrian, they would presumably have searched his house. Who knew what information they might find? Maybe they were on their way to my flat right now. Maybe they were already there, waiting. I imagined the waiters from the restaurant below peering out the window as the officers lined up outside. Jonty would answer the door and think that someone had died. He had once told me that at college in Cardiff his roommate had died in a car crash, and the moment the policeman knocked on his door to tell him had been the worst of his life.

When the truth was revealed, he'd be at first relieved, then shocked and hurt at my deception. Then, under questioning, things would start to make sense to him. *Yes*, he'd say, *she was quite secretive. She hardly left her room. She said she was writing a film script.*

In my mind I saw the police searching the flat. I had locked my door, as always, but the padlock was a flimsy thing that could be easily opened with bolt cutters. Once inside, the evidence wouldn't be hard to find. I had hidden the Tess stuff out of view—both the paper documents and those on my computer, as I did automatically—but it would take no time at all for someone to uncover them. The wall chart was just there, barely hidden by my posters.

I realized I had to get back home—if only to prevent Jonty from having to deal with the police. I crossed over to the other platform and boarded the next train back to Rotherhithe.

As I walked down Albion Street, the flat looked quiet, my curtains drawn as I had left them. I stopped outside, imagining the police inside waiting for me, squeezed together awkwardly on the sofa, grave and silent, with all the evidence laid out on the floor in front of them. As I stood there on the pavement, I remember thinking that this could be my last moment of freedom. I admit that I actually inhaled the air, sucking that aroma of fried chicken and exhaust fumes and the metallic tang from the barbershop down into my lungs. A teenage boy on a bike weaved along the pavement, pursued by another one who called after him, "Oi, twat!" A blast of music issued from a passing car. I looked up at the restaurant sign, above which I could see a sliver of my window, and realized I had never even noticed the actual name of the restaurant: Maharaj. The best curry house in Rotherhithe. Then I unlocked the door.

The flat was empty. Even Jonty wasn't there, the piles of unwashed pans in the sink evidence that he had finished his stew and gone out. In my room I sprang into action. First I made sure that all of Tess's files were on my memory stick, then deleted them and erased the Internet history from my computer. I knew that experts could find files that you thought you had erased, and that the only sure way of destroying information was to smash up the computer itself, but I wasn't quite ready for that. I decided that if I saw the police come to the door, as a temporary measure I would drop my laptop out the window into the restaurant yard, where the rubbish bags would hopefully both cushion its fall and disguise it from view.

I tried to rehearse my reaction for when they turned up. Should I deny everything? But if they had gotten to me in the first place, they'd have evidence that I was involved. And if my name was linked to Tess's, that would be that. It would be a matter of moments before they established that she didn't live in Sointula. Then they could check the IP address of the e-mails and trace it back to me. Then Marion would be told. Everyone would know. Connor would know.

As I sat there, waiting for the knock on the door, I scoured the Web. I put a Google alert on Adrian's name, and every few minutes my laptop bleeped with news. For the first day or so, it was just the same story, repeated all around the world. Even sites in Japan were carrying it. I sat at my laptop for many hours, only my fingers moving as I clicked the mouse. I heard Jonty come and go. Then, at six a.m. on that Thursday morning, there was a development. One of the newspaper Web sites carried an interview with the Red Pill member who had broken ranks.

Randall Howard was his name. I didn't recognize him, but that was no surprise, since most members didn't use their a real photograph of themselves, and it was quite possible that I'd had many conversations with him. He was a year older than I and had a fat, featureless face and short spiky hair. The photograph showed him sitting on a sofa beside his mother. She had her arm around his shoulders and looked angry.

The story Randall told in the interview was similar to my own. He had found Red Pill after a friend recommended it. "At first I thought Adrian was amazing," he said. "He was so clever and funny, and he really seemed to care." He described how, after being a member for a year, he had been approached by Adrian for a face-to-face. They had met in a London park.

The paper gave few details about Randall's "client." I know now that it was because the police were investigating and details had to be withheld. All it said was that he was a man in his late twenties, whom the paper called "Mark." At first, Randall said, he was committed to the idea. He believed wholeheartedly in the cause: that it was a person's right to commit suicide if he so wished, and the duty of others to assist if requested. He said he had asked Adrian whether Mark was mentally sound, and Adrian had assured him that he was. Adrian had put him in touch with Mark, and he had started collecting information by e-mail. Unlike with me and Tess, however, they had actually met in person. It was after this encounter, in a coffee shop in West London, that Randall started to have doubts.

"There was this moment when I looked at him while he was talking, and the chocolate from his cappuccino had stained his lips. It suddenly occurred to me what exactly was at stake. I realized that he was a real person." He also said that although Mark was "adamant" that he was sure about what he was doing, and he was of sound mind, Randall thought he could detect some reluctance. "He kept on looking away when I was talking, off into the distance, with a sad expression." He described how Mark's hands were shaking so much that he scattered sugar all over the table.

Randall had carried on with the project for a few weeks after that, collecting information, as I had done. But then one night, when Mark got in touch to suggest a date for checking out, Randall had had "an epiphany." He realized that this whole thing had to stop, and, moreover, I quote, that "Adrian Dervish had to be stopped." He went downstairs, where his mother was watching TV, and told her everything. She had immediately gone to the newspapers. Then the police had gotten involved.

"I don't know how many other vulnerable young people this despicable man has brainwashed," his mother was quoted as saying. Mark, apparently, had changed his mind about wanting to die, and was grateful at Randall's halting the process. "I can only hope that by coming forward, Randall has saved some other lives too," she said. The interview ended with Randall saying, "I once thought Adrian was a god—now I realize he's the devil."

I found the article unsatisfactory. Even if Mark had, as Randall diagnosed, "a manner that suggested to me that he really didn't want to end his life." Even if he had remarked on "how lovely the weather was," which, according to Randall, meant that he was still capable of appreciating the world. Even if it was true that Mark didn't really want to die—although, like I said, I didn't think Randall was qualified to make that assessment. Even taking all that into account, it didn't follow that the others Adrian had helped, like Tess, were the same. It was faulty logic.

The way Adrian was depicted also bothered me, but in a less straightforward way. I'd go as far as to say I felt conflicted, which isn't something I was used to. On one hand, I took some satisfaction in the damning portrait Randall painted; my abrupt banishment from the site was still fresh in my mind, and I couldn't disagree with the description of Adrian as "uncompromising" and "intimidating." I also admit to less rational feelings of aggrievement—betrayal, even—on discovering that I was not the only one Adrian had enlisted. Yet Randall's use of absurd, overblown language like "the devil" made me cross, and, beyond that, I still felt a deep-rooted loyalty to Adrian that made me defensive at this one-sided, hysterical attack.

Next to the article was a column on the same subject, with the picture of a solemn-faced woman at its head, in which she expressed her shock and outrage at the case. She called Adrian a "twisted Internet predator," a phrase that was picked up and used in many of the subsequent articles.

A debate started in the press over the case. Predictably, most commentators were negative, railing against the dangers of the Internet and this lost generation of young people, vulnerable little souls who were there to be taken advantage of. It was presumed that the people who had died—in those early days, there still weren't any figures; that would come later—had been coerced into it.

I found all this supposition frustrating. None of these journalists knew the reality of each situation, yet they all thought they had the authority to weigh in with their opinions, presented as facts. I hadn't read many newspapers before, and I was amazed that they were allowed to do that.

Over the next twenty-four hours, some of the coverage became more thoughtful and reasonable. One male journalist wrote a long article about how, although the full story was yet to emerge, and obviously it was indefensible if people had been coerced into suicide, the principle behind the scheme was not necessarily wrong. He, this journalist, was a right-to-die supporter, and he said that he agreed with the basic principal of self-ownership, and that people could do what they liked with their bodies. Another article suggested that it was wrong for us to automatically presume that the suicidal are delusional. Why could they not have just had enough of life, and want it to end?

Often at the end of these articles, there was a place for readers to post their own comments, and I must admit that, as I sat there during those endless hours, imagining the police were on their way, I couldn't resist adding a few of my own. I posted a message of support to the woman who said that suicide wasn't always a bad idea and argued rationally against the more negative posts.

At the same time, I was keeping up with my Tess work. That might seem strange, but to abruptly stop communications would have been more dangerous. Marion would get worried and start calling; Tess's friends too. Beyond that, it also felt wrong to abandon her just because things had gotten complicated. I thought of a sticker that our next-door neighbor had on her car: A DOG IS FOR LIFE, NOT JUST FOR CHRISTMAS. Of course, Tess was not a pet, but the sentiment struck a chord.

And, of course, there was Connor. He and Tess were in the habit of e-mailing each other several times a day, and when I didn't reply to one of his messages for even a few hours—as happened on that Wednesday evening, when I saw the newspaper—he would write asking whether something was wrong.

It didn't seem fair for Tess's friends and family to think that she was missing, and put them through that ordeal, only for them to then discover that she was actually dead. Much better for it to carry on as it had been, until the police knocked on Marion's door and broke it to her that her daughter wasn't living in Sointula but was missing, presumed deceased, a victim of the "twisted Internet predator" Adrian Dervish and the poor, vulnerable girl he had enslaved to do his bidding.

And so I carried on as normal, posting updates of Tess's lovely life in Sointula—Reasons to love this place, #358: You can get a massage for thirty bucks—and playing a silly e-mail game with Connor in which we took it in turns to make up a line of a song describing our respective days. I've accompanied a young felon to court, he wrote; I've walked sand all over my porch, I replied.

Meanwhile, I was continuing to monitor news Web sites, and on that Friday afternoon, there was a development in the search for Adrian that, for a moment, took the wind out of my sails: The police had discovered where he had been living, and had raided the premises.

Adrian Dervish was a false name, it transpired, and Red Pill had been registered in Brazil, so they couldn't find him through that. But apparently the endless reproduction of his photograph had reaped rewards, and a woman had told the police that a man who looked just like him had been her neighbor for the past week. There was a picture of the block of flats, a grim, run-down place near Gatwick Airport. When the police got there, Adrian had already fled; however, it was reported, they had seized a number of computers that they were in the process of examining. They had already found "significant information."

How long it would take them to trace me was impossible to predict, being dependent on how much information Adrian had stored and how well it was encrypted. Or whether it was encrypted at all. I thought back to our conversation on Hampstead Heath, when he said he was hopeless with technology. He'd made a basic attempt at covering his tracks by using a foreign IP address, but would he have bothered to protect me? I imagined a police computer expert rolling up his sleeves in preparation for a tough job and then laughing when he saw all the evidence there in plain view.

Who knew what had passed between Adrian and Tess— but, judging from my experience, I suspected she hadn't been too discreet in her correspondence. You've really found someone to help me die? You fucking legend. As for tracing me, they could pick and choose their method. I hadn't masked my IP address—Facebook would be able to see that Tess's account had been accessed from my computer. Gmail too. My credit card details were stored in Red Pill. Why had I not thought to take precautions?

Anxious as I was about an imminent knock on the door and the unpleasant formalities that would follow, my thoughts kept leaping forward to the moment when Tess's family and friends were told what had been going on. Or, more precisely, when Connor would discover the truth.

I mentally scrolled through various scenarios. Connor at work, receiving a call from Marion, his expression slowly turning from one of polite bemusement to openmouthed horror. Connor at home one evening, relaxing on the sofa watching an old episode of *Miss*

*Marple* (his guilty pleasure). The doorbell rings and he frowns at the interruption, and then panic grips him as he makes out the shape of a policeman through the frosted glass of his front door. (Of course, I didn't know he had frosted glass in his front door; I was just imagining.)

However he found out, I felt certain he would hate me, because he wouldn't hear my side of the story. He would assume that I had done it as a kind of sick joke, or for monetary gain. The thought of him thinking badly of me made me feel physically sick; I had to get down from my desk and bend double on the floor. And it was while crouching down there, staring at the crumbs in the carpet, that I realized I had to break the news to him now. I had to explain in person. If he understood why I had done it, he would forgive me.

Normally I carefully consider the pros and cons of major decisions, but the moment this idea came to me, I knew it was the right and only course of action. And I admit that I was anticipating more than just forgiveness from Connor. After all, if Tess was dead, there was nothing to stop us from being together. Once he was over the shock of the news, he would see that. Now he was free to love someone else, and the person he wanted was right here, in London, ready and available.

My anxiety morphed into impatient excitement; I wanted to see Connor right away. As I say, it was a Friday afternoon, so I decided I would go down to Temple and catch him as he was leaving work for the day. I put on the tight Tesco skirt and top I had bought for our previous, thwarted encounter and brushed my hair forty times. Luckily Jonty was out, so I didn't have to invent another excuse for looking so dressy; it also meant I could use the mirror in his room, the only full-length one in the flat. I had Mum's makeup bag, but there was no need for it: My eyes were shining and my cheeks were rosy all of their own accord. I looked as nice as I had ever done, I thought, and smiled at my reflection.

It was five past six when I reached his office. My normal bench was occupied by three middle-aged tourists taking the weight off their feet, but I couldn't have sat still anyway; I was too excited. I paced up and down the little park, mouthing to myself the opening line I had decided upon—"I have some bad news, and some good news"—and all the while keeping my gaze locked on the black door of Asquith and Partners. Just before half past six, Connor emerged.

He was alone, his leather bag strap across his chest, talking into his phone and walking briskly up the road. As before, the sight of him produced a lurching sensation in my chest and made my legs feel weak, but at the speed he was walking I had no time to waste. I gathered myself and started after him, struggling to keep him in view as he headed out of the cobbled streets of Temple and onto the larger road above, which was busy with cars and people. At the pavement he came to a halt, still talking on his phone. I was able to catch up, and was almost within touching distance when I heard him say, "Yeah, I see you."

I stopped and watched as he waved in the direction of a little red car parked on the other side of the road. In the driver's seat was a smiling blond woman, and in the back, waving at him enthusiastically, were two little children. I watched as Connor waited for a gap in the traffic, crossed the road, and got into the passenger seat. He leaned over to kiss the woman on the lips before turning around to greet Maya and Ben. And I watched as Chrissie started the engine and pulled out, and the red car merged with the traffic and disappeared from sight.

I don't know exactly how long I stood there on that thronging pavement. I was aware that the people walking past seemed annoyed that I was rooted to the spot, and pointedly pushed past my shoulder or clicked their tongues. If they had asked I would have explained that I couldn't actually move; my legs would not let me. My brain felt similarly leaden inside my skull, as if it had shut down in order to avoid processing what had just happened. It allowed only silly, tiny thoughts, like how it was a good thing that I had not put on any mascara earlier, as it would now be smudged down my face.

Eventually my legs started to work again and transported me to the tube station. The train was crammed, but a woman stood up and offered me her seat. I'm not sure why she did it, but I was grateful. Sitting down, I was aware of how short my skirt was; my lap seemed to be all bare thigh, the skin pale and mottled. Beside me was a man in a crumpled suit, who looked a similar age as Connor, slouched with his legs wide apart and tapping on his iPhone. The screen was in full view and I watched, as if from behind glass, as he composed a text to someone called Mila: I'll make it worth your while; you know that. I haven't forgotten what I promised at Ascot. . . . xxx. I imagined myself leaning over and typing P.S. Oh, and guess what—I'm married!

Back at the flat, I was relieved to discover that Jonty was still not home. I wrote him a note saying I was ill and not to be disturbed, and locked my door behind me. It hit me then that I was completely exhausted, and without taking off my shoes I lay on the sofa and fell asleep.

When I woke it was very dark, and both the street and the flat were quiet. Opening my laptop to check the time, I noticed I had forty-eight new e-mails, and was confused until I remembered that I had set up a Google news alert for mentions of Adrian and Red Pill. The Saturday newspapers had just been published, full of updates, analysis, and debates on the story.

I read the stories impassively, as if I had no personal connection with the subject matter. Another member, a boy called Stephen, had come forward to say that he had also been approached by Adrian to take over someone's life, but hadn't gone through with it. There were more reported sightings of Adrian, in England and overseas, in Prague and New York. One paper carried the headline IS YOUR CHILD PART OF A SUICIDE CULT?

In an interview Randall had been asked how many others he thought might have been enlisted, and had replied, "I don't know. God knows. Hundreds, maybe." The paper then used this as justification to ask a "respected psychologist" to compose a checklist of warning signs for parents worried that their child was one of Adrian's minions. The first question was "Does your child spend an excessive amount of time at his computer?" The second: "Does she keep odd, antisocial hours?"

Although I read the articles, I could not concentrate on them. All I could think about was Connor—or, more specifically, why had he done this? Why did he lie about being separated from Chrissie? Over the course of the weekend he sent Tess several e-mails, all as flirtatious as normal. When I asked him what he had gotten up to on Friday night, he said he'd gone out for drinks with people from work and then ended up at a party in Whitechapel. It was boring, because you weren't there.

I reread our past e-mails. Wondrous creature. This is a rare thing that's happening here, you know that? I feel I can tell you anything. Kiss me first. He had asked me once about my memories of being a child, and I told him about a memory of walking down Kentish Town High Street with Mum when I was seven—although I relocated the scene to Dulwich, where Tess grew up—and spotting what I thought was a little pink teddy bear in the gutter. I had presumed that some other child had dropped it and felt sorry for it because it was all dirty and forgotten. I crouched to pick it up, and it was only when I lifted it to eye level that I saw it wasn't a teddy after all, but a sawed-off pig's trotter. Aww, poor little Heddy, he had replied. That's too sad. I want to come and wrap my arms around you. Now that Mum was dead, he was the only person who knew about that.

Did it really matter that he was married? I wondered. Perhaps he and Chrissie were putting up a front for the children. One of Tess's unhappily married friends, Carmen, had e-mailed her once, We're doing the old "staying together for the kids" thing. Perhaps he was being selfless by staying married to Chrissie. And he hadn't told Tess because he suspected she would have nothing to do with him. *No more married men* had been one of her 2009 New Year's resolutions.

And people got divorced, didn't they? If they fell in love with someone else? And that other person was available?

These weren't the kind of questions that could be answered by Google, and, not for the first time, I wished that Tess were around to advise me. But then, I knew what she would say. She would tell me I shouldn't have expected anything from Connor in the first place. She thought that all men were, I quote, just *horny little toads* who would do exactly as much as they could get away with. She didn't say it with regret or anger but with casual resignation, as if it were just a fact, written into their biological code.

During one of our conversations I took issue with this view, pointing out that it was a sweeping generalization that didn't hold up on several points. By the same token, women should all share certain characteristics too, but Tess and myself were examples of how two people could share a gender yet barely any similar personality traits. I also pointed out that this "toad" quality was not much in evidence in her own dealings with men, most of whom seemed keen for more commitment from her than she was willing to give them. Actually, I said, from the evidence of her life and from what I could garner about the supposed differences in the sexes, it seemed that she was the one playing the supposed "man's role," hopping between partners.

I remember she was lying on her back on her bed as we talked, so I couldn't see her face for much of the conversation, but at that point she sat up and looked directly at the camera, her head tilted to one side and an amused look on her face.

*Babe, no offense, but I'm not sure you're qualified to advise on sexual politics,* she said.

But over the last few months I had realized something: that just because Tess said something with total conviction, it didn't mean that she was right. Back then, it was true, she was far more knowledgeable about relationships than I was, and I had little to back up a challenge to her assertions. Now, though, I had had some experience myself and did feel qualified to make my own judgments—and I just didn't agree that all men were the same and could not be trusted. Each person and relationship was complex and unique. And I knew Connor far better than Tess ever did.

I realized that I had to talk to him as soon as possible.

The next day I could was Monday. I considered going down early to his office to catch him as he arrived for the day, but decided against it; he was often late, I knew, and might be rushed and flustered. A better time would be when he left the office for lunch.

On that Monday morning I woke early, at ten a.m., feeling eager and nervous in equal measure. I couldn't sit still, and the prospect of waiting in the flat for two hours until it was time to leave was unappealing, so I made the decision to walk to Temple. I hadn't walked that far before ever, but this was an important, life-changing day, and it felt appropriate to be bold.

Once again I put on my new skirt, and brushed my hair until it rose from my scalp with static. Luckily, Jonty was away for a few days visiting his parents, so I didn't have to think of an excuse for my smartness. I left the flat and made my way down to the Thames path. It was a nice day for October; the city gleamed in the sunlight, and the air was fresh and invigorating—not that I needed energizing. The tide was low, exposing the riverbank, and just before Tower Bridge I noticed a group of people down there, using their hands and tools to dig around in exposed riverbed. I recall Jonty arriving home filthy one day and enthusing about a new hobby of his called mudlarking, which involved scavenging for artifacts from the Thames's sediment; perhaps that's what these people were doing.

Excitement made me walk quickly, and the journey to Temple took less time than my route planner predicted. . . . By the time I reached my bench it was only twelve fifteen p.m., at least three-quarters of an hour before Connor would venture out for his sandwich. I felt frustrated at the prospect of waiting, until it occurred to me that now I didn't have to. After all, if I were going to reveal the truth, it was no longer necessary to engineer a meeting with Connor; I could just go into his office and ask to see him.

I walked across to the black door and pressed the intercom. A female voice answered and I stated loudly and clearly that I was there to see Connor Devine. I was buzzed into a small, surprisingly shabby reception area. The woman behind the desk looked at me curiously and asked whether I had an appointment. No, I replied, I was here on an urgent personal matter. She asked my name, picked up her phone, and dialed a three-digit number.

"Connor, there's a Leila here to see you," she said, and at that, as I heard it so baldly stated, my confidence faltered. I stepped backward and opened my mouth to say I was leaving, but before I could speak Connor had appeared through a side door, as if he'd been waiting just behind it.

He looked at me and frowned, then glanced over to the receptionist, as if to say, *Is this her?* She nodded, and he looked back at me.

"I'm sorry; do I know you?" he said.

"Yes," I said. My resolve flooded back. "Come outside."

He frowned again, but followed me out onto the street. I walked a few paces away from the office, then turned to face him. Connor looked back at me and, absurd as it sounds, it was as if an electrical current passed between us. In just a few seconds I absorbed every detail of him: the pink tinge around his eyes; the thick, neat stubble; those wings of hair, covering the piercing in the top of his left ear that he'd had done while drunk in Thailand on his year off.

"I'm sorry," he said again. "Have we met?"

"Yes," I said, nodding firmly.

His eyes searched my face.

"Are you Tobias's sister?"

"No," I said. "I don't know Tobias. I'm Leila." I realized I hadn't really thought out how I was going to approach this. "I know Tess."

His expression changed, softening for an instant and then becoming more alert. He shifted on his feet and glanced around.

"Who are you?" He looked at me closely. "Haven't I seen you somewhere before?"

Perhaps best not to remind him of our previous meetings yet, I thought. "I told you," I said. "I'm a friend of Tess's."

"Is she all right?" he said. "Has something happened to her?"

"No," I said. "Well, yes. I need to tell you something. Can we sit down?"

I motioned toward the bench and we sat. I took yesterday's newspaper out of my bag and laid it on his lap. He gave me a quizzical look before picking it up and looking at the front page. It was only then that I noticed the ring on his left hand. Had it always been there, or had he taken it off when I met him before?

After a few seconds, he put the paper down.

"I'm sorry; I'm at a total loss as to what this is all about, and I'm very busy. Has something happened to Tess?"

"Yes. But first you need to know about Adrian Dervish," I said, indicating the paper. "Apparently encouraging people to commit suicide."

"Right," he said, impatient. "And?"

I had presumed our conversation would flow naturally, like it did online, but that was not the case. It no longer felt like Connor and I had a special connection; in fact, at that moment he might as well have been a total stranger. I felt panicked that things were not progressing as I had anticipated, and changed tack—perhaps too abruptly.

"Tess is dead," I said.

I watched his face carefully as I said the words. There was a twitch at his eyebrows, but his features remained impassive.

"What?"

"She killed herself," I said.

"When?" he said quietly.

I paused, knowing that after I answered this question, nothing would be the same. Connor had turned away and was staring into the middle distance, his mouth slightly ajar. It wasn't too late, I thought. I could just tell him that Tess had died that morning, in Sointula, then get up and walk away. But if I did that he would never know he had been writing to me. Our relationship would be over and I would almost certainly never see or hear from him again.

"When?" he said again, turning back toward me.

I laid my hand on his shoulder in a comforting gesture and took a breath.

"Four months ago," I said.

He looked up sharply. His eyes had almost disappeared, like they did when he was amused, only now he wasn't smiling.

"That's impossible. We e-mailed yesterday."

"You weren't writing to her," I said. "Well, that's not true. I mean, you were writing to her, but it wasn't her reading the e-mails. Or replying. It was me."

He stared at me, and when he finally spoke his voice had lowered to something like a snarl.

"What the fuck are you talking about? Who *are* you?"

His aggressive tone startled me. The image of him walking toward Chrissie and the children in the car resurfaced, and I felt indignant.

"I told you. I'm a friend of Tess's—a much better friend than you. I know her a thousand times better than you do."

"What are you saying?"

"I told you," I said, exasperated. "Tess is dead, and I—"

"Did you kill her?" He stood up suddenly and stepped backward, away from the bench, staring at me as if I were a dangerous dog.

"No!" I said. "I helped her!" My indignation suddenly dissipated and, to my dismay, I felt on the verge of tears. "Please sit down."

After a moment, he did, but again turned away so all I could see of his face was a muscle twitching at his jawline.

"I was only doing what she asked me to do," I explained. "She wanted to die but she didn't want to upset her family and friends, and so she asked me if I would take over her life, so that she could quietly slip away and—"

"And kill herself?" said Connor.

"Yes," I said.

Again Connor rose from the bench, but this time he didn't move away. He had his back to me, and I watched from behind as he produced a packet of cigarettes and a lighter from his trouser pocket. I heard a click and watched his slim shoulders rise and fall under his suit jacket as he inhaled.

"I thought you'd given up," I said, without really thinking.

The hand holding the cigarette paused in midair before continuing on its path. After several more inhales he spoke again, without turning around.

"Let me get this straight," he said. I could tell he was making an effort to keep his voice measured. "You're claiming that Tess was involved with that nutter, she killed herself, and you—whoever you are—encouraged her to do it?"

"I didn't 'encourage' her to do anything; it was her own decision," I said, and briefly explained about meeting Adrian and how my involvement with Tess had come about. I talked to his back, staring at the pinstripes of his jacket, willing him to turn around. "She was of sound mind," I added. "She knew what she wanted."

Connor was silent for some seconds, then dropped the cigarette.

He didn't squash it out with his shoe, and the smoke drifted in my direction. I didn't mind, as I usually did; somehow it didn't smell as nasty as other people's. Then, at last, he turned to face me and said, as if it had only just dawned on him, "You mean I've been writing to *you* all this time?"

I nodded and smiled. It wasn't surprising that he had taken a while to digest the truth; there was a lot to take in. Now, I hoped, the implications were becoming clear. He thought the person he had fallen in love with was in Canada, out of reach, but actually she was right here in front of him.

Connor was staring at me, but I couldn't fully read his expression. I tried to imagine what was going on in his head, and it occurred to me that he didn't know where he stood with me, Leila. He might think I was just doing my job when I wrote to him, that I couldn't care less about him.

"I meant it all, you know," I said. "Everything I wrote."

He didn't say anything, just continued to stare at me. I started to feel a little flustered, and found more words coming out of my mouth.

"I'm . . . I'm not going out with anyone, you know. I'm single. And available."

Finally, at this, his mouth curled into something like a smile, and he spoke slowly and clearly.

"Are you fucking insane?"

Now it was my turn to be lost for words. Connor looked me up and down in an exaggerated manner, still wearing that odd half smile.

"You really think I would go out with *you*?" he said.

It felt as if a balloon had suddenly been inflated inside my chest. My breathing turned shallow, and for a few moments I could do nothing except stare at Connor. He looked steadily back at me; now he was ugly, his face a stranger's. And then, just as suddenly, I was galvanized by fury.

"Well, I suppose it would be hard for you to go out with anyone, wouldn't it," I said, "since you're already married!"

Connor flinched.

"I saw you! You and Chrissie and the children, all cozy in the car. You said you'd split up ages ago! You said you were in love with me and wanted to be with me. Why did you say that? I—"

"What the fuck?" said Connor. "When did you see us? Are you stalking me?"

I shook my head, furious that he was trying to evade my point.

"You said you were in love with me," I repeated, loudly and slowly, as if speaking to a child.

"Shhhh," hissed Connor, before softening his expression for the benefit of someone behind me. I turned to see that a couple of his colleagues had emerged from the office for lunch and were glancing at us with curiosity. Connor gave them a nod and a smile, which was wiped off his face the instant they passed out of sight.

"You said you were in love with me . . . ," I began again.

"Stop saying that," he said. "I don't even know you."

"I'm Tess!" I said, almost shouting. How could he still not get it? "Don't you understand? *I'm Tess.*"

Connor gave a dry, horrible laugh. "I don't know what the fuck is going on here, but I'm sure of one thing, and that is that you are definitely not Tess."

"Of course I'm not *actually* Tess." By now I was waving my arms about, and anger and frustration meant my thoughts came tumbling out in no sensible order. "Those things you wrote—were they lies?

I told you about the pig's trotter! You said that you laughed in court out of happiness, just at the thought of me! Was that true?"

With each question my voice grew still louder, and I noticed passersby were looking over at us. Connor had backed away and was staring at me.

"Get away from me," he said.

The look he was giving me, a blend of disgust and fear, was too much to bear.

"And you're a . . ." I paused, because I couldn't think of just the right word, and then I found it—one of Tess's favorites, which I had never said out loud before: "A cunt."

As I hoped, Connor looked taken aback, but the word also defused my anger. I suddenly felt exhausted, and when I spoke again, my voice had returned to normal volume.

"Does Chrissie know?" I said.

"Of course not," he said.

"Would she leave you if she found out?"

He looked at me sharply. "Are you threatening me?"

"No," I said.

"Well, in answer to your question, I don't know. I don't know what Chrissie would do if she found out. I suppose she would leave me." He seemed far away, as if he were speaking to himself. "I can't believe Tess is dead. I can't believe you . . . I can't believe any of this."

"I'm not lying," I said. "You're the one who's lied."

Connor gave that cold, barking laugh.

"You're calling *me* deceitful?"

But I didn't have the energy to reply and start arguing again, and neither, it seemed, did he. His shoulders sagged.

"Who *are* you," he said quietly, but it wasn't a real question. And then, without saying good-bye, he turned and walked away, not stopping at his office but carrying on up toward the main road. I stood, watching, until he was out of sight.

I remained where I was standing for several minutes, before it occurred to me that Connor might return to work at any moment. I set off at a brisk walk that quickly morphed into a run, stumbling in my slippy shoes as I tried to escape from Temple. I lost my sense of direction, and what had once seemed a magical enclave now felt like a fortress, each of its cobbled streets confusingly similar and populated by men in suits who looked just like Connor.

Eventually I found an exit and emerged with relief onto Victoria Embankment. Lanes of traffic lay between me and the river, but I crossed the road without waiting for a sensible gap, dimly conscious of car horns and shouts in my wake. I leaned against the wall above the water. Now supported, my body went limp. It was all I could do to keep my head upright.

I didn't feel angry, or even disappointed with myself. It was as if I had been emptied of feeling. The word *gutted* entered my head—at school, people had thrown it around in reference to trivial events, and I had dismissed it as a slangy figure of speech, but now it was the only word that fit. I felt I had been completely gutted, and my body was now as useless as a banana skin.

The brown river glinted in the sun, the tide still low, and the breeze carried a dank tinge. On the opposite bank, I could see people leaning on the wall, as I was; unlike me, however, they all seemed to be in pairs, nestled close as they gazed out over the water. I turned my head east, toward Tower Bridge, and saw that the group of mudlarkers was still down on the riverbed. The tiny, crouching figures in their luminous jackets might as well have been on a different planet. Tess used to say that adult life was just an exercise in filling in time; if so, I thought, then maybe these people had the right idea. Digging around in the mud was absurd, but at least it was harmless.

I closed my eyes, but attempting to process what had just happened with Connor made my head hurt with a physical pain. How could I have gotten the situation so terribly wrong? How could something that felt so real to me have actually meant nothing?

I should go back to the flat, I thought, and pictured my laptop waiting for me on the desk, the tiny light on its power cord glowing in the shade of the restaurant sign. But the image no longer offered any comfort. What was the point, when there would never be any more e-mails from Connor? In fact, the thought of getting back to work, continuing to be Tess without him, now suddenly felt abhorrent.

What I did next was not due to anger or another form of high emotion. Rather, it was a rational decision, or so it felt at the time. On a practical level, I did not belong out here in society, and I could not bear the thought of the flat, with its associations. I needed somewhere else to go. Moreover, I could no longer trust my judgment, and without that, what was I? I had to surrender, and let someone else step in and take control.

I took out my phone and Googled the closest police station.

It was near Fleet Street, and in five minutes I was there. I hadn't been to a police station before, but it didn't look like I had been missing much. Although the outside was quite old and grand, inside wasn't more interesting than a bank foyer, with plastic chairs bolted to the floor and leaflet holders on the walls. There was a small queue at the front desk, and I waited impatiently behind a foreign couple as they falteringly explained that they needed to report the loss of their phone for insurance purposes and then conferred at length on even the simplest questions they were asked.

After fifteen minutes, I felt compelled to take action.

"Excuse me," I said loudly to the man behind the window. "I've got something important to say."

The policeman looked at me without expression. He had a tired, meaty face.

"Don't you all," he replied. "If you could just wait your turn."

Eventually, the couple moved away, clutching their completed form, and I stepped forward to the glass. The policeman raised his brow in weary inquiry.

"I wish to make a confession," I said.

"About what, may I ask?"

"My involvement with Adrian Dervish."

"And he might be . . . ?"

I sighed with impatience, and for the second time that morning produced my copy of yesterday's newspaper and held it up to the glass. The man glanced at it.

"You know this man, do you?"

"Yes, I do," I said. "Well, sort of. I mean, I don't know where he is."

He looked again at the paper. "Well, madam, if you care to take a seat, someone will come to take your statement in due course."

I was, I admit, surprised and somewhat disappointed by the lack of urgency and excitement shown by the police, an attitude that continued when, after a further twenty-minute wait, I was called to give my statement. A young blond policewoman showed me through a door and into a small room equipped with a table and four chairs. We sat opposite each other and she pressed play on an old-fashioned tape recorder with two cassettes. As I spoke she also took notes, holding her pen in the same way Rashida used to, with her hand curled over the top.

The woman was nicer than the man at the front desk and seemed to know something about the case, if not much more than could be gathered from the newspaper article. She started by asking a few questions—how I met Adrian, and so on—but when she realized I was going to give a thorough, chronological account of my dealings with him, she let me talk largely interrupted.

I had been nervous beforehand, but as I spoke, I found that the act of unburdening was quite enjoyable. It was also pleasing to have someone's undivided attention. But then, about half an hour into the interview, things abruptly changed.

By then, I had reached the point where Tess and I formulated her postcheckout plans, and was describing the setup in Sointula when the woman interrupted.

"Did Adrian Dervish at any point put pressure on you to carry out the scheme?"

I was confused and asked what she meant.

"When it became apparent that you were not going to go through with the plan, did Adrian Dervish try to persuade you to do so?"

She thought I hadn't actually done it. That I was just another Randall Howard.

It was like the moment earlier with Connor, when he asked when Tess had died—an opportunity to stop the full truth from coming out, with all of its attendant complications. This time, however, I didn't hesitate.

"No, you don't understand," I said. "I did go through with it. Tess killed herself, and I impersonated her."

There followed some seconds in which the sound of the whirring tapes seemed to have greatly increased in volume. Then the police-woman leaned toward the machine and announced that the inter-view was being suspended. She got up and left the room, returning a few minutes later. Then she sat down, turned the tape recorder back on, and said, her voice clearer and more formal than before, "I'm arresting you on suspicion of assisting or encouraging the suicide of Tess Williams."

|||||||||||

I said I didn't need a lawyer, but they didn't seem to believe me. Every half hour, DCI Winder would pause the questioning to remind me that I had a right to legal representation and ask whether I wanted to exercise it. After the third time, I asked him why he was doing this when my answer was always the same.

"We need to be sure that you're sure, and that you understand the implications of your decision," he said. Besides, he added, the interview tapes captured only forty-five minutes of recording at a time, so this way the warning was included on each side.

This prompted me to ask something that I had been wondering about since coming into the station: Why did they use old-fashioned tapes, and not digital recording?

"Digital is easier to tamper with," he said.

This, of course, made me think about the software I had used to imitate Tess's voice on the phone; however, I resisted mentioning it, as, again, I was going over everything chronologically and had not yet reached that part in the story.

DCI Winder was the investigating officer for the case of Adrian Dervish and had arrived at the Fleet Street station just over an hour after my arrest. During the wait, I had handed over the keys to my flat so they could search it, after using the phone call I was offered to call Jonty and make sure he was still at his parents'. I didn't want him to be alarmed by the police coming in.

Jonty confirmed that he was still in Cardiff and wouldn't be returning until the next day.

"Everything okay?" he said.

"Yes," I said, thinking on my feet. "It's just that I'm at a friend's house all day and Amazon was going to deliver something to the flat." As I spoke, I was disconcerted to see that the young police-woman was writing down what I was saying.

"What friend?" said Jonty, sounding amused.

"Must go," I said.

From then until DCI Winder arrived, I was largely left alone. At the beginning they offered me a cup of tea and I said yes, even though I don't like tea. The polystyrene cup now sat on the table, its contents untouched and stone-cold, and I gazed at it and thought about prison. I had seen pictures of cells on TV; they didn't look so bad. It might not actually be that different from being in my flat, I thought.

When DCI Winder entered, the atmosphere in the room seemed to change; I could sense the policewoman sitting up straighter. He was quite old, with mottled red skin and a bumpy nose, but had lots of dark hair on the backs of his hands. He introduced himself, speaking with some sort of accent, and then sat down and the tapes went on again.

Unlike my previous interviewer, DCI Winder knew a lot about the case and asked detailed questions about how Red Pill worked and what Adrian had said to me on the Heath and the exact terms of the arrangement with Tess.

LOTTIE MOGGACH

"Did Tess pay Adrian?" he asked.

I said I didn't know and admitted that the thought hadn't occurred to me.

"We have reason to believe that Tess might have given Adrian a large sum of money to facilitate the impersonation," he said, and explained that Randall Howard's client, "Mark," had told the police that he had given Adrian fifteen thousand pounds.

"If that's true," he added, "it means that Adrian was profiting from the death of others. Which would make this a very serious matter. Do you understand, Leila?"

I nodded.

"Did Adrian pay you?" he said.

I hesitated. "Not exactly."

"How do you mean?"

"I think he actually posted me the money, but it came from Tess."

"How much was it?"

"Eighty-eight pounds."

"A day?"

"A week."

He frowned. "That's a funny amount."

"It's just what I needed to live on," I said. "It was a full-time job, you see."

DCI Winder looked at me unblinking for few moments.

"Why did you do it, Leila?"

"Tess wanted to die, and I believed in her right to do so, so I helped her."

"And if you hadn't helped her, do you think she would have still done it? Or would she be alive today?"

"I don't know," I said finally.

Later, he asked about my own state of mind. Was I depressed? Had I ever considered suicide myself?

I answered firmly in the negative.

"Yet you empathized so greatly with someone who wanted to end her life that you were willing to risk being arrested for her?"

I had never thought about it in those terms, but I nodded. "I suppose so."

The two questions he asked again and again were the ones I had no answer to. Where was Adrian now? And where was Tess's body?

After three hours of questioning, DCI Winder said that was enough for the day. It was eight p.m. The moment he clicked off the tape, I realized that I was more tired than I could ever remember being before. I could have put my head down on the table and fallen asleep right there. Instead, they led me to a cell, and I curled up on a hard, narrow bed.

Then, what felt like mere minutes later, I was being shaken awake and told I was being released on police bail. It was the morning; DCI Winder had gone, and I was back in the charge of the young policewoman. I was not to leave London without informing them, she told me, and must report to the station each month.

"How long is this all going to take?" I asked her as I signed the bail form.

"I can't say," she replied. "You may not be surprised to hear that we haven't come across anything like this before. It's new territory for us."

That's it for now. The sun is coming up and I can hear the insects starting. I'm meant to be going home tomorrow—my flight is booked for three thirty-five p.m.—but I've considered changing it. Annie says she is going to stay for another week, and I think I might too: All it would take would be to go to the Internet café in town, amend my ticket, and e-mail Jonty to say I'll be home a week late. Annie says I can sand some more stools. I was thinking I might get a taxi to the Alhambra.

*I am on the Dorito-orange plane,* heading back to Luton. Or rather, not: We've been sitting on the tarmac at Málaga airport for the past forty minutes, and will remain here for an unspecified period. Apparently there is an issue with the "airport management safety measures," which I think means that not enough crew have shown up. The other passengers seem resigned to waiting, although the man in the seat beside me has made clear his annoyance at my using my laptop. It overlaps the little plastic table, and my elbows occasionally stray into "his" space. He's sitting with his thick forearms folded tightly over his chest, staring straight ahead. Maybe he's the same man I was sitting next to on the way over. This could be the same plane I flew in on a week ago; it certainly has the same malodorous atmosphere.

This was not the plan. Not the plane being delayed—I mean my going home now. Two days ago I was about to change my ticket and extend my stay at the commune.

I'm not quite ready to write about what happened yesterday and why I have had to leave so suddenly. However, I do want to finish my account of what brought me to Spain in the first place. It's not far from the end.

We had reached the point when I had told the police the full extent of my involvement with Tess and Adrian. Actually, what happened next is quite simply summarized: nothing.

By which I mean that after months and months of investigation, there was no legal action taken against me. Regarding the online impersonation, there was nothing they could charge me with. Apparently, prosecution is possible only if the impersonation is used to harass or commit fraud resulting in loss to a particular victim, and I had done none of those things.

As for her suicide, the fact that there is no body means that Tess was—is—officially classed as a "missing person," rather than deceased. The law states that if someone tells you they intend to kill themselves, you are not obliged to tell the authorities, but if you say or do anything at all that could be perceived as encouragement, you can be charged with assisting or abetting. The police asked me again and again whether I had said or done anything that could be construed as encouraging her. Absolutely not, I said. They combed through our e-mails but found nothing to indicate that Tess had ever wavered from her desire to take her own life, nor that I done anything to encourage her.

I didn't tell them about that time on Skype, when she cried.

The fact that I had received money from Tess complicated things somewhat, but I showed them my bills and calculations and they concluded that I couldn't be said to have profited from eighty-eight pounds a week. In the end, they decided it was not in the public interest to prosecute me. The person they really wanted was Adrian.

Since that sighting in Gatwick early on, he had disappeared, and it turned out he had covered his tracks quite thoroughly. As I've mentioned, the Red Pill Web site was hosted by a server in Brazil, to which Adrian had provided fake details, so tracing his IP address was useless. His passport was also forged. And despite his picture being plastered everywhere, they haven't been able to find him. As the news reports never tire of pointing out, there's nothing about his appearance to distinguish him from the millions of other stout, middle-aged white men in the world. *The devil in disguise as a manager of Dixons.*

Given this hysterical reaction, I can understand why Adrian felt he had to disappear. However, I was surprised that he did not pop up to give his version of events and explain the principles behind it. Using an IP-blocking application, he could easily have posted a video on YouTube or some sort of statement online without alerting the police to his whereabouts. Perhaps he felt that there was no point, that those who condemned him would not have their minds changed.

Still, I am disappointed in him. His silence means that there is only one side of the story, and the unchallenged consensus is that he is an evil man who took advantage of "vulnerable" people like me for his own ends. To try to say anything to the contrary has as much effect as shouting into the wind. Everyone presumes that I'm still under his influence—"brainwashed"—when really I'm just pointing out something I thought any reasonable person would understand: that just because Adrian made mistakes and handled some things badly, it didn't necessarily follow that everything he did or stood for was wrong.

By "everyone," I mean the police, and Jonty. I had told him what had happened when I got back to the flat from the station, after being released on bail. I didn't really have much choice, as he had returned from his parents' house before me, and I found him in my ransacked room, staring at the desk, where my laptop had been replaced by a piece of paper from the police detailing which items they had removed during their search. I couldn't think up a plausible explanation for that.

Jonty took the news surprisingly well, if melodramatically, his eyes wide and his hand clapped over his mouth as I explained the situation as succinctly as possible. Luckily, he had seen the newspaper story, so he knew the basics; although, of course, this meant that he had Adrian down as an evil predator. "Poor Leila," he kept saying, clutching my arm. "Oh, my God. That bastard. Poor, poor Leila."

That day I didn't have the energy to contradict him; besides, after my experience at the station, I welcomed his warmth and sympathy. But the following morning he brought the subject up again, and I had the chance to put him straight on how Adrian was not the monster the papers had made him out to be, and how I had acted out of my own free will. This time his response was more measured.

"Look, I'm not going to pretend that I'm not spun out by all of this," he said when I had finished. "I haven't got my head around it yet. But I know you're a nice person, and I'm sure you went into it with good intentions."

That was not the end of it, however. Indeed, such was Jonty's interest in the case, you'd think he was involved himself. He devoured the news reports and, because my laptop was still with the police, took it upon himself to update me with every development. "Someone thinks they spotted Adrian in Brussels," he shouted through the bathroom door as I was washing my hair. One morning, he came into the kitchen while I was making a grilled cheese sandwich and announced that I should consider seeing a therapist.

"Why would I do that?" I said.

"I was reading this thing on the Internet about Stockholm syndrome," he said, "when people defend their abusers. I think maybe you have it."

"Don't be absurd."

"You keep on saying what an amazing man he was and how you don't regret what happened—"

"I never used the word *amazing*," I said, irritated. "I've just made the perfectly reasonable point that the situation is not as simple as you and everyone else are making it out to be."

There was, however, one aspect of the case that I wasn't prepared to discuss: Tess. Several times Jonty started to ask about the details of my involvement with her, and I blocked his questions; eventually, he got the message. It was one thing for Adrian to be public property, to be the subject of speculation and gossip, but my Tess—I wanted to keep her to myself.

Weeks passed. The reported sightings of Adrian came to nothing, and, with no new fuel, the media moved on to be outraged at someone else. Behind the scenes, though, the case was still ongoing, albeit very slowly, as the sight of my bare desk constantly reminded me. It ended up taking the police nine weeks to return my laptop—although, when I questioned the length of time, the man admitted that for most of that period it had been sitting in a storage facility. He added that I shouldn't hold my breath for the results of the investigation; it was perfectly possible I wouldn't hear anything until well into the New Year. "It's a complex case," he said. "There isn't really a precedent for this sort of thing."

In truth, I had not missed my laptop that much—because of its associations with Connor. It was actually a relief to be away from it, at least at first. I spent a lot of my days sleeping, but I also opened a box of books that I'd never gotten around to unpacking and reread my childhood favorites. Not *The Princess Bride*, obviously. After a few weeks, though, the novelty of being off-line began to wane, and I asked Jonty to lend me his iPad.

|||||||||||

It was well into the spring when Jonty decided it was finally time to clear away the mound of junk mail from the hallway. It was something he had talked about for some time but never actually got around to—it had even become a kind of running joke between us—but on that Saturday he announced, "Today is the day," and took some black bin liners down the stairs. A few minutes later, he reappeared at my bedroom door, holding an envelope.

"This was buried in the pizza leaflets. It's for you. Looks fancy."

I wasn't in the habit of receiving letters, and certainly not old-fashioned, handwritten ones, with the sender's address in the top-right corner. Once I opened it, the first thing I registered was that it was a very short letter. The second was that it was from Tess's mum:

*Dear Leila,*

*I would like to meet you. Could we arrange a time for you to come to my home? Please call me. I believe you know the number.*

*Marion Williams*

I stared at it. Jonty was still hanging around the doorway.

"Come on then, come on then," he said. "Who's it from?"

I remembered something the girls at school used to say when the boys were pestering them and they wanted to talk in peace.

"Oh, it's women's problems. You wouldn't understand."

Jonty looked bemused, but he went back downstairs. I continued to stare at the letter. I knew so much about Marion, but, of course, I had never seen her handwriting before. The blue ink was neatly slanted to the right, with the occasional flourish, such as an oversize capital "P" and "L." After some moments, I forced my focus away from the patterns on the paper and toward the contents of the letter.

It was dated two weeks previously. If Jonty hadn't decided to clear up the leaflets, I thought, it would have stayed in the hall for another month, another year possibly. I could easily not have seen it. I could just throw it away. But I didn't entertain such thoughts for long. Daunting as the prospect of a meeting was, I knew it was the right thing to do.

I felt a rush of pleasure at making this brave decision, until I realized that the next step was to phone Marion. Although, of course, I had spoken to her before, as Tess, it had not been an easy call, and the thought of doing so again, as *me*, was excruciating. Instead, I waited until Wednesday evening, when I knew she would be at her book group, and left a message suggesting a day and time the following week. I gave my mobile number. When, later that evening, she returned the call, I let it go to voice mail and listened to her message immediately afterward. Like her letter, it was short and to the point. Yes, that time suited her, and if I was getting a train to Cheltenham I should take a cab and give the driver precise directions; otherwise he'd miss the turn. I scribbled down the instructions and was

Googling train timetables when something occurred to me, and my fingers went still on the keyboard: How had Marion found out my name and address?

||||||||||

I knew what the house looked like through photographs: a large, semidetached place with white walls, and ivy growing up its front like neat facial hair; a circular driveway lined with round bushes. One of Marion's sculptures, a spiky metal thing like a rake, stood on a plinth beside the front door.

As the cab crunched over the gravel drive, I saw that she was already standing outside. She was wearing slim red trousers, and I recalled one of the last e-mails Marion had sent Tess, before everything blew up. In it she mentioned she was considering an operation to get the varicose veins in her legs removed, but it would mean having to wear trousers until the scars faded. I wondered whether this now meant she had gone through with it, or whether she would have worn trousers anyway. This idle thought was immediately followed by a lurch of trepidation, as if the reality of the situation suddenly registered, and I had to resist the urge to tell the driver to carry on around the circular drive and head back to the station.

The cab pulled up where Marion was waiting, and I got out and stood in front of her. She said nothing, just looked me up and down, her face unreadable. I could see Tess in her bone structure and flat nose. She was sixty-seven, a lot older than Mum was, but she looked . . . not younger, exactly, but as if she had been made with better-quality ingredients. Her hair was dark and long, and her brown skin seemed tight and polished. Tess had told me she had had a face-lift. She wore a turquoise stone on a chain around her neck and was even tinier than I expected, her arms as narrow as rulers.

She told the cabdriver to wait—"She'll be about twenty minutes"—and turned and walked into the house, not looking back to check that I was following. The wooden-floored hallway was lined with paintings and old, dark furniture smelling of polish. You never let us touch your antiques, Tess had written in one of her accusatory e-mails. As we passed one open door, Marion moved to pull it shut, but not before I caught a glimpse of an ugly beige hoist, similar to the one Mum had. The house was silent and I wondered where Jonathan was, and whether I was going to meet him.

Marion led me into the living room and motioned at me to sit. The sofa was pale pink, and so dainty I was worried its little legs would snap as I lowered myself onto it. Marion arranged herself in an ornate gilt chair, about five feet away. I had expected to see more evidence of Tess's father, because in her e-mails Marion had often talked about him watching TV beside her. I had imagined a hospital bed set up in front of the TV, like Mum had, but I couldn't picture any ungainly plastic equipment in this museum of a room.

Finally, Marion spoke.

"So, you're the girl who pretended to be my daughter."

"Yes," I said.

"I talked to you on the phone."

"Yes."

"But you don't look anything like Tess."

It seemed an odd thing to say—why would I?

"No," I said.

"You're fat."

"I'm not that fat!" I said. "I'm a size ten."

There was silence. Up till then, I had thought Marion was near to expressionless, but now I could see twitches at her eyebrows, as if her face wanted to crumple but couldn't.

I decided it was time for the speech I had prepared.

"Marion . . ."

"Don't call me Marion!" she interjected.

"Mrs. Williams, Tess asked me to help her only because she didn't want to upset you. She went to all that trouble to *spare* you pain. I know that you and she had some disagreements, but I got to know her very well, and I know that deep down she loved you—"

"I spoke to you on the phone," she interrupted.

"Yes," I said, wondering why she was repeating herself.

"Did she ask you to write that e-mail? The one about us starting again, being friends?"

"No," I admitted.

"The police said you never met her," Marion said.

"No."

"Yet you claim you knew her."

I started to say that we had talked a lot, that I had read all her e-mails, but Marion carried on as if she didn't want to hear.

"Did you really think that I would be happy to never see my daughter again?"

"She said that you would be too concerned about Jonathan," I said. "That you couldn't leave him and there was no chance you'd be able to fly over to Canada."

"In the immediate few months, perhaps," she said. "But . . . forever? How did you possibly think it could work?"

"It was only going to last for six months," I said.

"And then what?"

I remembered what Adrian had said on the Heath. "I was going to gradually decrease contact . . . like a dimmer switch on her life."

Marion looked at me as if I were mad.

"Tess was hugely loved," she said, laying out the words as if to a simple child. "Not only by us. She had a large group of friends. Did you not think that at some point someone would have visited her, or offered to pay for her to come back over here? What about when her father died? Do you really think that she wouldn't have come back for the funeral?"

"No," I said. My voice was so quiet I could barely hear myself.

"I think you underestimated how much she was adored," said Marion. "Maybe you can't understand that. I hear you are a sad little creature. No family. No friends."

I flinched. How did she know these things about me? I opened my mouth to ask, but no words came out, and to my horror my eyes began instead to fill with tears. I looked down at the carpet. It was dark blue, and I could see a few white specks, like dandruff. I thought of what Tess had told me about Isobel, William's wife—how she put plastic covers on the backs of her chairs when Jonathan visited to protect the material against his greasy hair.

"And how did she meet that man?" she said.

"Adrian? I don't know."

"Stop trying to protect him."

"I really don't know," I said. "I had presumed they met on Red Pill."

"This Internet site? Tess wasn't interested in that sort of thing. She wasn't . . . like you." She paused. "Were they lovers?"

The idea was quite shocking, but I tried not to react. "I don't know."

"But I thought you knew everything about my daughter," she said meanly.

Another pause. Again, I looked away. On the coffee table was a neat stack of large glossy books and magazines and a small pile of leaflets and junk mail, presumably en route to the bin. They reminded me of my hallway, and finding her letter.

"How did you find out my name and address?" I asked.

Marion sighed, as if it were a boring question. "A friend of my husband's has connections with the force, and he made some inquiries."

"Oh—you must mean Uncle Frank!" I said, pleasure at making the connection temporarily overriding my discomfort at being investigated. "Frank, who wasn't really Tess's uncle and was a chief inspector until he was forced to take early retirement because he got accused of taking that money. . . ."

"Yes," said Marion icily.

Just then there was a noise from somewhere in the house, a sort of low bellow, which I thought must have come from Jonathan.

"Excuse me for a moment," said Marion, as if we had been having a polite tea party, and slipped out of the room. I heard her out in the hall, calling, "Helen!" I looked at the pictures on the walls, recognizing one of Tess's paintings, concentric green circles slashed with red stripes. There were photos of Marion when she was younger, looking glamorous in an exotic location I guessed was Chile, and some of Tess and William as children. Most of these I had already seen, but there was one of Tess that was new to me: a school portrait of her as a teenager, with black-rimmed eyes and her hair scooped high off her face. Her smile was similar to the one she had in that first photo I ever saw of her, the one at the party, where she was exchanging a knowing look with the photographer.

Marion returned and reseated herself in the gilt chair. She crossed her legs at the ankle.

"Is Helen your new caregiver?" I asked. "What happened to Kirsty?"

Marion's eyes slitted.

"It's none of your business what happened to Kirsty. Nothing that happens in this house is any of your business." Her voice rose, and I noticed that her hands were clenched, but her nails were too long to allow them to fully close into fists. "How dare you! How dare you! Tess was my daughter. You may think you know her, but you don't. You don't know her at all. I'm her mother. I know her."

It was on the tip of my tongue to correct her tense—*knew* her—but I held it in.

"You know, you haven't expressed any regret for what you've done," she continued. "For me. For all of us. For her life gone. Have you no heart?"

I swallowed and started to speak: "I believe in self-ownership over our bodies, and that it's our right to—"

"Shut up!" screamed Marion, her face flushed. "Shut up, shut up, shut up!"

There was a moment's silence. More than a moment, actually. I think the outburst shocked her as much as me. Marion wiped each eye with her finger, a bright red nail passing under her lashes, and when she spoke, her voice was again steady.

"Why did she go to Spain?"

I frowned, confused. "When?"

"On . . . that day. Last summer. The police say she took a ferry to Spain, to Bilbao. Then they can find no further trace of her. Where was she going?"

I tried to digest this new information.

"I didn't know she did that," I said finally.

"Oh, really?" Her tone implied disbelief.

"I promise," I said, feeling tears threaten again. "We didn't talk about it. It was the one thing we didn't talk about."

"Where's her body?"

"I don't know."

"How did she do it? What happened?"

"I don't know!" I said. "Really, I don't."

"I need to know," she said, but quietly, as if more to herself than to me. We sat there, not speaking, for a long moment, but it was different from the previous silences—not so much awkward, just weighty.

Then Marion said firmly, "Can you leave now?"

I carefully lifted myself off the sofa. Her hands were clasped in her lap and her head turned away from me, looking at the wall.

"I'm sorry," I said. I meant that I was sorry that she was upset, rather than sorry for what I did, and I considered making that distinction clear, but then thought better of it. I walked back down the polished hall, speeding up as I felt my chest heave, and just managed to make it outside and over to the flower bed before throwing up, just behind Marion's sculpture.

"Oh, dear," said the cabdriver as I got in the backseat. "Sure you're finished?"

I nodded, and he handed me a tissue.

The idea to find out what had happened to Tess came to me on the train journey home. I sat in a window seat as the train made its slow way through the dreary countryside, and thought about Marion's face: those twitching eyebrows, that *I need to know*. And I decided then that I would use my knowledge of Tess to calculate her most likely course of action after checkout and try to find the answers to Marion's questions.

The revelation that Tess went to Spain had thrown me, but I think that any discovery about her movements postcheckout would have done so. After all, I had presumed she had committed suicide very soon afterward, if not on the actual day itself. But I had another reaction on hearing the news that was, I'm ashamed to say, not in the least bit rational: a pulse of annoyance at Tess's sneaking off behind my back. After checkout, I was supposed to be in control. I thought her life was in my hands.

I no longer had Tess's e-mails to work from, because her accounts had been suspended when everything came to light. Still, I had my memory, and Google. I also had, I realized, another clue, which could narrow down the possible search area: the e-mail Tess had received, ten days after checkout, from her friend Jennifer, who said she had spotted her at the Alhambra in Granada. At the time I had put this down to mistaken identity and thought little more of it, but now, combined with the knowledge of her ferry crossing, it became highly significant.

The more I thought about the time discrepancy, the more it seemed plausible that there might have been an interval between checkout and the actual act.

It made sense for Tess to travel to another country to do it, somewhere she had more scope for disposing of herself in a manner that meant she couldn't be identified. And once in Spain, she would have been in limbo, free of her old identity: a nonperson, responsible to no one. In that situation, it wouldn't be unreasonable for her to spend some days alone thinking, coming to terms with what she was about to do.

Of course, the fact that she may have been spotted in Granada didn't mean she had stayed around that area. The city was on the opposite side of Spain from Bilbao, where she had entered the country; if she had already traveled that far, she might well have then gone farther. So, tempting as it was to concentrate only on that city and the surrounding area, I had to keep my options open.

Next, I considered what kind of place Tess would head to in Spain. The basic criteria were simple, as they were the same as I used to choose Sointula: somewhere basic and hippieish, the opposite of London. In this instance, though, I thought it was likely that Tess would be drawn to a place that had some personal significance for her, or that was guaranteed to have the kind of environment she desired. In conclusion, I thought it was probable that she had spent those lost postcheckout days at a place that was familiar to her.

Tess hadn't, as far as I knew, been to Granada before, but she had had "minibreaks" in both Barcelona and Madrid, the former with a short-lived boyfriend called Boris, with whom she had argued over lunch on the first day, calling him "a pussy" when he balked at sucking the heads of prawns, and the latter with a group of women for an "excruciating" hen weekend. After Googling those cities, however, I decided it was unlikely she would have headed to either. They were busy and built up, not obvious destinations for someone who craved peace. Yet, Googling *quiet + secluded + Spain* was clearly not going to get me very far.

With no firm leads, my quest quickly ran out of steam, although I continued to devote some time each day to it. Indeed, the breakthrough did not come for several months—ironically, when my mind was not on the task at hand. I was thinking about Connor.

Even after all this time, he still invaded my thoughts, despite the fact that we were no longer in contact. Since our confrontation there had been one final e-mail from him, sent two hours after he walked away from me in Temple. It was there in Tess's in-box when I checked it after leaving the police station, in what turned out to be the small window between my confession and the suspension of her e-mail and Facebook accounts.

It was brief and to the point.

Here's the deal. You don't tell Chrissie, and I won't tell the police. Okay?

I replied, I've already told the police, and I'm not going to tell Chrissie.

I paused. I had so many questions. But then I decided to ask just one. Where does "kiss me first" come from? What does it mean?

His reply came thirty seconds later: I don't know.

What do you mean? I asked.

I don't know, he said. Tess said it once, can't remember the context. It just became a silly thing between us, a private joke.

And that was that. Our last communication. But, as I say, in the weeks since, he had never been far from my thoughts. Indeed, it was as if there were a film permanently playing in my head of him going about his daily business, mostly composed of tiny, insignificant details that I had witnessed for myself or could vividly imagine: his hand guiding his mouse as he worked at his computer; his nod of greeting to the man behind the sandwich counter; the way he shrugged on his coat as he left the office. When it came to his life at home with Chrissie and the children, however, the tape went blank.

I relived our correspondence, mentally turning over his e-mails again and again to see whether there were any clues that I should have heeded, remembering how I had felt when I received a certain message or sent what I considered a particularly witty reply. This activity made me feel heavy with sadness, like a sodden towel; then, occasionally, I would experience sharp bursts of anger that had nowhere to go.

That morning I was at my laptop, the usual thoughts circling around my head while I ostensibly continued with my quest to uncover Tess's whereabouts. For some weeks now this had been reduced to Googling various combinations of words related to travel and Spain and Granada, and trawling through the results in the hope that I would stumble across a possible lead or memory trigger. I scrolled past a site advertising easyJet flights to Granada, a site I had seen many times before. That day, however, the name of the airline combined with that moment's thoughts of Connor to produce just that: a flicker of an association, which I concentrated on until it became a full-blown recollection.

In the early days of our correspondence, I—Tess—had sent Connor the standard e-mail describing Sointula, how it was full of "alternative" types and so on. It's got this really amazing atmosphere; I think it must be on a ley line. I feel so happy here, like I can think and breathe properly for the first time.

And Connor's reply had been along the lines of: But why Canada? At least before, you indulged your hippie tendencies somewhere served by easyJet.

At the time, I thought little of it. Now I snapped into focus. I started by looking at the list of destinations served by the airline, but that didn't help: Granada was one of dozens in Europe. After another hour of fruitless Googling, I concluded that I had no option but to e-mail Connor and ask him what he knew about this hippie place he referred to.

The prospect of communicating with him again produced a rush of adrenaline, similar in intensity to how I had felt seeing him in the flesh. I couldn't help but think back to before, when, despite the fact that we wrote to each other dozens of times a day, I'd still receive a stab of pleasure when an e-mail arrived from him; there was the feeling that we were members of a tiny club that was impossible for others to get into, that only we knew the rules of. For a moment, I experienced such a desire to be innocently back in that time that tears came to my eyes. Then the memories of his betrayal and the lack of feeling he displayed at our meeting in Temple came swarming back. I tried to concentrate on them, so that anger and hurt would harden me up.

Previously, of course, I had communicated with Connor through Tess's e-mail account, but that was no longer in operation. Meanwhile, my own e-mail address was in my full name and I didn't want to reveal that. So the first thing I did was set up a new, anonymous account. I spent a while thinking of a suitable name: It had to be attention grabbing, as there was the risk he'd write off mail from an unknown recipient as spam. I considered kissmefirst@gmail.com, but thought he might not open it if he knew it was from me, so I decided to use the name of a female singer he had told me he liked when he was a teenager: Carol Decker.

The subject line was Hello again, and my tone was businesslike, devoid of any reference to what had passed between us:

No, this is not really Carol Decker. This is Leila, Tess's friend.
We met a while ago near your office. Now, I need your help. I
am conducting some research into the possible whereabouts of
Tess for the benefit of her mother, Marion, and I would like you

to elaborate on a reference you made in an e-mail to Tess during the summer. The e-mail referred to a "hippie" place she had once visited that was reachable by easyJet. What was this place?

His reply came forty minutes later:

I have no intention of entering into a protracted exchange with you, so I won't comment on the immense irony of your noble mission to help Tess's mother find her daughter. But for what it's worth: Years ago, when we were together, Tess mentioned that she had spent the previous summer at some hippie commune in the Alpujarras. Skinny-dipping in the river, getting stoned around the campfire, communing with Gaia and earnest Frenchmen, that sort of thing. I don't know the name.

Okay?

Do not contact me again.

So exciting was this information, I didn't feel too hurt by Connor's hostile tone. The Alpujarras were, I knew from my research, near Granada, and a Google search revealed only one long-established commune in the region. Half an hour later, I had booked my plane ticket.

Then, it had all added up. I felt so sure that she had gone there, that the commune would hold the clue to her death. But it's come to nothing. Yes, a couple of people there thought they might have seen Tess last summer, but they weren't positive. That's not good enough. And even if I had ascertained for certain that she had been there, there was still the mystery of where she went when she left, where she died. I am no closer to finding her body.

I now feel embarrassed for having embarked on this mission, for not anticipating the obstacles. All I can be pleased about is that I didn't tell Marion I was coming out here, so she will not have had her hopes raised and then dashed.

We're in the air now, finally. I had to put away my laptop while we ascended, and when I looked out the window, for a moment all I could see below was white, as if the clouds had dropped out of the sky. Then I realized it was the greenhouses, a patchwork of white plastic obscuring the land from the mountains to the sea.

*I'm writing this from my desk* on Albion Street. It's two ten a.m. on Saturday morning and I've just heard Jonty come in. He's been out at a Halloween party, dressed as a newsreader, with a cardboard box over his head painted to look like a TV and a square cut out to show his face. He claimed that he was going to talk only in bulletins all evening, but I can't imagine that lasted too long, knowing him.

When I came back from Spain I was convinced that he would have gone. It wasn't a rational fear; after all, he hadn't left when he found out about what I'd been up to, so there was no reason he should have done so now. But still, I pictured myself opening the front door and my suitcase wheels bumping over his keys on the mat. His room would be empty, reduced back to just a single bed, the walls pockmarked from where he had taken down his pictures, the two holes in the plaster where he'd tried to put up that shelf, nothing else left of him. My suspicions appeared confirmed when I found the front door double locked, but then as I entered the hall I saw his duffel coat hanging on the banister, and relief flooded through me like a tap had been turned on.

After twenty minutes, he returned. I was at my desk, reattaching my laptop to the mains, when I heard his key in the latch and then, seconds later, the door to my room flung open.

"Oh, bollocks," he said. "I wanted to be here for when you got back."

He gave me an awkward hug—I found it awkward, I mean—and then proceeded to bombard me with questions about my trip. To my surprise, I realized that I did actually want to talk about it, so we went and sat outside. Jonty liked using the flat's "unofficial" roof terrace; he had found two chairs in a skip and arranged them on the lumpy tarmac. At first I was reluctant to go out there, but when I did, it was nicer than I expected. The view extends beyond the rubbish dump below; you can see the neighbor's back garden, almost entirely taken up with a vast trampoline, and balconies of the flats opposite, some of which had been cheered up with flowerpots. Anyway, we sat out there and I told him about the trip—everything except for the bit about Synth and Mum and the police.

Two months have passed since then. Now I'm sitting here, gazing at the screen, trying to concentrate. Jonty's blundering around—I've just heard the lavatory flush—and attempting not to disturb me, but I suspect he's drunk. I've made an important discovery tonight, but my thoughts keep straying to things that are totally irrelevant. What was the party like? Why do people get drunk when it makes them act like idiots and then feel terrible the next day? What would it be like to go to a party with Jonty?

I have the urge to go out and ask him about his evening, and tell him what I've discovered tonight. He's bound to be interested, as he's followed the story so far. But the flat is silent now. He's probably fallen asleep on his bed fully clothed. I hope he's remembered to take the box off his head.

So, I've just found out the answer to something that's been bothering me for a while. Actually, it's two things: where Tess and Adrian met, and where Tess was during that missing three months in the first half of 2008. But the answer for both is the same: a residential psychiatric clinic in West London called the Zetland Centre, colloquially known as "the Zetty."

If I hadn't heard that nickname I probably would never have worked it out. Since coming home I haven't made much progress with my investigations, but tonight the Google alert on Adrian's name delivered an item of interest. In a newspaper interview, a man claimed he had once shared a room at a clinic with the "twisted Internet predator" Adrian Dervish. Except that wasn't what Adrian was called, then; he said his name was Stuart Walls. And apparently, he didn't have an American accent then, either. He told this man he was from Worcester, which is in the middle of England.

Anyway, this man described Adrian—Stuart—keeping him up all night with his plans for world domination and never changing his jumper, and he also happened to refer to the clinic as "the Zetty."

The name rang a faint bell in connection to Tess. I went back through my notes and found that in 2008 the phrase cropped up in her e-mails. I hadn't been able to work out what it meant, and Tess had said she couldn't remember when I asked her during one of our question sessions, so, as I had considered it a low-priority matter, I put it to one side. My best guess was that it was the nickname of a short-lived boyfriend or friend. You see, she sometimes did that— put *the* in front of someone's name for no discernible reason. Shall we ask the Jack if he can deejay? she'd write; or, Sounds like the kind of crap the Big Mel would come out with. The unnecessary definite article—it was one of her habits.

So now my theory is this: After a suicide attempt at the beginning of 2008, Tess had been admitted, voluntarily or otherwise, to the Zetland Centre, where she had stayed for around ten weeks. And during that time she had met Adrian, another patient. They had stayed in touch—by phone, I suppose, as I never found any e-mails between them—and three years later, by which time he was running Red Pill, she had asked him to help her to die. Or perhaps he had offered. Maybe the other people, like Randall Howard's "Mark," met Adrian there too.

Obviously, I can understand why Adrian wouldn't want me to know about "the Zetty"—but Tess? She was hardly reticent, and had freely told me about other suicide attempts and breakdowns and unsavory sexual encounters. Why not admit she had been to this clinic? I can't believe she had genuinely forgotten. Or maybe she had. Maybe it had been a particularly bad period and she had blocked it out. I suppose I'll never know.

They still haven't found Adrian. To be honest, my interest in his whereabouts is fading. The last time I properly thought about it was a month ago, spurred by something Jonty told me. He had just had dinner with his sister and her new boyfriend, who was, in Jonty's words, a "conspiraloon." "He banged on and on about how Obama had been behind the whole banking crisis, that it was a false flag operation," he said. "I wanted to bury my head in the couscous."

I remembered a throwaway remark of Adrian's when we met on

the Heath that day, about how easy it would be to make up a conspiracy theory about Obama and banks. I was curious enough to
Google, and indeed a site came up that was devoted to that particular line of thought:

> In 2008, two momentous events occurred. Barack Obama
> became the most powerful man in the world, and the global
> economy went into meltdown. Coincidence? Really? . . .

The site consisted of little more than a hastily thrown-together
home page, and, beyond an anonymous e-mail address, there were
no details about the person behind it. Which, of course, if it was
Adrian, wasn't surprising. The only possible clue was a quote at the
bottom of the page—*The question isn't who is going to let me; it's
who is going to stop me*—by Ayn Rand, Adrian's heroine. However,
that's hardly conclusive evidence. And even if I did have proof that
Adrian was behind the site, I wouldn't tell the police. I don't want
to have anything to do with him, but neither do I want to cause him
to be found.

In his absence, Adrian has been variously diagnosed by the media
as both a "narcissistic psychopath" and suffering from "antisocial
personality disorder." I thought the latter didn't sound that bad—in
fact, it sounds like something I could have—but I looked it up and
it's actually quite serious:

> A persuasive pattern of disregard for, and violation of, the
> rights of others. Deception, as indicated by repeatedly
> lying, use of aliases, or conning others for personal profit or
> pleasure.

Adrian would have rejected any such labeling. He didn't believe in mental illness. He spoke about the subject in several of his podcasts: Doctors, he said, pathologized perfectly normal reactions to life in order to make money and control unruly members of society. I listened carefully to his argument and I subscribed to it too. After all, that's why I helped Tess: because I believed that her desire to end her life was a legitimate feeling, not to be denied or smothered with drugs.

But I thought then that Adrian was *rational*. That was the point. If I knew he had been diagnosed with a mental illness before he had told me that mental illness didn't exist, would I have listened to him in the same way?

I suppose I'll never know for sure. All I do know is that I don't regret what I did. It may have been Adrian who got me into it in the first place, but after that, during all those weeks of preparation before checkout, it was just me and Tess. However dismissive Marion was of me, I really do believe I knew Tess better than anyone else in the world, and aside from that single, understandable moment of fear on Skype that one evening, she never wavered in her long-held desire to disappear from the world. I helped her achieve that.

Not that a resolution has been reached with Tess—or, rather, not in the way I had been planning when I started writing this in Spain. I know nothing more concrete about her movements after checkout than when I got off the plane in Málaga in August. Her body has not been found. But now I have what I think is a pretty good theory.

But I'm getting ahead of myself. First I need to explain what happened to me in Spain, and why I left the commune so abruptly.

On that Wednesday morning, I was dozing under the tree when I heard the sound of first Spanish being spoken close by, then English.

I felt a hand on my shoulder, shaking me awake. Semiconscious, I assumed that it was Milo, but this grip was far heavier and more insistent, and I opened my eyes to see a man looming over me. The sun was behind him, so at first I couldn't see that he was wearing a uniform, and my first thought was that he was someone from the commune, perhaps sent by the annoying woman who kept going on about my not using the official toilet.

Then he said in heavily accented English, "Please get up."

I sat up and saw that there was another man there too, standing off to one side, and that they were wearing police uniforms. Such was my befuddled state, I had the notion that the account I had been writing of Tess had somehow bled into real life. After all, I had reached the point in the story when I was at the police station in London; by writing about the police, perhaps I had conjured them into existence. Somehow they had found out why I had come to the commune and were here to tell me that Tess's body had been discovered.

I got to my feet. They were both large, bulky men, wearing sunglasses and sweating in their uniforms. Behind them there was a police car and, beside it, a flattened rectangle of grass where Annie's van had been. One of them asked me to spell my name, and then informed me that I was being arrested on suspicion of murdering my mother.

Feeling like I still wasn't fully conscious, I got into the backseat of the car. Oddly, I didn't feel nervous. We drove back down the track and toward the main town. The two men didn't speak, to me or to each other, and the only sound was the occasional outburst in fast Spanish from the radio. When we reached the plastic greenhouses, I thought of my tent and belongings and wondered what was going to happen to them now. Apart from that, and odd though it may sound,

I didn't really think or feel anything during the journey. It was as if my brain were off-line. The air-conditioning was on full blast, and it was deliciously cool. Sitting on that cracked plastic seat, I was the most comfortable I had been throughout my week in Spain.

At the police station, I was taken into a room decorated with tatty posters warning of the dangers of thieves and time-share touts. Other than that, the setup was the same as it was in Fleet Street—a table, four chairs, and a tape recorder, which was even clunkier than the one in London.

As he stated the charge and read me my rights, the policeman's voice was flat, as if this matter were of no more importance than a stolen handbag. I had the right to an English-speaking solicitor; did I know of one? After he repeated the question, I found the strength to shake my head. Would I like them to find me one? I nodded.

I was told I could make a phone call and was shown to a plastic-covered phone in the corner of the room. The problem was, I didn't know whom to call. The only person I could think of was Jonty, but I didn't have his mobile number on me. So I phoned the only number I knew by heart, which was the landline of our old house in Leverton Street. A man answered, presumably the person we had sold the place to. "Yes? Who is this?" he said, and when I didn't reply, he swore and put down the phone.

I returned to my seat. One policeman had left the room, I guessed to find a solicitor for me; the other sat by the door, showing so little movement he could have been asleep behind his sunglasses. I looked at the posters on the walls, with their cartoon warnings against tourist crime—one showed a handbag hanging over the back of a chair with a red line through it—and thought that by the time people saw them, here in the police station, surely it would be too late for them to heed the advice.

I stared at the words BE CAREFUL! and thought about the flattened rectangle of grass where Annie's van had been. I wasn't disappointed with her for telling the police, but rather with myself and my judgment. I had gotten her wrong. *I understand,* she'd said when I told her, but she hadn't, really. Just like Connor had said, *I love you,* but he hadn't, really. I should have learned by now that people do not always mean what they say.

Then I thought about the word *murder,* and the idea of it being applied to what I did to Mum was so ludicrous I almost laughed.

And then, suddenly, I was very scared. I did not want to be locked up. That I knew with absolute certainty. When I had walked into the police station in London, I welcomed the idea of prison, but now things were different. The thought of it made panic course through me; I glanced at the nonmoving policeman and, for a wild moment, considered making a run for it.

Part of me felt that if I explained it all, they would understand—how could anyone not?—but I was not naive. Since Mum had died I had kept an eye on reports of euthanasia trials and knew that, while some judges were sympathetic and showed leniency, others did not. The fact that Mum had not been a member of a right-to-die organization and had never publicly registered her wishes would not count in my favor; nor would the fact that I was the sole beneficiary of her estate.

Suddenly I missed my mum so much it stopped my breath. I pictured the door opening and her rushing in to rescue me. She would hold me and take care of me, just as I had taken care of her. We would burst out laughing; it had all been a terrible mistake and she was fit and well again; we were back in Leverton Street, me sitting at the table, her jiggling around to Radio 2 while she cooked. I was safe and loved, and when they bullied me at school she would be waiting at the gate with a bag of doughnuts from Greggs, the bakery, and she would hold my hand tightly, just as I held hers when her own breath finally stopped.

The policeman looked in my direction. I gripped the plastic table and inhaled deeply, trying to regain control. Then the door opened and the other policeman reappeared. Behind him was someone else, but it was not an English-speaking solicitor. It was Annie.

She had Milo and the baby in tow and looked even pinker than usual, her hair damp and plastered to her face.

"Are you okay?" she said.

I looked at her in astonishment and nodded.

"I was at the supermarket," she said. "When I got back, I didn't see you, and then I heard that you'd been taken away by the police."

She said it was Synth who had told her, and that she could tell by her expression that it was she who had called them. Synth must have overheard us talking at the bonfire.

"I've been explaining to the police that there's been a misunderstanding," she said. "Synth's English isn't good, and she misheard what you said. You didn't mean *killed*; you meant *died*. You meant your mother had died naturally, as a result of her illness." She looked straight into my eyes. "I told the police that you'd be prepared to make a statement confirming this, and that you'd cooperate fully in giving them details of your mother's death so they can corroborate the facts."

I just nodded. Annie then addressed the police, speaking in fast, complicated Spanish. I didn't know she could speak so fluently.

Annie and I were in the police station for another three hours. They found me an English-speaking solicitor, a thin middle-aged woman called Maria, and I repeated Annie's story. I talked them through the night Mum died, omitting my involvement, and gave them the name of Dr. Wahiri, who had come in the next morning and signed the death certificate stating that she died of complications arising from MS.

They said they would have to phone England and check the story. While we were waiting, Annie pulled up a chair beside me. We didn't talk about what was going on, but she kept up bright, cheery conversation about other things while Milo wandered around the room, kicking at chair legs. At one point she gave me the baby to hold. It was the first time I'd had one in my arms; it was the same weight and temperature as our old cat, Thomas.

After an hour, Annie went out to buy us some drinks, and while she was gone I heard the sounds of raised, angry voices through the door, coming from the front desk. I became worried, but when Annie returned she told me that the altercation had nothing to do with our case. While she had been grappling with the vending machine in the reception area, two men had been brought in, charged with assault. It was some argument over water, apparently.

"From what I could hear, one of them's a farmer," she said. "He's been siphoning water from those greenhouses, the ones near us. He says it's his water because it goes through his land. Everyone's getting desperate because of the drought."

I didn't think much of this at the time. I was still too preoccupied with the police phoning Dr. Wahiri. You see, that morning, when he came in to examine Mum, and I was telling him about waking up to find her dead beside me, he had given me a look. It was very brief, a fraction of a second, and at the time my reading of it was: *I know what you did, and I understand.* But perhaps yet again I had misunderstood, and the look was one of suspicion.

Another half hour passed and I grew more and more worried. The baby started crying, so Annie pulled up her T-shirt and started feeding it. Milo was whining too, so I tried to amuse him by doing the peekaboo game through my fingers, the same one Mum used to do with me. It worked for a bit—he actually laughed—but then he got bored again and tugged at his mother's skirt.

Then we heard footsteps approaching. Annie had finished feeding, thank goodness, as the door opened and the older policeman came in. He spoke in Spanish to Annie, who nodded. I couldn't tell from her expression what he was saying. My heart thumped.

She turned to me and said, "Dr. Wahiri has confirmed that the death was natural. Because the accusation against you was based on hearsay and there's no supporting evidence, we're free to leave."

‖‖‖‖‖‖‖‖

It was dark by the time we drove back to the commune. Annie asked what I was going to do now.

"I think I should probably go home," I said.

Early the next morning, I packed up my tent and Annie drove me to the airport. We didn't speak much on the journey. It wasn't an awkward silence, though. At the airport, she parked her van crookedly, blocking the taxi lane. I said good-bye to Milo and then, to her, "Thank you very much."

She waved it away, as if it didn't need to be said.

"Good luck out there." And then, as she started the engine and I walked toward the airport entrance, she called after me, "I'm on Facebook; look me up."

‖‖‖‖‖‖‖‖

Three days ago there was an interesting development.

Annie has Facebooked me several times since my return from Spain—chatty, inconsequential reports of her and Milo and, once, an invitation to an exhibition of woodcraft that she helped organize in Connecticut. For my reply to that I recycled Tess's response to Connor when he first asked her out for dinner: Would love to, but not quite worth a ten-thousand-mile round trip.

This latest message, however, contained some real news: Have you heard that it hasn't rained in the Alpujarras since we were there? It's the worst drought in living memory, apparently. The river has entirely dried up and there's been more trouble between the farmers and the agribusiness. It's the poor wildlife I care about.

I checked Spanish news sites, which confirmed the ongoing drought in the region. As I was doing so, a small item caught my eye. It mentioned that a female human skeleton had been revealed on the dry riverbed, about four miles from the commune.

I sat there, thinking, for some minutes, until my laptop logged me out.

Once, on the phone, Tess had mentioned drowning. She had just seen a film about a writer called Virginia Woolf, who committed suicide by walking into a river with stones in her pockets. "It's the best way to go, apparently," she said. "You struggle and panic at first, but then when your oxygen runs out you surrender and then there's this moment of bliss, and that's the last thing you know."

Of course, it may not have been her. The skeleton could have been there for years. It could have been a walker who got disoriented in the heat, a murder victim, another suicide. It could be an illegal immigrant, one of the workers in the greenhouses, somebody who would never be missed.

But it could have been her. A scenario took shape. On checkout day, Tess took the ferry to Bilbao, and from there either hitchhiked or took the train to the commune. There she spent a week, punctuated with her visit to the Alhambra in Granada—*Visit the Alhambra before you die!* I read on one Web site—until she decided she was sure of her decision and ready to proceed. That evening, she would have walked to the river and, after disposing of her possessions, waded in. Perhaps she waited until darkness fell.

It would appeal to Tess's romantic nature, I thought, to disappear like that. I pictured her in the moonlight; she would most probably have taken some alcohol with her—a bottle of tequila, perhaps. I pictured her listening, for one last moment, to the sound of the crickets in the trees.

After two days of deliberation I e-mailed Marion. I told her about my trip to Spain and what I had discovered, laying out my thoughts about the drowning. I left it up to her to decide whether she wanted to investigate further. She hasn't replied, but then, I didn't really expect her to.

I'm glad, actually. I don't want to know whether they find Tess's body. Because that would destroy the other possibility: that she's still alive. Maybe, during that week at the commune, she decided against it. Maybe she thought that now that she had shaken off her old identity, life would be bearable. She could reinvent herself, start afresh as a new person, and this time get it right.

Maybe, when she left the commune, she just hitchhiked to another one, and is still there now, sitting around a different campfire, making something out of feathers and string, discussing the price of bread with some ratty-haired Australian. Maybe she has fallen in love with a man and is now roaming the country with him in his camper van. Or maybe she has left Spain altogether; when she was in Granada, she might have gone into a bar and asked a shady-looking person to make her a false passport, and gone anywhere in the world.

Maybe her new name is Ava Root, and she is my friend on Facebook.

The thought occurred to me only a few days ago. As you know, I presumed Ava Root was Adrian, using an alias so that we could communicate about Project Tess undetected.

When everything blew up at Red Pill, I sent a message asking where he was and what was going on, but heard nothing back, and that was the end of our communication.

But last Sunday, I put up on Facebook some photos taken the day before, when I had joined Jonty and some of his friends for a walk in Brockwell Park. The park had been thick with colorful autumn leaves, an attractive scene, and one of the pictures showed Jonty's friend Saskia throwing a handful of leaves at me as we walked. I didn't mind—the gesture was meant in a friendly way, and in the picture we're both smiling.

Several of my Facebook friends had "liked" the photo—Jonty and Saskia, and another girl from Jonty's drama school called Betts. And then, yesterday, I saw there was another "like." From Ava Root.

Of course, it could have come from Adrian. But I suspect that liking a photo of me having leaves thrown over me in a South London park would not be at the top of his list of priorities.

So perhaps "Ava Root" was Tess all along. Perhaps she decided against killing herself and, once settled in her new life, couldn't resist getting in touch. Maybe she was bored and wanted to play with fire; maybe she just wanted to check that I was all right. And when she realized that I thought she was Adrian and was telling her details of how the project was going—how her friends and family were doing, what was happening in her new life in Sointula—well, I can't blame her for not letting on. She couldn't have resisted hearing about that.

If Ava Root wasn't Adrian, it would certainly make sense of his confusing attitude toward me when we met in Westfield, several months into the project. It wasn't that, after all these attentive messages, he suddenly didn't care about me and Tess. Rather, he had lost interest long before that, probably as soon as Tess checked out. *Proneness to boredom* is a key psychopathic trait, I read.

Ava Root's profile is still completely blank, and I'm still her only friend. I've been considering sending her a message, asking her outright whether she is Tess, but instinct tells me that would be a bad idea and I would never hear from her again. I think I'm starting to accept that life isn't black-and-white, that there isn't an answer to every question. Some areas will always remain gray, and perhaps that's not a bad thing.

I have got some other new Facebook friends too: I'm now up to ninety-seven. They're mostly friends of Jonty's, whom I met when they came around to the flat. The latest is a girl called Tia, from his acting school. She's nice. Two nights ago I joined her and Jonty in a pub by the river and had quite a pleasant hour drinking elderflower cordial and hearing about the travails of being a wannabe actor in London. She told me that she has a job temping in offices with an agency that allows you to work as much or as little as you like and take time off at short notice if something else, like an audition, comes up.

"The work's not thrilling," she said, "but it gives you freedom to do other stuff too. It's mainly just actors who work there, but I'm sure they'll let you in."

"Ah, I'm sure Leila can pass as an actor," said Jonty, and winked at me.

Tia messaged me their number, and I'm going in to see them

next week. The woman on the phone thought she had misheard me when I said I could type ninety words per minute.

Jonty, meanwhile, has given up on acting. "The last thing the world needs is another shit, out-of-work luvvie," he said. He's decided to train to be a London tour guide, working on a boat that goes up and down the river. For my birthday he took me out on it. I was glad of my decision to keep my hair short, because in places the boat went quite fast and the passengers with long hair got it whipped all over the place.

Jonty wasn't leading the tour himself, because he was still in training, but he kept on adding his own commentary to the official one. "Poor old Cannon Street, the dullest bridge on the Thames"; and then, as we passed a theater on our left: "I've just realized—if I'm not going to be an actor, I don't have to go and stand for four hours watching Shakespeare at the Globe. Result!" At the London Eye: "A little kid was sick in our capsule when I went. Longest forty-five minutes of my life." On and on he went. He seemed to have had an experience at every landmark we passed: his own personal tour of London.

The boat went right down to the Houses of Parliament, and we passed the spot where I had stood the day I confronted Connor, just before I went to the police. As I glanced at it, I thought: I could give my own commentary. For a moment I considered telling Jonty about Connor, but decided against it. It's so complicated to explain. Besides, there are other things to talk about now.

## Acknowledgments

This book would not have been finished without the tireless bolstering and wise counsel of my mother, Deborah Moggach. Its publication is thanks to my agent, Antony Topping, and editors Francesca Main, Jennifer Jackson, and Bill Thomas.

I am also indebted to Chris Atkins for his love and technical support, Hannah Westland for her editorial input, and Tom Moggach, Victoria Hogg, Mark Williams, Laura Yates, and Nicola Barr for their notes. Alex Hough, Alex Walsh-Atkins, and Cameron Addicott gave invaluable advice on medical, legal, and police matters. My friends Sathnam Sanghera, Susannah Price, Alex O'Connell, Flora Bathurst, and Vita Gottlieb saw me through years of writing angst. Encouragement from Lucy Kellaway and Craig Taylor meant a great deal; Craig also told me about Sointula. Kevin Conroy Scott was an early advocate of the book, and a grant from Arts Council England was a huge help at a lean time.

I'd further like to thank everyone involved at Macmillan, Doubleday, Greene and Heaton, and beyond, including Paul Baggaley, Geoff Duffield, Emma Bravo, Jodie Mullish, Jo Thomson, Alison Rich, Nora Reichard, Nita Pronovost, Adria Iwasutiak, Brad Martin, Kristin Cochrane, Chris Wellbelove, and Hellie Ogden; Dean Cooke and Suzanne Brandreth at the Cooke Agency; and Sally Wofford-Girand at Union Literary.

A NOTE ABOUT THE AUTHOR

Lottie Moggach lives in London. This is her first novel.